THE LEDE
TO
OUR UNDOING

The Lede
to
Our Undoing

Donald Mengay

Saddle Road Press

Saddle Road Press
Ithaca, NY
saddleroadpress.com

ISBN 978-1-7365258-9-0
Library of Congress Control Number 2023938278

Design and cover image by Don Mitchell
Author photograph by Hrvoje Slovenc

Contents

Part One

Part Two

For Channing Sanchez

PART ONE

Grounding

As a final straw they buried me in this traffic circle under cover of night. The soil was in the jaws of December, though I'd been in a freeze of another kind for months already. They were able to pull it off because the panhandlers and druggies that usually track by, they and the beat cops who tail them, beg off that time a year. And yet the relocation didn't go without a hitch. Just when they figured things were going smoothly an officer from the Parks Authority picked up their scent and issued a citation. For illegal dumping. Nothing about him said, Don' do this. Instead, it was more, I got a quota t' fill. But never mind. They carried on, ticket in hand, Wren and Jake with Donald colluding. They hemmed me in one of the flower beds of this roundabout, just across from the beds coiling the museum.

That winter I rattled with the semis passing by. I whiled away the time under that blinking eye overhead, the one that signals caution to the flow of cars breaking from godknowswhere to godknowswhere. The vehicles shot past the place I wanted to be, in the company of the ever-musing one on the museum steps. That brazen nude. A thinker like me. It was there that Jake and I used to kill time when he should've been in school.

The ground around me has softened now. The blanket with the chrysanthemum pattern that they wrapped me in has begun the process of decay. I sense the root of a daffodil breaking through, feeding off me. If Harry were here he'd howl, Stop your barkin'! But he isn't here. Not him, Florrie or Diana, nor Jake for sure. It's just Wren and Donald who pay their respects. They and the little one do their best to stop by somewhere in the vicinity.

Jake, meanwhile, is in another state, one a mile high, that paradise he up and hightailed it to. His exit from me was an expectation of some kind—an expectoration is more like it. Hacking up, ridding himself of his life here. Or running for running's sake. Granted, a death is a tough nut to unshell, but the important thing is what comes after, including basics like soil and water—it won't do to go looking for a better version elsewhere. I mean demons follow you everywhere, to any soil or water, like the kind all around me. Unlike so much in life they're uncancelable, like the memories that haunt me.

I've heard April is the cruelest month, and it's true in a way. The rain drops down like tears, trapping fluorocarbons as they descend here in the Forest City. But the sun shows through from time to time, making it a hybrid state that I inhabit. I'm attuned to the world it creates that's awash in blooms.

In this year of the plague, the first of two in his time and the one most people overlook, Jake considers himself lucky. Does he thank me now that he realizes, finally, that I had something to offer? About staying alive most of all—not just him but others too? They thought I was clueless, that I didn't see color, that I existed in a world of gray, as though that were a bad thing. I'd argue it's better than seeing things in black or white, or, worse, seeing only color.

Jake with a new-found vision, allowing him to notice me finally, which I sense all the way here. Those moments when he spirits himself into town I recognize his shoes as he jogs by, though they avoid darkening the ground where I am. It's such a change from the way he and I were tethered for so many years, that is until he ran off and unleashed the others on me. As if he'd lost faith in his own kind, beginning with his own family. God forbid it should be just the two of us, a long-awaited meeting of souls—or soles as the case may be. Usually he spills from Donald and Wren's, faking ignorance of my presence as though that night in December never took place. I know not only his tread but those of the others, though he assumes I'm oblivious. A mere swelling in the ground. A place-marker for what was. A memory interred. Anything but myself: a thinker like him.

I make nothing of it. I inhabit a different reality, tucked away from the pain and inertia, the weight loss and lesions in Jake's world—run, Jake! What is there to recall me by anyway? A daffodil like any other. It too will droop. Toast it'll turn. It'll peter out in the sun. A ring of daffodils, a wheel of light, a circle of bulbs beneath the earth, and me among them.

If Jake can't find me it's because they never bothered to leave a stone. I heard him tell Wren that the one he found, just above, black and shiny and pooched at one end, the rock he pocketed unbeknownst to anyone, reminded him of me. To which I replied, Your heart, my dear. No, there was no stone or cross-sticks planted during that makeshift ritual— god forbid! He would've never stood for that, for cross-sticks most of all, which by then he'd renounced entirely. When the clouds don't bathe me they bless me, stone or no stone, cross-sticks or no cross-sticks.

Objective time abandons me. Now—a thing that doesn't exist up there—has assumed jurisdiction. Meanwhile the grind of freezing and thawing dogs the soil. The rock below levitates upward, threatens to dislodge me, heaves into and irritates my side like a prod. The only relief I get is from words—from me of all people, the one they refused to believe capable of both language and thought when I was up there.

On this rock I read tales almost too raw to relate, about personages faceless as sparrows yet not without countenance. Consequence too. The rock's untold tales and me, Molly— the two of us have taken up residence down here. We are too close for me to consider forgetting, just below the surface, the story-stone and me in a drawn-out conversation. It shoulders, threatens to dislocate me permanently to the land of silence if I don't speak. So I engage while I can, a mute with something to say, never mind the mire and whatnot around me. No one sees or notices, but I recognize me. I spy this ancient erratic, product of a world I never knew. Mottled as a killdeer's egg, it's neither jade nor diamond— it's more a bone to console me where they plopped me down this rabbit hole.

My only other consolation is I know I haunt Jake still.

For him my heart failed initially. I ranted about his rocky heart, stuck as I was in that electrifreeze, tossed among the other stiffs. And from well over a thousand miles away he heard—he came back! How could he possibly recognize me, I wondered at the time, with years and miles between us, not to mention a chain of events that held him after he reached the city of inversions, a mile high, stuffing a shoe box with cocktail napkins, drawn with phony names and numbers? I let it be known I was holding out for the whole enchilada, a proper visit and not a mere passing through, not to mention an apology for having abandoned me the way he did. But when I whiffed my boy's circumstances up there, standing on a field of a different kind of passing than the one he fled here, that melted me. Caused me to realign my position regarding him and our past.

We've come to terms, Jake and I, in mortality if you will. On the prairies and mesas or whatever they're called, just below the foothills where he lives, where they season piety with three shakes of fanaticism—They're a bunch a crazies

out here! he declared. Much more religious than back East!
All the way in the Forest City I feel the beat of the mariachis
around him. I move with the pulse of the placita Tommy's
from. I sense the beat across fourteen-hundred-odd miles
the way I never could back then—

—My gringo. What does he know about drumbeats or
heartbeats, or any kind of beat quite frankly? Regarding
Tommy most of all, the one he's got his eye on. The two of
them check every food label they encounter, tot up vitamin
and fat contents, he and Tommy both. The money he used
to blow on the lottery he now sinks into running shoes.
He listens to Spanish conjugations on his cassette player,
mows his nails over verb tenses, hidden sugar contents,
and unnatural dyes. When he's visiting Wren he avoids the
solitude of what nature there is here as he jogs by—is that
what the Mile High City has taught you? He buys ever more
cushioned sneakers with thicker soles to separate himself
from the earth. He's moved to a trailer park, he told Donald
on a power run. Fronted by a fiberglass cowboy, giant, free,
and eternal.

At a certain point there comes a time when you have to
cease your yapping and commence speaking logically. I'm
not there yet. Though I hope to be. To exist in a more
systematic idiom. In the meantime I vow to try and organize
my thoughts, impose a semblance of structure on memories
that harry me—I beg indulgence a little while still.

Marriage was a state Jake thought about often—it must
have been a hundred times, concerning him and Romeo first,
then Peacoat. Of course like everyone he was birthed into it,
the buzz of matrimony, given how ingrained it is, decades
before anyone ever dreamed of the thing he had in mind,

dreamed of the plague too before it was christened with a name. In truth, in his heart of hearts, he was into imagining Romeo, and like I say Peacoat after, as weddable. Spouses. He insisted on it in his monologues with Wren and me both, never mind the word denoted a certain kind of currency. For that reason it's something else to glean his reaction to you, Tommy, who first brought the subject of marriage up, unfortunately after his soul had been vacated here in a sense, after he up and shot far from the Forest City. Tommy said, It'll do buenísimo by me, marriage—that is whenever he caught Jake pooh-poohing it. He said, Don' knock it, to which Jake made no reply. So friends they remain, leaving the two in a limbo of the flesh, not to mention a limbo of the State, cohabiting without a shilly-shally piece a paper.

What we have won't fade the way a legal documint does, Jake assured Tommy finally. The way a page brittles an' dies. To which the latter quipped, Don' be so sure. Unwritten intentions also fade. Turn to shreds. I think that was his drift. They crisp like an aborted bud and drop off, like these blooms around me will do that are now celebrating a moment. Yeah, I planned on a kind of early Fall between those two given the dogged nature of Jake's opposition, never mind his track record. And yet he dragged his novio here, I assumed to meet me, to see his twin again too who'd already met the guy, out there. Come to think of it that was before they plopped me here—he and Tommy jog by me daily now, on yet another visit, cantering from Wren's, stopping from time to time. Faking a rest.

You're too big picture, Tommy grouses.

Well wha's more big picture than a lifetime commitmen'?

But it's only a prollem if you make it one. Less juss try an' get through each day.

Tommy seemed to sing the words, his intonation lilting then falling. He fretted they'd never make it considering

Jake's stubbornness. Then he outed in an row another time, T' you, relationships are sacerd cows. But we're just human.

At which point a bolt seemed to spike through Jake because it was then that he began to rethink things, even if he was only ready to agree to table the discussion until a future date. So, new ground rules having been set, with the rapidity of two mutts mating, they returned to the house above the embankment where Donald, Wren, and Billie reside. Until another day when they track back here, this time to face what Jake had been evading like taxes: a mess of festering memories regarding yours truly. From time to time they sit not far away, along the flank of Martin Luther King, né Liberty, Boulevard, where Harry and Florrie refuse to tread because of the possibility of running into Wren or Donald, or the little one, to this turf and its Ellis Island of failed white dreams, its absentee landlords and houses boarded up. Yeah, Jake made it back after assigning me here, sometime into esa cosa with Tommy. And now here he is—with Donald, Wren, Billie, and the others standing witness, practicing a few wine-induced I do's, not far from the Thinker, mon ami over there, though not I do's of the federal kind. That's for breeders, Jake quipped, inducing Wren to caress her third chakra and Donald to caution, Easy bro.

Tommy couldn't help himself, truces be damned. Why sh'we settle for second best, amigo? He was rebelling against the state of things that made their I do's moot. And indeed he swung hard when Jake threw his fast ball, though far afield, called him straight male, always trying to possess a body. Tommy rejoined, You could label me worse. Whiteboy. Like you. And the irony is, the guy could pass. Not for a minute. About as easy as Donald, for whom the thought of aping a whiteboy is sure to bring on a curse.

Meanwhile back at the ranch, the Civil-War-era, shot-gun-style affair that Donald and Wren call home, the place they purchased for five thousand bucks from Midge, Donald dusted off a volume of the encyclopedia to prove that white, pigment not light, is achromatic—the complete absence or, as Tommy put it, the nada of color.

Se me hace que es así, mi amor. It's true.

They were talking over a pair of mechanical voices from either corner. He wouldn't stop driving home the point, that that's how it seemed to him, until Wren conceded, OK you two win!

Blood on the leaves and blood at the root.

White doesn't exist! Tommy crowed, Para nada! though he looked a bit incómodo afterward, riding Donald's coattails like that.

Scent of magnolia, sweet and fresh, Then the sudden smell—
—Hey you two—
Here is a strange and bitter crop.

For Donald to have forced Wren to cry uncle was no easy task. It was Tommy though who disculpa-me'ed Jake later when the two stood alone. He apologized for "the general force" of his words "if not the gist."

General indeed, Jake complained. General Tomás. That is when you're so cock-sure.

You mean when you're stonewallin', Tommy returned. Refusin' to lemme get a word in. Listenin' to what I have to say. Then he, like Donald with Wren, gets to terrorizing poor, innocent whiteboy.

It was after the debate about color, or noncolor, that I believe Jake developed a distaste for mirrors. He talked himself—a self-declared lover of reflection—and Tommy too, into getting rid of them—or at least he tried. There're totally too many, he complained. Everwhere y'look. People're too obsess with what's on th' ousside. He came out with it after smashing up the glass in the faux gilt frame in the living room of their trailer, on a wall that now features an empty rectangle, wrought with scallops and acanthus leaves. After that he and Tommy peered into it to perceive what they could. A window that looked in—or did it look out? An opening in any case, just what they needed for scanning interiors under baked and unbaked skin.

The wall-length jobbie on the back of the bathroom door, the one they kept, is where Tommy likes to approach Jake desde atrás. It reminds them of their differences in the most naked terms possible, differences that can enhance, or so my boy likes to say.

The back-and-forth in front of the thing may be working, at least at present—but—Oh! the stone! Butting into my spleen, like Jake into Tommy in their private film before the glass. Only now I see—here he comes again, the two of them—speak of the devil! I hear them hum as they pass, Jake and the person he labeled for Wren, in that unironic tone of his, his "life's jogging partner, no matter what happens." A person who will never know me except for these daffodils arced in an O, signifying nothing to most, that and a patch of trees budding all around. The two are getting drunk on pollen—It's a time a rebirth, Jake remarks profoundly—I heard him say it just like that. Do you think Tommy rolls his eyes the way Donald does at Wren? But wait, it's two, four, no it's six sets of feet passing through, here in Martin Luther King Circle, with the traffic hunting by, as if to taunt me with memories that won't quit.

It's winning, I know, the stone with its insistence I speak—tell everything from the beginning—as though they were knowable, beginnings. Well, a start of sorts, one that commences naturally at the end. Tommy slows the group's steps to a crawl, dawdling I'm sure. He feels me. After all, his heart lodges not up in the airy reaches between his ears like Jake's but a good deal lower, nearer the earth and me. Yet do I say anything? Do I bark or do I curse? You've got to get up pretty early in the morning to find me is all I have to say, and the sun's long ago achieved its peak. I'm now all sense. Down here I'm reminded of everything, including my former dependence on things human, a knowledge, to be sure, that I never escaped when I was up there.

Overkill of cherry blossoms hounds this place. Petals confetti the air, blanket the walkways. Pollen drifts with the torrent of cars rushing by mechanically. Obliviously. Darkness shields Jake and Tommy now that the others have left—they steal a kiss. The beds of otherwise disinterested tulips take to ogling Tommy as he plants two lips on their target when he assumes no one's looking, between the fits of sniping. Yeah, I eyed them, trapping Jake. Tommy knows I'm here, I'm sure of it. He all but verified it when Jake's friends Cin and Diablo were along for the run earlier.

Diablo (slowing, taking Cin's hand): Is it here?

Wren: No, I think it's here.

Jake: What does it matter where it is, th'exact spot?

Cin to Wren: See how he is?

It was Tommy who stood bang overhead, the only one I'd never met. He courted me in his way, soles to earth, as though hankering for a blessing. A word or two of wisdom about how to handle the boy. In the process he thumped me hard into this rock here, the one with the lines chiseled on it, inscribed by a glacier a mile thick as it coaxed the stone south, setting it to rest, a product of eons—it's worse than a blade. Tommy remarked, I think Donald said th'other day that it's aquí. And indeed aquí *it* was, just beneath the blooms.

But what do I care? How could they begin to imagine where I am, even if they were to exhume the residue they call me? It would be not-me. Now-me—go, Tommy! Run for Jake's hand. Three's a charm they say. As I say you're not taking on a late bloomer. On the contrary—there were two before you. For your sake hold your brooding eye for

Numero Uno; the other keep for my boy with his million hesitations, rooted in loves lost.

So you discovered that whiteness ain't what it's cracked up to. That it's more a cardboard cut-out, a projection like that Oz guy. I mean, what would my boy understand about a beauty like you—how could he possibly? You two have a lot to explore on your private terrain, a mile high, with my boy issuing from whiteness to whiteness, Peacoat notwithstanding. For all his big talk he's only now beginning to catch on to Wren and Donald's world, the twins both learning to chuck aside a mountain of old chestnuts.

Can you feel me, a thinker like you? Kin in the capacity to suffer? Overlook my idiom, the old saw about whether I've a mind—maybe they're the deficient ones. Wren rose highest to that challenge. Jake tried, though he fumbled— if not, he would've stayed. Or, better, he would've taken me along. The others shot nearer or wider the mark. Cin and Diablo got it, sort of. But the others I'm not so sure. All except Florrie—she surprised me. What are all those screaming matches of my boy's now, the ones you said Jake spurred because he felt guilt? Gilt is more like it. A privilege worn thin. That's what those loves were to him— life without them opened on a leaden world. I was there then as you are here now, Tommy, piercing me, killing me with a certain kind of kindness, catching my drift I hope, a bit more than Jake who never seemed so mindful. He's been pierced the same way you're piercing me now, only a stone's throw from that traffic light and Le penseur—I beg you to stop so I can think.

Voiced or voiceless, I feel you and the whiteboy—shall we call him Jake II? Sequel to the First? The one I'm about to story for you now? An altered copy at the very least—that's how I read the stone, shouldering me out of myself. The one mapped with arteries of a life. Three.

OK a handful. A constellation is more like it. One I'll try to chart for you, sketch in the way Jake attempts to catch Tommy on paper and canvas, which is to say a failure in advance as all representations are, because the real thing lives only once. Hopefully. The minute we try to nab it— the original, that is, as in the real Jake—it's lost. It morphs into a second-order thing, a new original untwinned with the first, though potentially as powerful—or even more. So enjoy your shot at him, just don't, I ask, dislodge me. If you do your Jake is done for because there are truths he'll never tell, and the stone threatens to smash like plastique if I don't speak. I'll unpack for you the lede to our undoing since you dragged me from sleep. Only promise once I start you won't look back.

THE UN-WORD, OR THE DINOSAUR IN THE LIVING ROOM

JESUS CHRIST! PLEADS HARRY. He wheels down his window, spits, then jesuschrists again. I could kill that goddam son a yours—I could kill the bastard. Lightin' out and puttin' all this on us. He gazes in my direction when he says "all this," then back at the road. He sets a cigarette on fire and the smell of tobacco burning, cremated's more like it, freaks me out. The smoke tornados across the windshield then breaks into pieces.

She's shaking, Florrie announces, and in response Harry reaches over and backhands me. Cut it out! he yelps, and the woman, the one he habitually refers to as his old lady despite her age, starts crying again. Her look melts in tears.

Meanwhile along Liberty the sycamores spider by, their leaves brittle and crack under bald tires. I can feel the dryrot creeping in. C'mon! Florrie enjoins, now in that steel-plate voice of hers. Pull yer head in, Precious! As if in a momentary lapse she musters her other self, the one she struggles to paper over though it's never far from sight.

I can't help myself—I'm no simpleton. I know the drill. I wait for the softer Florrie to return. Trapped in an arboreal web the length of Liberty I try to read the sky. The branches above slim to threads and end in filigree. In a flash Florrie toggles back to her practiced self as if on autopilot. She reorients her whimpering, so much so that I think her old man's gonna whack her too.

Jake can' help how he is. Just leave 'im be.

We pass under a stone arch with a curtain of ivy chaining by. Yellow bricks line the underbelly of Superior overhead, and the world shades dark as a memory, one trapped under the abutment of the past. To live here in this place, to protract a moment to an age, halt the restless universe, or better yet, back this baby up, say, five, six years—just long enough to alter things, the present most of all, but—. We roll on. We pass below another curtain of green then sail back into the light.

Leave 'im be, Leave 'im be—that's what you always said. And now look 't what you got.

Well things ain't like they use t' be. Things're changed.

The lady's located the sweet spot. I lower my head, spin my neck to the side while she works. Harry exhales. Another cloud of smoke mushrooms up and engulfs us, obfuscating the landscape.

I can tell you one thing, and that is ain't nothin' never change. The more you think it do, the more it stay th' same. That son a yers—he ain't never gonna change his spots.

Well—

—You ruined him.

Me?!

—Well there's a limit. To think a the excuses.

You oughta be ashame.

Me?! Th' hell. You're the one oughta be ashame. It sure as hell weren't me turning out no son like that. Not in a million years.

I know this conversation by heart. If I've heard it once I've heard it a thousand times in the years since Jake vamoosed, left me high and dry. I can recite chapter and verse, what will come next—I feel its immanence. He's your son too, Florrie will wail, and then like well-oiled clockworks her tongue unhinges. Down steal the tears, pained scrunches the face, out flaps the hankie like an albatross, the sniffles winging in air. Harry hacks up phlegm then rolls his window down and spits. Just as quickly he windmills up the glass, sniffs, and Florrie and me look as if in unison past the window, checking the mottled trees as they float by, their skins peeling into the street as if to say exteriors aren't a thing. Harry swerves, unsuccessfully, to avoid an animal shooting from the curb. The guy in the next lane bleats his horn.

Asshole!

Without saying a word, that is with that mute, momentary glance that Harry reads so well, even from the corner of his eye, Florrie admonishes Harry, then retorts, Why don't you watch where you're goin'? You wouldn'a hit that squirrel if you were watchin'.

Florrie's silence from then on all but hurts it's so high pitch, so Harry does what he always does at times like this, he clicks the knob, turns on the happysound.

Ninety-nine point sev-en....

Dis broadcast brock to you by "For-ess Cid-dy Lum-burr" ....

The chippy voices deafen, but not as much as Florrie's no-talk. Harry inches the dial further as the vehicle comes to a stop. A light overhead blinkers off and another flashes on, and once again we're flying, until out of the blue Harry up and cries, *goddam!* The car jerks to the side and he repeats his retort, as if it were news of a death or a touchdown on TV—*Goddam! Goddam! Goddam!*

Hold on, he advises as Florrie cranes toward the spot behind, kittycorner to Harry's side of the vehicle. Hold *on!* Do you hear me?

Ohhh, boy. Ooooohhh booooy.

Hold on! Harry barks once again, as though Florrie possessed no ability to suss the situation on her own. I said just hol' *don!*

We're definitely holding, limed like sparrows to a limb. We're not going anywhere, though other cars hum and stampede sibilantly. I start to stamp my feet, look at the crack where the door should open whenever the car comes to a halt, gaze back at Florrie, panting, then back at the spot where the door should open—back and forth I turn my gaze, stamp my feet. I register my desire in no uncertain terms.

Settle down, Precious! You ain't goin' nowhere.

Goddamit! Don't neither a yous move. An' lock the goddam doors!

Harry slivers himself out the driver's side, barking repeatedly, Stay put! before slamming the door in my face. I tried to make a break for it, wrestle myself from Florrie—I tried to get free—but the old man hemmed me in. I look around and the view out the back disappears. Florrie sighs, moans, Oh, dear lord. Lordy, lordy. Last thing I need on a day like this—. C'mere baby.

It feels as though she might embosom me to death, but then something inside clicks, and just as before she turns cold, and there's no soul in her embrace. A space of mute emptiness opens up within the confines of the car. She seized me, it seems, not to endear me but to cover something up, as though something had slipped out. I kiss her obsessively, whine, and she turns her face away. An age passes before I hear her bawl, Oh, Precious, I can't bear it! It must be a sign from god! She's perspiring in the fall air—I can smell it. Sweat overlaid with essence of orange, hibiscus, and rosewater—

—Oh lordy, why is life so—?

—Who cares? I wonder.

I wanted out—what can I say? But did I persist, did I hound Florrie?

Well, OK, I eyed, I gave her the wet nose, a bit—I admit. I caught the web of clouds and branches overhead parting, the sun showing off some kind of glint, a rarity this time of year—so, yeah, I dogged her. After all, Flo was lost in her lachrymose world, and despite the fact that her face forecasted Armageddon we in fact were headed to Nowheresville, which was fine by me given the world all around. Her fingers were running the beads while her wristwatch *tick. . .tick. . .tick*ed robotically, all the while as free a universe as you're ever going to meet called from outside, enticed, pleaded with us, beyond the glass.

Florrie burps. To be stopped here in this place, the one that always fades by, this long, serpentine park where we never break or stop to look, let alone picnic—god forbid! This place where we only steal by, practically flee—we shoosh. We've passed along here a hundred times if it's been once, with Harry always barking, Lock th' doors! *I said, lock the goddamn doors!*—he always says it the minute our headlights turn toward Liberty Boulevard. Too many a *them* around here, he complains, each and every time we're here, as though on cue, like it's hardwired in his brain, despite the fact that we're just driving—like I say, never stopping by.

Leastwise not until now. We and godknowswhat plans rooted in the heart of man, woman too, are halted, even as the other cars continue to river past. I whine, cry, stamp my feet until Florrie finally comes to. She escapes the tug of her thoughts, surfaces, then pockets her beads.

Enough already with yer jibberjabberin'! she remarks. And then, as if miraculously, I hear the click I've been waiting for.

What the *hell* are you doin'? Harry howls as Florrie jackknifes the door. Stay the *hell* in there! It ain't safe out here. But Florrie isn't paying him no mind.

God will take care.

She and I skittle over the curb then spread out like the spot on the seat, the one I couldn't help given all the fuss. We lace the grass back and forth and Harry shoots after us, though he doesn't want to leave the car sitting like that, a downed duck, floating so far out. His face has that look that foreshadows a conniption, ruby and sclerotic, his forehead furrowed like the brow of god. I look away, first at a shred of moldered paper, then a stray clip of bone. Now here's a flattened can meshed with lines of smog and soot coughed up from the lungs of what was once, over a century and a half ago, unironically minted the Forest City, which I'm assuming reflected the state of things at the time.

Florrie seems as happy as I am to escape that mess Harry's tending to, that and whatever thoughts might have nudged her from her seat. Still I can't help but shoot back a glance, divine if Harry's still there, and I notice the vehicle has its tail still lifted and he's extracting a cross, though not the kind Florrie clings to.

C'mon, Molly, she bleats over the traffic, let's do a little esplorin'. I sense, perhaps even more than she, that I've been granted some kind of reprieve, a stay from my undoing. In the distance I watch Harry bow before an iron crucifix, a truncated swastika, pagan symbol of eternity at a time when patriarchs ruled. He's genuflecting, turning the cross as he does, as though lost in his own version of a meditation, though a service to a mechanical lord. Meanwhile me and Florrie arrive at a lake—OK, hardly a lake. A hollowness. Sooty and gray as a lunar gorge, the crusty floorbed sinking before us for quite a distance. The parched bottom is cracked, like Jesus's tongue as he slumped on the crossbar, as Florrie likes to remind us every time we gaze at the picture on the living-room wall. The lake is like a puncture wound in the landscape, as far as I can see from my vantage point.

I use to canoe here when I was a kid, she reminisces. Midge and me use to come.

But I'm only half listening. The castoffs here are endless. I'm tooling for something a little meaty, fit for an omnivore, though god knows not for Wren or Jake. Preferably not too dry. What I chance upon instead is the stuff of readymades, cadged together by some conceptualtist bent on killing tradition, elevating the banal, some commercially-made nonobject to brandish with a lower-case A. I spy a pacifier, a Crazy Straw, a discarded beret. There's a gat-tooth comb, a Batman toothbrush, and a penny page of S&H Green Stamps. I find a nailpolish bottle that plays host to a spider, a common garden-variety washer, a plastic carnation, and a Barbie head, all deposited offhandedly or dropped unconsciously, like the work of a collective. Not *luxus* but *fluxus* perhaps, the end of the world as we know it.

We come all the way from Forty-Fourth and Bridge.

A rusty nail. A flattened soup can. A streamer from a bike handle—never mind the bits and bobs of mummified food too dry to bother. There's this poor soul too, shriveled and gray and practically guillotined by a spring trap, snagged in a house above or carted here from the suburbs, then tossed from a passing vehicle. Florrie looks at me and I knit my brows.

Now look at it—

Just over the edge of the retainer wall lies a matted diaper that has long ago given up its vapors.

My, my, my. We been by here how many times? Yet still an' all, Molly, it's like I forgit all about this place. I find a rusted heart pendant, a busted Indian bobblehead, and a lead soldier.

Gosh, we use to have fun.

She puts her hands on her hips then pulls them away, straightens her blouse where the hem has inched up the lovehandles. The colored gems adorning her sandals— the glass rubies, sapphires, emeralds, and diamonds—are trying to muster a little sass, but the gray sun only half cooperates. I find a piece of wan bun wedged in a divot but

Florrie checks me, warns, Don' touch 'at! She pulls me away as though I'm about to ingest my own mortality. Further along we find a rusted barbecue with a leg missing, Ahab-style, and beyond that an old mattress and magazine.

What are you gettin' yourself into?! Florrie queries, waking from revery, jerking to the present as if she cared about my wellbeing after all. She chains after me, stands on the rim of the lake like a settler, the mistress of all she surveys, this urban park and the memories it hacks up, and yet she peers at a waste land. She spies the figures in the magazine, the one with pages spread wide as a pair of naked thighs.

Oh, dear Jesus! If he ever would a lived to see this. It would a killed him. To think a the way people abuse somethin' so sacerd. She pauses, shakes her head, and we continue around the edge of the lake. To think a the ones that's gone now. Miss Glasby, Peacoat, my Wrennie, and Jake—well, seem like they're gone—

I stop. I can't unstick my mind from the idea of Florrie invoking Peacoat's name, never mind Wren and Jake's in such a vein, even as I spy Harry retreating into the landscape, into negative space, which Jake is—correction, was—always going on about, during his sketching tours with Peacoat, while Florrie looms larger with each step we take. It isn't like her, I muse, to strike out on her own, but then again as Miss Glasby used to say, You never know what t'expect from a Tuesdy. Meanwhile I chance upon a couple of T-bones, the kind Harry places akimbo on his plate, shooting me a glance as though underscoring a point, though these bones hang on the brink of fossilization. There are leathered bits of pork as well, only partially edible I'm guessing. They're covered with sand and grit, half-archeologized bits of flesh, and yet I still toy with the idea.

Unh-*uh*! Florrie tugs, sucking her teeth. She doesn't even need to raise her voice before I drop the thing. You li'l imp!

Don' even *think* about it!

Well I was only looking—no harm in that. Who wants an old chop the dimensions of a postage stamp after all, a commemorative, tiny portrait on an envelope, featuring the mug of a guy in a wig saying he hasn't begun to fight? Flo explains, It's for yer own good. Like I'm a simpleton or something.

I look up: the sycamores. They stand the length of the boulevard, from end to end, tall bodies ancient as gods, impressively bulky even when you consider the constant shedding of skin. I think it's just me who notices them, but then Jake pipes up in the middle of a conversation, interrupting the flow—Does anything say old world more than a sycamore? The past in the person of a tree.

Why d'you say?

He's sketching as we roll along, despite the herky-jerky path we're on along Liberty, despite Harry's gassing and breaking on account of the ice and flakes unleashed from the clouds. Jake tugs a tattered book from his knapsack and plops it open; it lands immediately on the page he's looking for. He tosses it in Wren's lap.

Take a look—

Oh prutty! It looks like somethin' you did.

You mean somethin' he stole, pipes Diana.

That's not nice.

Well he doesn't draw nothin' new. All he does is rip off dead guys.

Jake peppers another page with a series of lines. Diana comments, Give it up, Jake. It don' look nothin' like the pitcher. The flurry of marks continues until he suddenly stops, yanks the page, crumples, and tosses it on the floor.

Screw you!

No, screw *you*!

Stop it you two! Florrie cranes her head, squinting at the pair from the corner of her eye. For a minute they sit dormant, until Jake can't help tossing in his two cents, the ones no one was asking for.

They oughta put *you* in that place!

What place?

The nuthouse—that's what. He recites the name of the place in the painting Wren has been studying, the one with the sycamores in a row, just like the ones here along Liberty, and she replies, It's a prutty name. Then Jake recounts the story, the one he read in the museum guide.

They're trees, counters Diana. Big woop.

Wren, don' you think it's somethin', that these-here trees are the same ones he painted over there, almost a century ago? Like the whole city is one big nuthouse.

And you're the king nut, issues Diana. All you do is mark up page after page then tear it up. You never finish nothin'! She fingers the ends of her curls, resumes twirling them in the way she did before Jake up and changed the subject to dum-dum trees.

He wheels the window open beside him and looks at the landscape, including the empty lake passing by, as if he's trying to glean something. A flake slips in like some back-door man.

It's *cold,* you idiot!

Wren remarks that when she sees these trees she thinks of a giant cockroach.

A *cock*roach!? exclaims Diana.

You know—like in ol' Prague. It was raining, and the trees were jus' outside his room—he makes a point of it. At least that's what it says. Branches clawin' at his window. The same spotted trunks, shedding their outer layer. Just like this.

Jake muses they make him think a Temeschwar, a city behind the iron curtain.

You two don' know what you're *talkin'* about! You were never in Russia, you lurp, and *you*—jabbing Wren with her finger—you were never in Austria!

Romania.

And Czechoslovakia.

Check-a-slow-whatever!

Diana!

Jake protests that he, Wren, and Harry saw them on *Jim Doney's Adventure Road,* on an installment about a once-German city in what is today a Soviet satellite. In the old part of the city, fronting the cathedral, there's a line a them, over a hundert years old! These are old-world trees for sure, the dead-old world passing, though not without a fight. Trying to hang on—I give you exhibit A.

Florrie comments that nothing good can come out a the Soviet Union. That godless place? Nothin' but empty shelves and long lines—it's a bankrupt state! A bunch a godless people elbowing each other in line at the store, waitin' hours for nothin', a single chicken leg t' feed a family a four. Nothin' like we got here.

Wren remarks that she read a book in school about a guy who was accused of being a spy, after he was captured by the Germans in World War Two. He was put in prison for ten years even though he was innocent, just like the writer, who was sent to Siberia because he didn't like Stalin.

That's a dumb story!

All them Ruskies like Stalin, Harry pipes in. No matter what no book says.

Atheists, all a them!—Florrie shakes her head. No wonder they're penniless. Serves 'em all right.

In Wren's lap lies a copy of a painting of plane trees in St.-Rémy. Like limbs they stretch misshapen, jutting from what looks like snow, or like Satan in the seventh ring, stuck in ice, upside down, head hidden—like the picture in her world lit book. The ankles branch out, the toes scratch the sky, as though, she adds, it were the lid of a coffin. They're Bohemian trees, for sure, insists Wren, trying to mask a grin.

They're th' same ones we saw on *Jim Doney,* Wrennie. Around the streets and squares of Temeschwar, one hundred, two, three hundred years old, though the place is called Timişoara today. Lining the streets of the old world with its ancient beliefs, just like here, the new world be damned. The same ones that put the painter in that place, just cuz—

—What in the world are you two *talk*in' about?!

Jake peers out the window to his right. Wren shifts her gaze toward Jake and the two grin at each other with their eyes in the coded language of twins. Wren returns to the museum guidebook in her lap, the one with a permanent crack in the binding that opens automatically to *Large Plane Trees (Road Menders at St.-Rémy).* Diana clears her throat— *Tit-hem!*—then resumes jostling her curls. I do my best to smooth things over, reach my head and place it on Jake's shoulder, feel his hand absent-mindedly caress my back, shoulder blades, neck, and forehead.

Seriously, you two are clueless. A tree's a tree. Look at it and shut up!—

—A tree's not a tree, especially one that's always shedding its skin, untreeing itself as we speak.

Whip!

Pustulan'! One thing's for sure—you can't help but think a biddy old nuns when you spot a sycamore. You'll be right at home in that place, ancien' as sin.

Like a buncha moozlm women with their hair coverd, pipes Harry.

Retard!

Diana! yells Florrie.

I was talkin' about Jake. Both a them.

Don' ever use that word! To think that Ruby an' Miss Glasby are gonna have to put up with the three a yous.

Well, them two started it!

Wren remarks that it's interesting nuns still cover their hair, and most a their faces, just like some Muslin women— they too were on *Adventure Road,* on an episode about old Hungary.

Th' young ones don't! protests Diana.

But plenny do. Same's they did a thousan' years ago.

Long live the dark ages! intones Jake.

They covered their heads for a reason then, instructs Florrie.

Diana should too! Jake glances at his sister, seated just behind Harry. Do us a favor an' cover that mug.

Wren says the purpose wasn't to cover but to keep men from impure thoughts.

Then she ain't got no worries.

Not another word, either a yous.

You'll make a fine pustulant.

Florrie plants herself on the edge of a reflecting pool gone dry. Something is happening in her head, but exactly what is your guess as good as mine. She peers at the lake bed, dotted with detritus, then belches air that seems to have been trapped since we left Laurentine. A man does more than approach, he purposes by, holds out his left hand while grasping a child's with his right. Binoculars hang down from his neck. Florrie sees the hand but pretends not to notice, as though we were strangers whose paths crossed by chance in a vast, open space. At the point she realizes it would be rude not to recognize him, to ignore the outstretched hand or, worse, just walk away, she stops and starts. After a pause she extends a limp paw.

Meanwhile the man and I exchange less complicated greetings as I mull the fact that Florrie chose to engage at all, however wary she is of doing so without Harry. I give father and child a friendly whiff, though the girl shies away as though I were going to bite. As if to reassure it's all right, father and daughter advance. He kneels and offers a familiar hand, oogles, Molly baby, then adds I'm looking a little—I think wizened is the word he used. Florrie complains, *Wiz*ened—*ha*! Goodness, no, I can' keep up with her. She's into *everythin'*—she's definally a handful. Full a spunk t' beat the band.

Truth be told Florrie pales beside the guy, like a yolk from an industrially-caged hen beside the ones Wren enjoys from her bug-eating brood.

The more they center their conversation around me the more I wonder what I have to do with the three of them, knowing I'm just a diversion. So I break free, launch out on my own while the woman's distracted. I'm amazed at what I uncover as I dodge here and there, evading Florrie and godknowswhat spilling from her, like the memories that jod in my brain, willynilly and out of time. Back and forth they go. I want them to stop, truth be told, allow me to rest a bit. But they motor me away in a memory-car without a driver, a fever dream indistinguishable from the moment.

We're definitely rolling, then we brake. Then advance. The new-budding canopy above casts orange under the streetlight, its top flirting with the low clouds. Below the canopy the half-clad branches diminish the light some.

Jake struggles behind the wheel as though in a fight. He jerks the Valiant fast and then slow and sometimes I, OK not just I but the others too, think we're gonna crash.

The way you drive! Romeo complains in Jake's ear. Here an' there and everywhere—I swear we're gonna *crash!*

Rauch remarks that Jake drives the way he works. Off an' on.

You hush, shoots Cin.

Wellllll? brays Jake.

Yeah, Romeo intones. Jake works. Sometime. Then he disappears.

It's always about you, ain't it, loverboy? Marks grumbles. For two months he splits while we-all struggle to cover his behind, and you're the one complainin'.

The two a y'uns just hush, orders Cin.

Rauch can't help but put his two cents in. Romeo's right, Cin. Where is Jake when you need 'im?

Let it go.

Jake studies the road while the others' eyes shoot back and forth. Well, I'm back now.

I ain't gonna bank on it, Romeo grumbles.

That's all that matters to you, ain't it? complains Marks. What you can bank on.

I was a. . .stone, Rauch intones, in semi-sync with the radio. . . . *If the cause. . .I'd leave. . .on the road—*

You're lucky th' big guy took you back, Rauch mutters, glancing at Romeo.

The big guy, echoes Marks, glancing outside. The big guy.

Shuuuuuud uuuup, whines Romeo.

Won't you just leave the boy alone? pleads Cin.

I was a heart. . .beating for someone—

Like I say, I wouldn' count on Jake.

Don't give my Jakie a hard time, Rom, warbles Diablo.

You call that a hard time? Rauch queries, reaching back and poking Diablo's shoulder. He swivels around fully in his seat then leans close enough to breath in her face and mine.

The Laurentine section of the graveyard shift at Geist Manufacturing jostles back and forth, on tenterhooks. Just about everyone but Jake shoots a look at the light we just sailed through, as though for him each one were green, or as though red were for all the other drivers, or as though he were color blind like me.

We're all just waitin', anyday, for the axe to drop, gripes Rauch. And you pal, you go and nix yourself.

If you only knew the half of it, I think to myself. To nix oneself. Turn oneself to *nichts*. An empty shell—if you only knew.

But the times. . . I say the more—Rauch continues to croon and then stops. It's a miracle the ol' man took you back, he remarks.

Rauch! With a voice like that you better keep your day job, quips Diablo.

The big guy, Romeo grumbles, as though Marks's comment a minute ago just registered.

I'm surprised Jake wanted to *come* back, adds Rauch, filling out the bucket seat next to the driver. He ain't exactly a lover a the nine-t'-five.

Or the four-t'-midnight, as the case may be.

You're a one-track wonder, comments Diablo, glancing at the back of Rauch's head. Like you've made it your mission to set Jake straight.

There ain't nothin' gonna set Jake straight.

Come to think a it, I wonder why th' big guy *did* take you back, muses Marks, glancing at Romeo. No offense my boy, but any a us could run circles around your count. He peers now openly at Romeo. It's almost as though someone's pulling for ya.

Diablo has me on her lap. I can smell the lacquer in Cin's hair next to me, the chalky chemicals rubbed over the bumps of Diablo's skin. I whiff Romeo's cigarette breath as well, all the way on my side of the vehicle. Diablo has a hand on Cin's knee yet nobody notices but Cin and me. Rauch lights a doobie in the front seat that emits a cloud, one that tumbles back and engulfs the five of us. He hands it around.

Want some, baby? Cin offers after taking it, before putting it to her lips.

Not the type, eh? offers Diablo, leaning forward and planting a kiss on my cheek. You're a good girl, aren' you, Mollykins?

Diablo, stop corruptin' America's youth, Rauch hisses, then joins in the lyrics on the radio, *PHIL—FREEDOM!. . . ON A DAY I. . .ON MY KNEES TO A—*

Rauch, you're gonna deafen us all, complains Diablo.

At Rauch's rewording of the song, Marks, usually Mr. Serious, musters a smile. He's shoehorned between Romeo and me, his knees pressed between Romeo's behind and Diablo's knees. Meanwhile Romeo's hands clench the back of the bucket seat in front of him, apparently for dear life, his cheek all but making love to the back of Jake's neck.

The car careens along the boulevard. We don't stop for anything, despite the traffic on Lake Shore, unusual at this hour. I turn to my right and detect the Great Lake stretching out like a reflector, in both directions as far as the eye can see. Finally we arrive at a break in the road, and Jake turns wide then glides down a long, winding driveway to the parking lot we know so well, even at this hour, or maybe especially then, aiming us in the direction of what seems like eternity—over the asphalt we roll. He shinnies the jalopy into a spot between a pick-up and another old clunker, killing first the engine then the radio.

I like that song! Rauch whines, switching the knob back on.

Can't we just listen to the end?

I want *out*! demands Romeo. I've had enough a Jake's drivin'—and this rattletrap!

Me too! Marks concurs, with Romeo of all people. He adds, I've had enough of the butt a this one here, squishin' me.

With a look Romeo distances himself from Marks, as well as the others in the group, as if to say they'd stick out in any crowd, and not in a good way, that his being here was a mistake. Knowing what I do about him I surmise there are other things sticking in his craw as well. To put it another way it's as though a cloud were tethered just above his head, the reasons for which are reduceable to two. One, Romeo is never a back-, always a front-seat driver. And two, something brings him to this gathering unlike all the rest, whether he likes it or not, to this reunion that Cin and Diablo organized—OK, cajoled, shamed, and threatened the others into. "For Jake's sake," I heard her say while Jake accompanied Rauch in the all-night liquor store. Otherwise Romeo wouldn't be caught dead with this group—or in this car.

Romeo groans, We've had enough a that song!—Rauch, open th' damn door! We're packed in here like sardines and that was one crazy ride.

But it only has a minute to go! argues Rauch.

You like it so much you don' even know the words! Romeo complains.

I want out too! Marks demands. He's reliant on his pal Rauch to make a move, crack the door and then remove himself, followed by the rest of us. But he's in no hurry. Put another way, all of us back here make up a chain of sorts, dependent on an errant link, the only one who can set things in motion, followed by Cin, then me and Diablo, Marks—before any of us can hope to get out, with Romeo following up the rear.

Out, out, *out!* cries Diablo.

Back and forth she and Rauch argue in earnest, their usual posture about things, about whether to listen or notlisten to the rest of the song, but also about much more than either's passion or dispassion for any verse—god knows they play the song enough. After awhile I take advantage of the rift Diablo creates when she literally hurls me forward, almost suffocating Rauch. While he's distracted, Cin, on cue, reaches beside him and tugs on the handle, and it's me who flies first from the Valiant like a renegade from the underworld, just as soon as an opening has been created wide enough to fit.

Finally free, it's hard not to feel relieved after that snafu, there at the end, not to mention after being shoehorned in a car pocked and scabbed with rust, its driver-side door bashed in, heaving back and forth on account of Jake's driving, that and the verbal back and forth we can never free ourselves from whenever either Rauch and Diablo or Romeo and Marks are in the mix. But never mind. Again I'm relieved, uplifted even, to be out, despite the late hour, because of what's before us. My thoughts flock to a horizon, liquid and burning from the city lights. Turn toward the sense of a beyond and what it enfolds at the line defining the limit between sky and water, a body pregnant in some sense and about to give birth, be it live or still. Never mind the carbonated clouds overhead, sparked by earthly lights, an omen of sorts after the graveyard shift.

I look beside me and spy Rauch, who was so insistent on remaining in the car but now seems to sport his own sense of wonder, almost a curiosity even. He's speeding ahead of me and everyone else, lumbering, trampling the grass beside the path in the direction of the dunes below—as if all of a sudden taken by an urge. Eyeing him, Marks wonders while turning to Cin, I swear he's never not lookin' for a trick.

Goin' back to the days at St. Andy's. I mean the boys he use
to—

—Spare me! interjects Diablo.

Romeo tracks behind. I glance back and see him eyeing
Rauch as he skulks toward the dunes. He gripes in that FM
voice of his, Oh my god. People are pigs. Look a' all this!

I and the others glance down at our feet, and the otherwise
lofty scene shifts to something prosaic.

Yuck! complains Cin.

What a mess! echoes Diablo.

Marks, immersed in thought, has tooddled along last.
When he catches up with us and the conversation, he
grumbles, My god, it's not the end a the world. What a bunch
a babies.

F-U, dissents Romeo, tracking in front of Jake and kicking
sand at my heels. I mean, seriously. What're people thinking
when they pull this kind a crap? I mean, someone's gotta take
responsability. It's foul, he bleats, surveying the trash hiding
the sand. Why should we have to look at other people's mess?

It's a class thing, instructs Marks, and Romeo shrieks, Oh
god, here we go! He barks, Yeah, they don' got none a that,
the lowlifes. Class, that is. And Cin pleads, C'mon, Rom—
don' get him wound up.

Jake yelps, Never mind him!

Through all this back and forth I manage to keep my
mouth shut. What would I have to say anyway, and would
anyone listen if I did have a view on things? What would a
discussion about a world overrun with debris have to do with
me, Molly? As though nature and I were one or something.

Don't put your bourgie values, lover boy, on the shunned
and shunted.

Khhhhh! carps Romeo. You're a broken record. He kicks a
stick then picks it up, draws a line in the sand, then pointing
it at me fake-hurls it.

Do we have to have this conversation again? implores Cin. We punched out half a hour ago.

Face it, some people're pigs! Romeo squeals. Completely irrasponsible—he glances at Jake while he speaks.

What's a little chazerai?

What if everyone did it? Dumped their crap everywhere like this. What kinda world would *that* be? I'm following the stick in Romeo's hand, eyeing it as he switches it back and forth as if in a wind-up, until he at last chucks it at some distance, but not without batting the air, taunting me. In the shake of a tail I've retrieved it.

Oy. It's not people, Marks jabs, wrestling the stick away from me and hurling it. It's classes.

I trot back this time to find Diablo chugging from one of the green-glass bottles Rauch purchased and Cin passed around. I'll drink to glass—I mean class! She swills the wine, drinks again, then wipes the spillage down her chin with the back of her hand. Here's to the oppressed!

Here, here!

Oh god. Y'all got it figured out, don't ya. Who's OK and who's t' blame for this mess, an' everything.

At that moment Rauch pads back to the group, pleading in that long-grass voice of his, C'mon, y'all, keep it down. I could hear you a mile away! Can't we leave all that BS behind? Romeo, Marks, you're ruining a good—. He coughs, having taken a hit on the cigarette dangling from his hand. The words squeak out like the voice of an insect. Then he takes another toke, holds it, exhales, and once again smoke drains out. You two need an off button. We ain't at work no more.

And yet the conversation, started in another context but not unlike what's in front of us here, keeps rearing its head. I think to myself how the past never really dies, not because the problem at our feet is new—it's more a matter of scale than anything—but because back and forth they battle in wars of some kind, apparently about class, such as everything seems to have been reduced in these recession days, but maybe more about a whole different subject or subjects that I expect never can be explored let alone resolved.

Until finally the group, OK Marks and Romeo, manage by hook or by crook to pry their hands from the talking stick, let it rest a moment, giving us all a breather, only to take it up again, though on an alternate topic, as often happens with those two, after another interlude or two of keepaway between me and them both.

No really, Marks postures after I return from fishing the branch out of the water. They're pacifying us. That's all they're doing.

C'mon out with it! Right here, dares Romeo, huffing and puffing. Let's have none a your games. Tell us how you *really* feel. *"They"*—he crooks two fingers as he blurts the word.

It can't be anything with a singular face, chirps Cin. He doesn't deal in such things. Collectives only.

Don' take him so literal, Cin, snorts Rauch. To put a singular face on it, how 'bout Jake's? That's singular. A cloud of smoke tumbles from his mouth as he belts out a laugh.

Be nice, complains Cin, plopping on the sand next to Jake, patting his thigh. Jake who wore the hurt openly.

Cin, stop playing mother, harps Rauch. Jesuschrist he's twenty-two years ol'.

Don' tell me what t' do. What would you know about mothering?

Rauch's a mother for sure, quips Diablo.

Ha! You should talk.

Let dead dogs lie, you two.

As though it were possible for dead dogs to lie.

My gaze shifts to the heart of the lake, this waterless wonder, toward which Florrie and I make our way. Her friend has disappeared, but not before she spilled all kinds of beans on a host of topics—as I approach I can tell by the look on her face, the guilty expression she gets when she's gone and said too much, about Harry most of all. The way her voice plays the violin while narrating his life. Shedding light on key topics, including his language and view of the world, which includes Donald and Wren. Florrie, the free encyclopedia regarding all things Harry, especially his past, how it affected him, and all delivered in a flood of words. Abhorer of a vacuum she is, and Donald wasn't talking until they were about to part—I could see from a distance. Willing to spill at a hair's trigger she is, without the asking, ultimately in the expectation Donald would respond in kind. Because what in the world did she know, Harry too? About anything? Wren most of all. The kid, their grandkid.

All that aside I can't get over the basic fact of Florrie stepping up without Harry, someone to muffle her the way Jake's public advocate silenced him at the inquest. Harry, who would have nudged her when she'd gone and committed one of the worst crimes in the world according to him, that is shot out the truth, namely that he and Florrie miss Wren?

I couldn't believe it either when she paused her monologue long enough—I spotted it slantwise—to baby-talk the kid, the source of everything in the first place, as though a child were to blame. Oogling her beyond what manners required, before revolving the conversation back to herself, couched as her conversations are in the confessional mode. And since we're on the subject of disbelief, I can't believe many things about today, including the way Florrie, even before the encounter with Donald, took the plunge down here with me, set her bejeweled toe onto that old, overturned bucket, acting as a stairstep to a carriage, then later lifted herself back up in order to meet the two on their own turf, up from that fossil of a lake that seems to be calling my name.

The duo having departed, and Florrie having resumed lugging her guilty thoughts, I'm leading her around the fountain shunted to the side with its massive, rough-crumbling bowl, host to a micromeadow of dandelions, shepherd's purse, and golden alexander.

The water used to trickle down ever so delacately, Florrie informs, running her finger over the stone as she speaks. From the sound of her voice and what I'm eyeing the waterfall seemed less a trickling than a weeping. She brushes the side of her face, then burps. Harry and me use to rent a paddleboat. Nickel a pop. We use t' paddle like ducks and reach our hands out—like this. . . . Like it was rainin' money, a sign a things t' come. Her sandals dodge a couple more magazines, their pages fused, as we continue to circumvent the fountain. She remarks, Whooda thunk it woulda all come to this—whooda *thunk*?! To think you take it all for granite. Nothin' never pans out like you figure, Precious—but what'd I know? I was just a kid.

After having circled around, the group has now landed, and we're ringed in a drunken circle. While we're settled physically though, our idealogues-in-residence are intent on tangoing still. Squawks Marks, raising his chin toward Romeo, He's the one unable t' let dead dogs lie! All that bull about the company going to the dogs because a the aconomy on its last legs.

It's true, cowboy. The country's more like it. Takin' a nosedive fast.

Rauch interjects, I think it has t' do with them foreign bigshots. Suits with greedy pockets, suckin' the life outta us here.

After having the life sucked out of him as well, or was it his wits, Jake chimes in with his own two cents, declaring, It's a paycheck nosedive—referring to what the company offered when they agreed to take him back. Never mind the nosedive a the soul. That starts the moment you're born. He gestures toward Rauch, Any a that left?

The keeper of the light, Rauch begrudgingly strikes a match, and a spark, noticeable from space given the darkness where we've settled, flashes on Jake's lips, as though spotlighting them for a deaf divine. He inhales then leans on the bank behind us. He pulls me close.

Nosedive a the soul, Rauch hisses. Christ sake, Jake, don' make me laugh.

Jake mums like the wind that's died down. He takes another hit from the stub—Molly, he rasps, expelling a thunderbumper at me. My Moll.

Meanwhile the air from Ottawa nips you, even this time of year when winter is technically a goner but which threatens to return. Jake warms me. He was looking at the behind of a barenaked sky, at something really, while I caught out of the corner of my eye a waterlogged shoe not far in the distance.

Shall we do another? Rauch asks, setting another tip alight. I juss happen to have one. Cin croons, Wouldn't that be luverly, and Diablo lilts, Luvvv-er-llly—luuuuu-verrrr-llly.

Lu-ver-ly my ass, Rauch coughs after swallowing a hit.

After taking a puff Romeo croaks, Seriously John, juss what d'you propose? After which Marks rehearses again a position as practiced as religion.

Well, we can't just sit back and take it youknowwhere, juss like 'at. It ain' right. The crap's gettin' worse, and they're not even postin' that bad a loss.

Romeo wisecracks, If I were you, cowboy, I'd be happy just to—

Ha!

—Yeahyeah, we know, echoes Marks. You're a goddam broken record.

Just to—

—Just *to*, adds Diablo.

Well you won't even have a job if they get their way, admonishes Marks. The bastards.

Cin and Diablo glance at each other wide-eyed, as if to remark, Did he just *say* that? To his *face*?

One implores, Let's not talk about it. It's bad karma. It's crappy enough we have to kill ourselves every night—well most a us. He looks sheepishly at Romeo. But another rejoins, It's a bigbig problem, what they're doing—also glancing in Romeo's direction, though their eyes don't meet. Our livelihood's at stake. Damn straight, concurs another. They're out to protect their asses at any cost. By puttin' the pinch on us, finishes a fourth. Meanwhile Marks, the group's Serious Sam, dogs Romeo, even as he addresses the rest of us—You ain't very rational, are you?

Cin sucks on what was a fresh-rolled doobie and that has now become a roach. Her partner, the one Rauch labeled a common devil—not to mention a thief! stealing a person like that—rests close, shivering slightly. She traps the joint in the V of her fingers as Rauch reflares the tip, a tip as bright as a flame from below.

Jake comments while gazing at Marks, None of it amounts t'a hill a beans. Economics schmeconomics, he poetizes. Who really cares?

What would you know, cowboy? To you life's a big joke. Only one you care about's yourself.

Temper-temper, rumbles Marks with his baritone voice.

We're trapped on a sinking boat, jobs on the line, because of a recession, complains Rauch, And you, Jake, you rescue yourself, leaving us to bail on your behalf.

Diablo glances first at Rauch and then Jake. Cool it, you two. Juss cool it.

Leave it alone, echoes Cin. He's back in our loving embrace.

After which, as so often happens in human conversation, after so many threads have been knotted until they reach a dead end, we sit in prolonged, I would say blissful, silence. .

. . . .
. . . .
. . . .
. . . .
. . . .
. . . .
. . . .
. . . .
. . . .

Gazes cast sand-ward for awhile. Then they begin to stir and ultimately rise. Eyes resume darting, rendering the quiet as short as the jay Rauch gave up on finally. We sit waiting for a shoe to drop, and it's Rauch this time who extends his arm and lets it go. He opines, It was those young hotshots they hired from overseas. Education out the behind but can't run a company to save their life. They ended up bumping off all them old farts when they came over, or almost all—glancing at Romeo—the old, diehard white-shirts who never sat college a day—right Rom? Couldn't even write pratically, let alone spell the word college—right Rom? Forget the fact they managed to start a company, built it—ain' it so, Rom? Then these stickupthebutts come falling on us from over *there*, like they was a gift a god, and now look at what we got, our jobs on the brink.

Marks counters, My tuchas, Rauch! That don' make a lick a sense. It's true the new guys are a nightmare, but the homegrown farts were just as bad, the whole damm lot.

Romeo scrambles to his feet now, ready to take on Marks then and there. He bellows, I can take your *tuchas*, no prollem!

To which Marks now springs up, followed by me registering my disapproval at the turn of events. Cin leaps to her feet too, imposing herself—she and I between the two of them.

That's the lover-boy we know, ain' it? sputters Marks, not backing away. Th' apple don't fall far from the tree, do it? If you can' join 'em, beat 'em. Word is about your daddy—

Marks, warns Cin.

I have a right to my opinion.

So do I, cowboy.

Them old farts were only hiding their fangs behind their stupid, DP grins—who said anything about your old man? They were thinkin' about their fancy homes along the lake, featherin' their nests. In the long an' short of it they weren't no better than these new DPs.

I don' live on the lake.

Close enough. The *whhhhole* thing was rigged from the get-go.

Them is fightin' words, whispers Diablo to Jake, looking in Romeo's direction but aiming her comment at Marks. It's one thing for you to vent your spleen, John, but if you don't watch out yer gonna get us *alllll* canned.

Old DPs, new DPs—.

—None a us ain't a DP. Or wasn't once, interjects Cin.

Diablo counters, Don't tell Peacoat that.

OK—'cep' Injuns, Cin allows. An' maybe them too.

Jake looks up and registers the gaffe, issuing from Diablo's lips, having gone and uttered Peacoat's name, around him.

Can' we *pleeeaaase* give it a rest? pleads Cin. I thought we were comin' here t' have fun! But look at us! I mean we haven't been tagether, all a us, in ages!

Maybe never, adds Romeo. Now that I think about it.

What a thrill it's been, remarks Marks.

Really you guys, warbles Jake. Give it a rest.

Romeo looms toward Jake. You're the one bent on forgettin', cowboy. You go tramping off as though I—as though we—don' exist.

Weeeelllll—?

Drop it, twitters Cin, looking to her side. Anyone here would a done the same if—

—We all knew it was comin', ventures Rauch.

Shush, all a y'uns!

We hear nothin' about nothin' except downsizing, and Jake downsizes hisself.

One thing you can be sure of, Marks adds. Is last thing them new guys are gonna do is sack themselves. They'd slaughter the company first, and all a us with it—including you, lover-boy—they'll be goin' after management next, you and yer daddy both, juss to protect their own behinds, though not without robbin' the reserves, doling out big fat bonuses to themselves. For them there'll always be somethin'.

It ain't no laughin' matter, remarks Romeo. Worse recession ever.

Worst recession, ha! Brought on by a crook of a presiden'. A veritable thief.

Watch out, warns Jake. That's his hero. He trains his gaze on Romeo as he speaks.

After all them years a hoarding, rakin' in profit, the company shootin' like a mushroom, then all of a sudden they start the BS about the business collapsin' under it's own weight. That th' fat needs to be trimmed. And that we're the excess poundage—it's never them—god f'bid! Fat cats don't never talk about themselves first when it comes to slimmin'.

We ain't gonna solve any a this now, counsels Cin.

Stop it with the fat references, remarks Rauch. He leans in Cin's direction. Want any? I happen to have found yet another. He asks with that chenille voice of his all of a sudden, as though trying to win himself back in Cin's graces. Save her from solidifying the mistake of a lifetime—Take all you want.

I'll take some, pleads Jake, hankering after the light.

You don' know when t' quit, do ya, pal?

Rauuuch—

Rauch juss wants to save some for the gals, don't you Rauch? comments Romeo.

For da wid-dow wa-dies, mocks Diablo.

Rauch makes a show of kissing Cin on the cheek then grouses, Never mind Jake never pays.

Do you ever stop paying? carps my boy, though no one cracks a smile.

Here's to the end a payin'! toasts Diablo. She pushes Rauch away and slides her arm around Cin. The boy's got a point.

Sitting erect now, Rauch natters, He's so wasted on freebies he don't even know 'is name. But the waves kick up, drowning his comment for most of us here. The breakers encroach against the spit of sand we're on, forcing us to move farther up the beach, toward a band of discarded or washed-up trash that we passed when we arrived.

How can I forget? complains Jake when we've finally settled. He opens his eyes as slowly as a serpent. Demons never stop remindin' me.

As if he'd been mulling all night over the timing, Rauch drones, I miss the good old days when Peacoat—

This time the mention of the name is impossible to overlook. A round of sighs and awkward looks circulates. Oh, Christ, murmurs Romeo. Even I ain't that cold.

We circle around the fountain with its turn-of-the-century, cracked-and-crumbled urn, standing like a monument with contour shapes dancing on the side where figures made their mark once but have been flaked away by weather, smog, and buckshot, a friend to no generation.

The water use to spill from up 'ere, she comments, pointing as she speaks.

She lifts me so I can see. Where a watery burbling welled up, raining into the lake below, the urn is stuffed with earth and debris, including hamburger wrappers, doll parts, and an errant straw, one end pointing toward heaven and the other toward our reality down here, with a column of air between.

These planters use to be filled with petunias and vinca vines. Daisies too. First time I met Harry—

—I look in his direction, toward the place where he bowed before the iron cross a while ago, which has now disappeared. When he dropped it I felt the echo in my bones, as if in waves washing this way and that and bouncing off the urn. Meanwhile Florrie waxes poetically for awhile about her youth, set as she is, statuelike, as though she were embosomed by the past and unwilling to escape it, until present circumstances interrupt.

I hope Harry don't gimme heck. I squirm then leap down. I din' wanna be—couldn' a been—rude. There's no excuse for that, Mama Ruby use to say. The two stand there, Florrie and the shadow of the figure she was talking to. I watch as she rehearses a series of excuses for having engaged him, how she'll justify her actions to Harry, given that lying isn't an option. Maybe a little stretching will do—by the time I returned to her and Donald earlier she'd already unleashed her hankie and started blathering about this and that—What could she do once Harry'd made up his mind? That everything was outta her control—a man is the king a his castle after all. How she missed her Wrennie. That a wife's duty was a mother's sorrow, which never ends. I'm the real victim, I heard her say as I approached. Donald for his part was offering a quarter's worth of consolation, maybe fifty cents, because it was clear she needed reassurance. For which he received little for the gesture in the form of anything to tell his wife, other than the strange likelihood of the encounter in the first place.

As I approached the trio Florrie was already coming to her senses after having made the decision to strike out on her own. She was backing away without offering anything so much as the thought of a visit, solo or with Harry. So the man retreated, though I could tell their departure wasn't without a few tugs of emotion. Florrie and I observe the crumbling urn. Having taken me up again she hugs me while I survey the landscape from that vantage point, scanning for a bite or two. She commences to nibble her cuticles while chaining me to herself, glancing in Harry's direction.

I mean a all the coincidences. Where in the *worl'* did he come from? She peers back to the place where she and Donald met. And now—of all times! Of all the people t' run inta. Though I spose it's his neck a the woods after all.

Why she's saying these things I have no idea, as though I was demanding an explanation. She's fearful of judgment—that's clear—but from me? As though I already had a foot in the other world and was about to meet the grand arbiter. She rationalizes yet again, It's not ladylike to be rude. It always comes to bite you in the behind. You gotta give a man a penny's chance, she pleads, even if—

She holds forth for some time about why things turn out the way they do, about fate versus chance, things ordained by heaven happening for a reason, in a speech as lengthy and persuasive as those times around the dinner table, appertaining to nothing in the conversation to that point, when she used to pipe up and remark that "they" discovered boys who were "that way" were better off marrying a girl and settling down—"they say it's good ther'py." Which always caused the conversation to come to a dead stop. Whether or not good therapy was needed was one thing. It was the abrupt shift I always found interesting, wondering where it came from. The way her thoughts jet-stream just as they are now, regarding the coincidence of the meeting with Donald and the little one, just happening by, just like that, how it begged a charitable attitude on her part, toward a figure I can still see retreating, his daughter's hand in his, binoculars suspended around his neck, up the hill to where Miss Glasby, Ruby, Midge, and Leo used to live. After marvelling for the umpteenth time that god works in the strangest of ways Florrie ceases talking finally and, glancing toward Harry then back, she bids Donald Bye! in a voice as loud as the jalopies rumbling past. Then, as though wanting to get the inevitable over, we start moseying back over the wall, across the crabgrass and debris and toward the Falcon.

We stop at a distance safe enough from godknowswhat. When we're within a stone's throw it's clear Harry's fit to be tied, that he might even spontaneously combust, like the Cuyahoga River not that long ago when a volatile mix of chemicals, spilling from the factories in the Flats, slicked the surface and was ignited by an ordinary August sun, splitting the Forest City in half. Harry's even saying the crying word, and Florrie warns as we approach, I ain't gonna put up with no talk like that, mister. If yer gonna go on that way I'm gonna *walk* back to Laur'ntine, me and Molly both. Or maybe I'll march right up the hill to Wren's.

Maybe Harry doesn't hear because he rifles off the crying word yet again, the word pinging like a phone wire, roost for a murder of crows—it's the one word Florrie says sets the virgin to tears because it degrades god's most precious gift. It's a word that never passes her lips, because it sullies god's great gift, which should be spoken of, never mind engaged in, in a sanctified way, and only within the context of a marriage.

And yet out it flies again from Harry's mouth as he reorients himself to the task at the edge of the auto stream. Fuck, fuck, fuck! School after school of metallic fish shoosh by and disappear, nearly drowning him out. Meanwhile he's lit a red candle, and the flame blazes as it burns a groove in the asphalt. A driver's forced to screech to a halt because there's no place to go. Out of frustration at having to touch her brake she lets out a series of honks.

Fuckin' idiot! screeches Harry, as loud as possible, then speaking the way he does when Florrie isn't around, he adds, What the fuck am I spose to do?

The lady near me falls into a lapse in hearing, as if to say, Let it go, jus' let it—. In some serious way she isn't herself today, though I'm not sure why—she never doesn't hear in moments like this, and she never doesn't protest when he goes on that way. Yet she's doing just that, failing to perceive, which, granted, isn't difficult to imagine, I suppose, under the circumstances, what with all the traffic coming and going and Harry trapped in the worst kind of hell, stuck on this spot along Liberty, and in a newly drycleaned leisure suit, rolling the old, dirty tire from the trunk of the Falcon, the one that he repaired after a blowout because he didn't have enough to buy new, the one that will make it possible for us to get going again—Paff! it bounces on the street as he picks it up and drops it in a test, then backs away to protect his suit. He exchanges it for the tire with the flat edge which he's already lugged to the trunk.

Goddammit! he yells, abandoning his task and rushing toward us. What the hell were you doin', talkin' to *him*?!

Florrie backs away. He was very polite, she explains, increasing her distance. There ain' no excuse for rudeness.

The hell! You oughta know better. Talkin' to him like that! You're worse than a kid.

Well he weren't nothin' but nice.

A regular, first class—

—Harry! worries Florrie. At home's one thing. But not down here—of all places! One a these days you're gonna be sorry.

The hell—

—Wren said it's not even a word, that it ain't even in the dictionary. Well, never mind. He seem perfec'ly nice. He says they're all settled now.

[Somethingsomething], says Harry. Shall we say I couldn't hear?

Seriously, Harry. He was tellin' me about the way he walks the kid down here every afternoon, to look at birds of all things, under these grand trees, after he picks her up from school. I din' even know there were birds here, did you? And he was talkin' about the trees. Victory planes—that's what they're called. He knows more about em' than we ever did. There's a nice sound to that, don't y' think? Vic'try planes. Like it's a play on words. They come up with the idea even before the boys come back from the war over half a century ago. Imagine that. He says they din't dig the lake til later though, in the twenties. D'you even remember what this place is called?

Who cares?

I'm serious—I forgit too. Funny, ain' it? Midge and I use to come here all a time as a kid, and I never know half a what he tol'. Or maybe I did but don't no more. You get up every morning and you carry some things, others jus' fall away, like off th' earth. Like they never happen—they desert you, Harry—gone. Jus' like 'at.

Let's get the hell outta here. After snapping on the hub Harry returns to the back of the car, slamming the hatch gently despite his mood—as if it's the only baby he's got left. Then he rubs his hands with the rag he keeps for moments like this. He tries eliminating the smudge on his palm but it's stubborn and won't budge, so he gives up, walks the staggered line on the other side of the car and orders Florrie and me back in the vehicle. The two are speaking in an increasingly normal register now from opposite sides of the car.

Grab 'er! he orders, raising his chin toward me. You don't want her gettin' ran over.

Florrie remarks, It's all a sign—everything. That we should abandon our plans and head back to Laurentine. Do we really gotta go?

Diana'll have a fit.

Still, Harry, she'll understand about this happenin' an' all, that we just couldn't go through with it. She gazes at me as she speaks then lifts me against my will.

Let's get it over with. Last thing I wanna do is hang 'round here.

Florrie's quiet for a time, clinging to the curb, unwilling to move—she's keen to discuss something. Don't you even remember back then? she pleads.

Back when?

We're in the car now, sitting and peering out the windshield.

Wayback when. You an' me.

Harry glances at Florrie. Way back when's the thing. What's the point?

But Harry—

Don' Harry me. He puts the keys in the ignition and the engine sparks on.

Florrie tears up and Harry barks, Enough a'ready! Don't get yer britches in a twist. Nothin' ain't never gonna change.

Who's talkin' about change? Who's sayin' anything 'bout that? I'm talking about the pas'.

Well, look a this place. *They*'ve gone and took it. Past, presen', an' future. Stole it all. A army a sharecroppers from the south come and ruin it. Ever'thing we had—a good life! They stole it all.

That young man din't do nothin'. He knew all about this place, goin' way back, all the way to the time you and me—. He was telling me about some bird called a kinglet, that he couldn' even see—but he knew it was there cuz a the sound. He said it's a straggler, after the peak migration.

Don't let 'im fool you. He's part a it, him an' his whole fam'ly. Everything that's wrong with this place.

But he know all about it. More'n me. Don't that say somethin'?

Let's get outta here.

I'm looking in the direction of Liberty's arid sea. Even Harry is too, as if he can't avoid its pull. Then we hear a thud—a *ka-thut!* is more-like—a distant cousin of Peacoat's thumb, thwapping the side of his guitar, paired with the lurch of our bodies forward. When we turn around Harry yelps the crying word again, and Florrie cries, Stoppit! Then she turns too.

Jesus Mary and—

Again Harry repeats the crying word.

The cars, which were used to sluicing with the current, clearing our vehicle, are now starting to snag as in a net. In no time they're pooling in large numbers—caught they are with nowhere to go. They straddle the length of Liberty. Car horns start to blare. The two cars, ours and the other involved in the crash, sit perpendicular to the flow of traffic.

Peacoat's lost, echoes Rauch, glancing at Jake, who appears to have nodded off. I think he run off for good. Which is weird. God knows he didn't have no enemies—well, OK, maybe one. He and a couple others gaze at Romeo, as though waiting for space debris to fall in a fireball, right in the middle of the group, that or an explosion from Jake. But it never comes.

We use to pal around all a time, adds Diablo, gazing toward Jake and judging the coast clear. Me and Cin and him. He was still the same guy, it's just he—

—Same guy, my ass, complains Rauch. He use to be such a good *deal* a fun. Trust me. But then he changed once them holyrollers got 'im.

At least we saved Jake. Cin pats his thigh.

Or unsaved him.

A muffled chuckle circles the group.

Ha! "Unsaved 'im."

Maybe you did, maybe you didn't, I think to myself.

Well, he probly had a little too much fun back then, declares Diablo. He could outdo all of us. Maybe he was just takin' a rest with all that hallelujah stuff, taking a rest from us too. It ain't a crime.

It's true, affirms Cin. He could outparty any a us back in the day. Maybe he did need a break. Maybe he had second thoughts about his life here.

Maybe he was waitin' for the secon' coming.

Who doesn't want a secon' coming?

You. . .shush! Everyone but Jake erupts in laughter, including Romeo.

Skipped out to figure things out.

In search of a different mounting-top experience.

C'mon you guys, it's serious! It's unlike 'im, and I miss him.

I miss him too, complains Diablo.

He became a comp'ny man, complains Marks. That was his downfall. Once Bradford got at him that was it.

Maybe he grew up, s'all, suggests Cin.

No it was Bradford. All that Jesus mumbo-jumbo, the mind control—it change Peacoat.

Jake raises his head. I'll kill the next one that mentions his name. He pulls me close, roughs the nape of my neck. What the hell would they know? he mutters in my ear, as though we were in on something.

I spy the shoe again, no more than fifteen, twenty meters away. I break free from Jake's clutches and venture off in the direction of a toe, pointing at me. Leathery and black, especially in this light. I trot closer, give the thing the once-over, heel too, arch, and instep. The eeldark flesh of the legs, arms, and torso, jellying out, once held in by a firm border that has now become permeable, prey to the elements, a porous contour easily crossed. I lickitysplit a return.

Jake! I motion. Jake! He reaches for me once again—

My Moll. . .Moll, Molly, Molls. Don' ever leave me, baby.

I break away, approach Diablo and Cin. I address them—Former Ladies of the Convent!—never mind how long it's been—we speak a similar language—we women can handle things better'n these louts, and I got a doozy for you, just meters away. Won't you listen?

The two enthuse, Molly baby! simultaneously, like a couple of choristers, then laugh—Owe me a Coke. How are you dear heart?

Such a cutie patootie!

Save it, I reply. I got something of immense—. But I leave them be. Marks, Romeo—even you Rauch! Anybody!

But nothing. They show affection in spades, almost as if I were a person, one that just happens to be mute. A dark lady that never speaks. It's sweet and all, the way they cutiepatootie me, offer attention on one level while ignoring me on another. It doesn't requires an ear, just an eye for gesture. They cassandra me, incapable as they are of grasping an idiom other than their own, but are they really trying? Instead they mollymollymolly me, wear my name out. Even Romeo, in his way, everyone but Rauch for whom I simply don't register.

When I pad toward Jake he again pulls me close. He continues to peer or halfpeer at the the cloud-bottoms with vacant eyes, a vacant soul too, lately, facing the great navel above—Mollymollymolly, he sighs, as though I could crack the code on what's up there—. How can I reply, A giant vacuum? But more to the point I'm focused on what's at our feet, right below our noses on this trashed patch of earth, so near it's practically on top of us.

Cin declares, Why don't we start a fire? and Rauch, keeper of the flame, in solidarity replies, Capital idea, my dear. You find sumpin' and I'll torch it.

You go—I'm *coold*.

Why don' somebody else do it?

There are no takers initially, until Jake rouses himself from semi-consciousness and moans, *I'lllll* go. I need t' pay my respects to mother nature anyhoozy. C'mon Moll, he mutters while lifting himself from a horizontal state. The two of us shamble over the debris and down the beach, horizontal to the edge of the lake, though we're tracking in opposite directions.

Not that way, Molly—over here!

I wanted to head east, in the direction of the shoe, the foot—whatever—but Jake is lumbering west, toward the place we used to meet Romeo—how many times was it and how long ago? Too many and too long to guess. He's kicking up sand in the direction of Romeo's ghost in a sense, a kind of Romeo-void, while the still-embodied version traces not far behind. In fact I wonder why he wants to tail us given the blow-up last time we were here, the three of us alone except for a zoo-full of animals, but there he is, shadowing us. Even if he weren't physically present and gaining on us, he'd be haunting us still—OK, he'd be haunting Jake, and me too in a way given how memories write themselves on a place, indelible as a tattoo and impossible to avoid.

The two converge now, stand beside each other in the manner men do without uttering a word. Jake sends a stream that is exed by Romeo, like two coyotes marking the spot. But it doesn't take long to realize it isn't like before when things were a whole other kettle of fish. They glance at each other while nature does its thing and I read the shorthand in their gazes—you don't need words to say the most complicated things. On the contrary—what's going on is read easily enough. Namely that tonight makes it clearer than ever, no matter what either of these two might have wished or half-wished, hoped or half-hoped, dreamed or half-dreamed, that they could resurrect things-as-they-were. Jake knows the terrain better now, for one, in contrast to before; I sense it dawn on him that the old Jake isn't the one standing here, never mind the fact they're both there. The old Jake couldn't be resurrected even if Romeo could split himself in two, lead a parallel life, pre-Peacoat and pre-marriage, rewrite what happened next to these breakers, concrete monstrosities dropped here to hold back the lake. I get the sense too that Romeo's looking for some spectral Jake, which is no doubt why he chose to come here in the first place, waiting for a chance like this, not to change things but to pick up where the two left off. Jake would have never agreed to come if it were just the two of them.

Again I want to say, you're headed the wrong way, the two of you. There's nothing here if you're looking for old heroes, west of the group, under the fake orange of the streetlights atop the cliff, shadowing our steps as we tumble over nature and culture's debris, the spume and driftwood, rotting perch, carp, and lake trout, mixed with the glory of industry. There's the waveground glass and rusty pipes, the ubiquitous plastic and occasional wad of TP. Romeo all of a sudden seems to overlook all of it, his eyes trained on what's before him.

Nothin' big enough here to bother with, Jake comments finally. Nothin' to make a decent fire. He's recalling their mission and in doing so breaking the silence. Clearly on edge, even on the verge of nervousness, Romeo reaches forward and plants a kiss on Jake's lips—he grabs my boy's crotch.

We need t' go back.

I motion mutely—Let's go the other way! But Romeo persists, clearly on a mission. Let's go that way, he motions, farther in the direction of the past, which seems to have turned to sand.

We could only find this dried-up thing, Jake explains when after an age and no small struggle we finally return to the group. He drags a holiday cast-off, discarded over the cliff, and rolls it into the center of the ring. Aleast what's left of it.

That's one sad tree.

Burn it! Rauch rejoices.

It's better'n nothin'.

Out comes a match, but winds are blowing from Ontario, and the flame whisps out, like a dashed lover's breath. Another try, another snuff-job. Then another. I want to comment that this seems to be a site for snuff jobs, for lost sparks of one sort or another, but I leave it be. Jake's still so close to some kind of edge, his brain steeping in too many realities to process much, snuff jobs most of all—

—Can we get a little light down 'ere?

Lemme do it, yelps Diablo, and in no time all of us here from the graveyard shift, plus one, we're burning.

Cin comments, Leave it to a lady, and Diablo crows, Here, here! Study it an' weep boys. Then she adds, with not a little bit of pluck, Jackie, come to think of it. . .we never see you with yer sketchbook no more.

His eyes close.

To be honest all a us use to make fun a you with that thing, your face in it all a time. At work. In the lunchroom. In the bars. Drivin' us all crazy, tellin' us t' hol' still. Yellin' will you please hol' still! In that rattletrap a yours in th' parkin' lot. Everwhere. And now—nothin'. Like it died with the Jackie we use to know.

The one that drove y'all crazy.

If Peacoat were here he'd play for us, Rauch rasps, affected by the smoke he's been taking in—he says it quietly enough for the dead to hear. Jake covers his ears.

Well, who could take that holyroller music he was into? carps Marks. Oy! That sappy, religious crap. And t' think a how he kicked ass in the days before, the stuff he use to play.

Rauch rejoins, That Monny Carlo a his weren't just a car—it was a pleasure dome on wheels. We use to pull up at work on a Monday at three-forty-five and it was anyone's guess who'd pile out. Diablo glances at Cin. Whoever it was, the lot hadn't slept a wink, all weeken' long.

Can it.

Don' be a demon.

That was then.

And—I mean, we all go t' Sandusky for a couple weeks and return to find he ain't th' same. Talkin' a whole new language. Dressin' and lookin' different. Like some kind a zombie.

No fun at all.

God forbid he wern't no fun, grumbles Jake. It's unamer'can.

Don' be judg*mint'l*.

Well you, Rauch—you act as though it's the only thing that matters. Gettin' off one way or another. With this one or that one, girl or boy. When you're not workin' you're—zonin' out. Or workin' the dunes. An' mos' a time you're doin' both.

Flakes ramp up, then fall. White felt splinters from some iceberg in the sky, as if to inundate us. Put on the dafroster, advises Florrie, as if Harry's reflexes aren't honed to a sharp enough point. As though, to put it baldly, he doesn't know he can't see.

Whose drivin', you'r me?

But the visability. We're gonna wind up in a accidint!

Th' visblty, nuttin'. Harry takes a swig and rests the bottle on the seat between his thighs.

The eyes of each of us not on the banquette in front are trained on the black beyond, on the windshield too with its ice layer encroaching from the world out there. The group of us in the back huddle, trapped as we are in this fun-house on wheels. Behind the tempered glass we advance, not unnaturally fast but unnaturally slow. The car behind honks and Florrie peers at Harry.

Lemme drive—.

Wha'd'y'mean?

For all of Florrie's pins-and-needle grins in our direction, her glances toward us in the peanut gallery, not to mention her repeated belching—Everyone OK back there? You doin' Ohh *Kay*???—for all her uneasiness it's difficult not to notice the beauty of what's beyond the glass.

It's pretty! declares Jake, breaching the usual wall of silence in the car during times like this, when matters outside and in have converged in an uneasy quiet despite the fact that no one has ever commanded, Don' nobody talk!—or, Not a word!—or, No more idle chatter about trees, kids, while Harry and these road conditions conjoin in this way. No, no one has ever-never to my mind stated such a thing, though a cloisterlike quiet reigns, during what has suddenly become a slippery winter ride. Diana's jibes and Jake's rebuttals have ceased, his and Wren's both, including the chatter about the painting at the museum, that marble marvel, the beaux-arts beauty that we're not far away from at the moment. Even the comments about Diana getting the divine call—all of it has been snuffed by something no one can name, let alone express out aloud.

Ultimately it's Jake who breaks the silence. He tables his usual trash-talk about the Forest City, the comments that cause Wren's eyes to top like the banks of the Shagaran River during the thaw—his bad-mouthing, which he throws down just about every time we pass along Liberty, either on our way to Gramma Ruby or Doctor Feher's, dissolving as he does in grumbling about the failing of not just this place but the whole metropolitan area, which stretches from Plymouth-on-the-Lake to Sandusky and which everyone knows includes Laurentine. He carps not so much about the age and condition of the buildings, the trash everywhere, the plywood-treated windows up the hill, but of a fatal flaw unique to the entire area, maybe the state or the region, in a series of complaints that fall away only when he visits the museum, when he should've been in school. But not tonight.

I agree it's beautiful, Jake, asserts Wren. I don' know why you'd think otherwise.

Whatever, replies Diana. Are we almos' there?

Wren, let's get out and walk the rest a the way. Check out the lake.

Kid, yer'n id'yot.

Harry.

With all this snow, it's so pretty! Jake swoons, having put his sketchbook to rest, apparently because of the lack of light, though it also could have been the developing situation outside the car. But now he's enthusing about the glow that patinas everything, the frozen-candle warmth from the streetlights. He declares it's a moment when everything on earth—when nothing needs altering. When whatever is, is all right.

Diana wonders if Miss Glasby's gonna make potroast, and Wren replies, I hope it's p'tata salad!

P'tata salad!? Only retards think that's a meal.

Diana—

Jake concurs, I love Miss Glasby's p'tata salad!

If it ain't potroast I hope it's ham.

I can tell Jake isn't focused on the menu though, including his usual complaints about the lack of nonmeat options, reducing him and Wren to bird food. Honestly the boy's had a look about him today, unlike the pout he usually sports when we're driving to Ruby and Miss Glasby's, which is to say Leo's as well. Indeed, he hasn't been himself since last night. It's true he parrots his usual complaints, that he doesn't like going to Gramma Ruby's, and that he, like Wren, the two of them, object to the meat fest.

But I rully like it tonight.

I like it anytime, Jake.

Howd I evr endup w'the two a yous?

Daddy.

Who ast you two?

It's like a world reborn, Jake suggests with a lilting voice, mooning over the glow of everything, the silvery darkness brought on by the glow of the streetlamps on what has become one of the snowiest nights of the year. Jake with love liquor in his eyes, caught in the midst of the storm.

Wren repeats, Jake, I prefer it here. More'n Laur'ntine.

Yer a id'yot lil' girl.

She's your—

—Who'evr hearda sucha thing, an' frm my ownkid? After all we—

—Never mind.

After turning off Liberty finally and driving a ways on Chester, Harry trains the wheel in the direction of the flakes. We creep a few blocks, make a pitstop at the corner store the way we always do then retake our way, catching every light until finally we reach the *K&M Tool & Die* and *National Fittings Co.*, the signs we've been looking for. Under thickening ice their opposing shipping bays threaten to eat us as we slide here and there. Despite that, Harry struggles nonchalantly with the wheel, along the lines of going with the flow, because his uncle taught that lesson early on, at thirteen, just after his father died— Always turn the wheel in the direction of a skid. How many times have we heard it said during times like this? The upshot of which is there's nothing for a driver to do because you should just go with the flow. Do that and everything's fine.

So here we are at the entrance to Ruby and Miss Glasby's street, threatening to slide into either the *K&M*

or the *National,* until somehow, miraculously according to Florrie, we make it past the shipping bays, managing to hold our ground without losing a shade of our crew. We pass along the red, brick street, a road low on its luck on a good day. Once-proud structures watch, their window screens askew, some boarded against the elements, and the cops. Harry does his best to navigate this remnant of the streetcar era with its rails still ribbing the center, stiffening the road like the whalebones in Miss Glasby's corset, the one she wore in a different era that she keeps in her drawer, still, only to bring out when Wren requests yet again, What was it like back then, auntie, when you were my age? Meanwhile we've passed the main obstacles but the Falcon with its balding tires still slips here and there as it rumbles over the paving stones, the ones so uneven the plows avoid them on nights light this.

Thank god, murmurs Florrie when she eyes the drive— Thank you, Jesus! She burps air in earnest now, having caged it—it's been over an hour and forty-five minutes, for a trip that usually takes us twenty, twenty-five minutes, max. The car veers left, glides, and then slides. It lurches into Ruby's driveway just inches from—OK—*tut!*—right up against Midge's bumper.

Harry sighs, Ohhhhhh Kaaaaay, fumbling as he does with the door handle.

We glance at each other in the back.

Ain' you gonna turn it off? Florrie queries, opting to sidestep the matter of the bump.

Once inside, shoes stomp the mat. Harry steadies himself against the wall, and the rest shed the snow, the car karma too.

Jake, don't fergit to clean Molly.

Mollykins! enthuses Midge, approaching us. Come 'ere girl! Give us a kiss!

I oblige her excitedly whether or not I—

—How are you Molly dear? inquires Ruby too. Good to see you.

They pass me around, and I kiss one and all since it's my job. I aim for the lips but end up with a cheek, a chin, a forehead, or a neck. Already I know what we're having for dinner.

How're you mama? Florrie asks, peering at Ruby.

Leo breaks in and performs Hellllloooo, bowing and smiling with the sincerity of hired help.

No complaints, returns Ruby.

Leo, put a shirt on, Midge orders. He's prancing about with a rug on his chest. No peach-fuzz lad like Jake, he's more like Harry, though half his age. And take the coats!

Is Miss Glasby here? queries Wren, and Midge replies, In the kitchen, Wrennie dear.

Nice shirt, interjects Leo, glancing at Jake when he hands over his wrap.

Don' be mean, exhorts Midge. It's cute.

Me and Wren circle Midge as she limps toward the couch, toward anywhere she can take a load off. We make a beeline toward the kitchen at the back of the house. The scent thickens as we tool along the length of wainscoting in the hallway, Wren flapping her fingers in the grooves as we pass, the countless layers of paint under a 2-D riot of pansies, poppies, and roses just above. At the far end of the hall we spy Miss Glasby bent over in the frame of the door, basting a bird, the roaster blackened from use, witnessing decades and the demise of hundreds, maybe thousands of fowl.

We brought Molly! announces Wren, and Miss Glasby, catching her hand on the side of the sink as she straightens, replies, Yes, dear, I see.

Help me with this, will you, Wrennie dear?

Tasked in that way, Wren of all people takes the frayed potholder from her hand and coaxes the bird back into the heat; the door complains as she wrestles it shut. Miss Glasby leans, steadies herself, then lengthens her back.

Good to see you, Wrennie dear. She extends the lips that Diana says remind her of death, and Wren kisses her in return. Here, she says, turning over a neatly-ribboned box. I brought you this!

I abandon the two, realizing only pleasantries are on offer and nothing edible, after which I happen on the insular world of Leo's room, halfway along the hall where the boy regales Jake with his physique in wordless ways. He dumps the coats on an unmade bed, struts and flexes his muscles, extends his crop of chest hair, showcasing it. He stretches fingers at the end of two dark arms, shows off the ring that he—not just he but Romeo too—recently got, a band that weds them in a way, in a society of men, the real kind and not, Leo implies, some facsimile like Jake.

It's for life, trumpets Leo, showing off the ring again. It's mine. No one can ever take it away. It ties the knot between him and posterity as well, he implies, a fact memorialized in the names on the plaque in the Hallway of Champions at Saint Andrej's, just beside the principal's door.

We were ten and O!

When 're we gonna eat?

It's only turkey.

Diana saunters in and queries, Who's a turkey? Must be Jake.

Leo glances toward her then repeats, Nice shirt, Jake. He says it's more for a girl—Isn't it?—and Jake addresses Diana—Get thee to a nunnary!

Turning to his cousin, he comments, No really, Leo, that's great.

The latter persists—the games the wins the games the wins—Leo Romeo, LeoRomeo, leoromeoleoromeoleoromeo. The two sparkplugs of the team, explains Leo in so many words. And, Words words words, Jake seems to say—I know that look. Romeo, Leo's bosom pal.

Diana's gonna be a pustulant, Jake announces.

Jake!

Florrie and Midge mosey in. Diana dear? *You*?! Who woulda ever—?!

Diana swears she's gonna kill Jake—He wasn't 'pose to say!

Florrie remarks, Well never mind. It was just a matter a time *any*way, and the women start to back out of the room—we hear Ruby calling them. Jake? Midge inquires before leaving. Did Leo show you his ring? But before he can reply she steps back in, reaches her head back so her face is aimed toward the parlor where Florrie has already taken a seat—Flo, come back an' get a good look a this thing. The boys got their rings!

After some muffled dust-up with Harry in the parlor over the goods he picked up on our way here, Florrie lumbers back along the hall, though she seems to have left her head behind.

How nice. She takes Leo's hand and raises her head as though she were wearing bifocals. Good for you—Jake, how could you?

How're things in the Glee Club, Jake? inquires Leo, and my boy responds, I'm not—. But Leo cuts him off, belly-laughing to distraction, and Midge yells, Harry! Come an' see Leo's ring! Show Harry the ring, Leo, and Harry counters from the living room, Cn I git a ope'ner?

Glee Club, Art Club—whatever, remarks Leo. What in the world are you gonna do with that? You can' make no livin' from it.

We're about to eat, announces Miss Glasby, passing by on her way to the living room, in a voice reminiscent of a ghost. Come take your place.

Come 'n' pick yer seats, quips Harry, tooling toward the kitchen for an opener. So we cn eat.

Leo, how many times I gotta tell you, put a damn shirt on?!

It's hot in 'ere. One thing I ain't puttin' on is no shirt like Jake's. It's for a girl.

If you're hot then open a winda.

It's like some trickster arrived and rearranged the scene. The flow of traffic is halted, though it isn't supposed to be like this—even I know that. It's all jowled up with nowhere to go. The cars screech in waves to a halt. They honk like geese though nobody's flying—we're all earthbound.

Stay back! cautions Harry. An' keep her the hell outta here—pointing at me. He charges, his pinstripes pointing to heaven, that place Florrie prays to, pointing down, too, toward the place Harry claims he's headed, where he swears he's already got a foot in. Watch yourself, frets Florrie, but Harry isn't listening. He's in the middle of the cars now, disappearing from sight.

I try to get Florrie to advance a little—C'mon! You an' me. . . . It'll be OK. Really. I'm no simpleton, I know the drill—I understand the deal of an object in motion arrested. There's nothing moving here, neither the river of traffic nor Florrie now for some reason. Like she's decided it's best to do as Harry says, stay put where we are, though I flank right as far as the tether allows to get a look at what I might have missed. I whine and cry some, so Florrie picks me up, then I take notice of the mechanical sound that casts a spell on me, making me howl—I can't help myself. It's been working its way toward us for some time, growing louder, to the point of being ear splitting as it makes a path among the welter of cars, like fish caught in a trawler's net, revolving lights circulating above the cab, coming toward our car and that of the stranger who smashed into us. An old man hobbles from between the vehicles when the first man in black ventures toward us, a man who's several shades darker than Jake in the summertime and who makes Harry look as pale as the unwatered grass in our lawn. The other driver too. Round and round the darker man goes with Harry circling behind. Another siren approaches and then another. More dark men, a coffeecream too, bringing together the two blades involved in the crash. Together they present an array of tones on a spectrum, leading me to observe that for all I hear about black and white, I don't see a single one here who fits the description, except for me, and living in a world of no-color I ought to know. Instead they're all, every one, some middle tone along a band of gray. But never mind. Back and forth they shift, and Harry is taking the lead all of a sudden. He shows one of the men the black marks in the road. He kneels down, points to where the flame burned and where it flickered out, touches it, sniffs his finger, and lifts the remains of the light.

I see a breaded wing I didn't spot before with nothing but a bite or two out of it, cast from the window of a vehicle on the move. I consider it seriously, strategize how to nab it, but when I jump down and try to make my move Florrie jerks me back—Leave it! she barks, then scoops me back up. I look down—the morsel's only feet away—and start to cry, and Florrie replies, Never you mind, Missy.

It's not my fault, assures Harry when he rejoins us finally, as though we were accusing. That walking stiff over there got the ticket, thank yer lucky stars.

Thank you, Jesus. Is he a'right?

The ol' fart's shaken up is all, but he should a been watching where he's goin'.

We got a call the 'surance company when we get back, remembers Florrie aloud, and Harry replies, No way!

All they gonna do is jack the bill.

Well lord knows we can' afford that.

It's totaled. Frame bent like a pretzel. I guess it was a piece a crap to begin with, that old thing.

Even if the guy's got no 'surance can't we get a little cash outta 'im? Florrie sets me down, having punted the wing out of distance with the side of her sandal—it took a few tries.

The old codger don't even got two sticks t' rub. Before the fuzz even got a chance to ask, first thing come out a his mouth is, I ain' got no money.

Well what a we gonna do?

The fuzz is gonna call a cab.

I mean about the car.

It's dead. We ain't gonna do nothin', 'specially not this late in the day. The fuzz is gonna call a cab and were gonna go home, simple's 'at. While the two talk on, a pair of tow trucks work their way along the shoulder, up to the plot of grass where we've been standing on the sidelines.

Florrie peers at me. What about *her*?

It's gonna have t' wait after all.

Florrie bends down, reaches toward me, kisses my face— she Preciouses me. Bless the lord, she chants. Bless the lord! Then she turns serious: What're we gonna tell Diana?

Harry replies, We gonna have t' think about that. Come up with a plan.

Don't you think we should a tried to get somethin' out a that guy?

Did you see the rattletrap he's drivin? You seen how he's dressed. Y' can't squeeze water from a rock. What's done is done. Even god ain't gonna change nothin'.

Maybe the guy ain't as down's he seem—ever think a that? You can't judge a book by the cover.

But he's a union man. He tol' me. All you gotta do is look at 'im to see he ain't got two pennies t' rub.

The street's still not clear. The men in black continue to hold the cars at bay while the two crumpled vehicles head toward and away from the freeway, in opposite directions. Overalled men descend from tow trucks and slide their brooms over the road before driving their rigs where all the glass had been. *Shuuuuuush shuuuuuush shuuuuuush* move the bristles over the metal bits, glass shards, dandelion fluff, and grizzled leaves on the pavement, that and the remains of a squirrel, flattened by modernity in a sense and dried like jerky, coming toward me. I jump away from Florrie's arms when she tries to take me up again, having spent a fortune in energy, squirming to get free in the first place. I see better here, closer to the earth.

Come here you imp! Florrie orders. But I'm at the side of the boulevard, heading toward the thick of things, sussing the situation for myself—who knows what might be in that pile?

Get the hell back there! carps Harry from the yellow line, his usual good humor swept away with the debris. Did the fuzz call a cab or not?

Diablo remarks, Peacoat was jus' findin' hisself. She swears, I'll always have a soft spot in my heart for 'im. He's the one brought us together—gesturing toward Cin. Never mind the way he turn out at th' end. She glances at Jake who appears zonked as Peter in the garden, unable to prop his head for love nor money. Oops, she whispers. Well. . .never mind. I hope he found what he's lookin' for.

For that we pray.

You pray, Cin? chides Rauch. I thought you abandoned that ages ago. Way you did me.

—Leave it—

—It was a comedown, that crap Peacoat was spoutin'.

Diablo studies Jake then ventures, He was a dear heart if ever there was one. We'll always be kindred spirits, even if he backslid a bit. Later on, during the car ride back, she'll smile as she repeats to Cin, *sotto voce,* the joke she made despite herself—Even if he backslid a bit.

Who cares, asserts Romeo cynically.

Who cares, echoes Cin ironically.

Who cares, repeats Rauch sincerely.

Who does care, ponders Marks philosophically.

No really, *who cares?!* asserts Romeo, dead-seriously. The hell with y'all! Why d'you always go on about *him?* he grouses, looking at Jake. He storms off in the direction of the surf.

He's gone and left us, Diablo laments. Peacoat, that is.

Disappeared from the face a the earth is more like it, Marks observes. No matter what—he was our buddy. He jus' vanished.

The fire goes out finally and dark returns. If only Peacoat were here to get us something to burn, insists Rauch. Can't you find somethin' else, Jake? He nudges him with the toe of his shoe.

Yeah—the conversation.

We could sing away the blues, suggests Diablo.

That's right.

The blues are here to stay, Marks muses.

Amen to that, Brother.

Seriously, Jake, repeats Rauch. Can't you and your Romeo there—nodding toward the figure in the distance—can't you find nothin' else t' light? It's cold and the fire's just about skipped out on us.

I don't wait for Jake. I track away on my own to look with or without him—he doesn't pay me any mind anyway in the state he's in. I've been through this plenty of times. Jake with the stuffing coming out like an abused teddy. I observe a hand outstretched, a torso straight, nose flared and jaw ajar, eyes godstruck but empty. Arms legs toes and nails, all once animated, now waterlogged and leathery, almost unrecognizable, though born of a mother once, just like me. Like you, Tommy, and Jake too—the whole blessed lot gathered in this traffic circle, an animal no matter what you say, set loose in a world or a lake, only to end undone.

From a distance Romeo sees me then whistles. I glance in his direction, let him know I'm tracking something. My instinct is to try again to rouse the group, so I head back even as Romeo heads toward me. I see the bush stirred miraculously back to life by Rauch, watch as it flares before a final die-out. He fans it repeatedly with a moldered cereal box—it's clear Jake won't be looking for any more trees to incinerate, despite Rauch's or anyone's pleas. The night is no longer young. For all that, we can easily keep going until the day returns, even in the cycle of shorter days this time of year, the bone chilling nights, shortening a minute or two each passing day, lengthening the light.

Jake's trying to get a different kind of flame going, including a reason to truck on, enlisting me in his campaign, as well as Rauch Diablo Cin Romeo and Marks. The setting too, where we used to come, first with Romeo and then Peacoat. Again it was Cin and Diablo who insisted on this reunion—"For Jake's sake. Now that he's back from the brink." Of insanity I added to myself. Brought on in part by starvation, which may have had a thing or two to do with the disordered thinking. Why not enlist the gang despite their grumbling?—that was Cin's reasoning. The others, now that they're here, despite their objections and the complications, they'd be more than happy at the moment to be warmed now that the breeze has again kicked up. Though no one seems interested in abandoning this circle, the wind from Ottawa least of all. It seems I'm the only person casting a vote for a nice warm bed, a bit of pile carpet, anywhere but the cold sand, now that the warm spell last month has been shown to be a fluke. Jake in an underworld sleep, it seems, where Rauch and the magic smoke have led him. As for the rest of the group they lounge around, lamenting Peacoat's loss, the winds tailing us like bad news.

There were rumors 'bout them two, stagewhispers Rauch—he gestures toward Jake with his jaw. Despite the Jesus talk.

Wha' d' you mean, *ru*mors?

Rauch's belly shakes as he laughs.

My boy in lahlah land—C'mon, boy!

Yeah—they were no rumors.

Is this all you got? Pressing your cheek against the sand while people bandy you in earshot? I near him and he looks at me, asks in a daze, What time is it? In the soft, sandy surface near his chin he inscribes a C with the tip of his forefinger, a C and a backward C, the tails relaxed.

Marks reads the dial. Four fifty-six.

Jake nuzzles the earth as though it were one of Florrie's folds when he was still Jacob. Good old Molly, he mutters when I near him, and then I lose him again. I stretch out beside him, but it's like cozying up to a stiff. Cin draws me close when I give up finally. I venture by, and the two Mizzes, Lee and Morales, enfold me. Their nylon jackets warm me in feminine heat. Meanwhile I see Romeo wandering aimlessly back from the east, heading toward the spot I circled not long ago, having fled the conversation about Peacoat, which is to say about him and Jake. One thing's for sure and that is he isn't avoiding Marks, contentious as their conversations get, because he draws too much pleasure from it, as does Marks—truth be told. Instead, Romeo wanders with no goal in sight, or kneels as the case may be. When he finally lifts himself from the sand the rest pay no mind, wrapt as they are in the open secret of those two, a secret muttered about, about what transpired, or expired. They noticed the way Romeo made off after all that Peacoat talk, the mere mention of his name, as though the topic bored him to death. So he disappeared to the east where I wanted to go, in the direction of the sun, or son, to me at least, his current state notwithstanding.

Jake raises his head and again tolls, what time is it? Again Marks reads his arm.

Four fifty-seven.

Again Jake nuzzles the earth.

Diablo starts to hum a tune, one of the ones, she informs after Jake has nodded off, for sure this time, that, as she puts it, My Pea used to sing.

Your Pea.

Oh Kay, *our* Pea, Cin. It's just a song.

Sing it, encourages Rauch.

As I was talkin'—no, that's not it. *As I went walking*— That road—no. *That ribbon of highway*—that's it—

I saw above me—

—What time is it?

That endless skyway.

I roamed and rambled and I've followed my own footsteps,

—Four fifty-eight.

Over the edge where the erosion was starting to take its toll I spot Romeo's head pop up as he climbs the bank toward us.

As I went walking I saw a sign there,

And on the sign it said "No Trespassing."

But on the other side

It didn't say nothing—

While Diablo and Cin fumble with the words, Romeo tromps in our direction, his feet shooting sand and debris—

—You guys!

In the shadow of the steeple,

I saw my people—Marks has now joined in with his *basso profondo* voice, drowning out the rest—
By the relief office I seen my people,
As they stood there hungry,
I stood there asking—
Guys! You guys!
No person living can ever stop me,
As I go walking
That freedom highway—
You guys!

By the time Jake has roused himself, the band we're islanded on is cast in gunmetal gray. Dim as it is, there's no need for anything to burn—there's plenty of hot light now, twirling like a lighthouse, flooding the scene in the shape of two far-reaching cones. I approach the man by the car, nose and inform him, I saw first! But he disregards me as though I were mute, mindless, or both. Romeo is only now returning from the boulevard, back from the door he pounded on for some time in search of a phone.

Who saw it first? the big guy asks, speaking of a body, the big guy that Marks refers to *sotto voce* as a pig, Jake the fuzz, and Romeo, when he returns, as officer. He's still out of breath as he takes credit.

I saw it first.

That's right, agrees Rauch, either to incriminate Romeo or protect me. Mr. Geist here saw it first.

Diablo, Cin, Rauch, Marks, and Jake most of all, shift back and forth in the chill air, entirely mum. In fact Jake is only now waking up to what-for, failing to beg the time. I inform him anyway that it's over an hour until full daylight, though per usual he doesn't register the comment.

The man in black starts to walk away. The chains near the firearm jangle, tormenting me, the keys and accoutrements dangling like charms—his bulk is Jake times two, and maybe three.

My boy gasps, I can' b'lieve it! And Rauch responds in his devil's-food-cake voice, That's life, pal. Get use t' it.

I mean it's far *out,* comments Marks.

Thank god we finished the stuff. What the hell would we a done?

They ain' looking for none a that! complains Diablo, trembling, and Cin charges; How can you even *think* about that in a time like this!?

Well, lookin' or not, Rauch says, it ain't nothin' you wanna have on you. ' Specially now.

Oh god, agrees Romeo. 'Specially now. To get caught, the police on top a us, the fuss that could a caused—

It's always about you, ain't it?—Marks shoots that look. God forbid anything might happen to the family image.

You guys! It ain't no joke! screams Cin, sobbing. Like Diablo, she's shaking.

Really! echos Diablo, who's turned sickly, in some ways more than Jake, for whom, truth be told, the scene doesn't seem to be registering.

A thing like that-there, muses Cin. It's impossible t' dig.

Fluff from a stand of cottonwoods collects around our feet, nesting in the grass like snow.

I'm nosing along the squad car with the devil's eye. A bigger, boxier vehicle left some time ago, carting away the stiff. The policeman's mouth is pressed against the radio.

It was some cracker. Must not a knowed how t' swim.

I shadow Florrie. When Diana spies me she grouses at her, padding sheepishly up the stairs from the landing, Oh my god, yer useless! What the hell's she doin' back?

Don't ask.

I'll tell you later, mutters Florrie.

I wanna know *now*!

You hush. I said I'll tell you later. Florrie speaks in low tones but Diana doesn't respond in kind.

I won't hush! I wanna know! You couldn' go through with it, could you? Diana demands, and Florrie starts to cry.

It's bad enough without havin' to put up with your guff.

I don't see what's the big deal. You had a easy task and you flubbed it! I should a took 'er myself. I told myself you din't have it in you, an' I was right! Such a simple thing. I mean I can't believe between the two a yous you dit'n have the gumption.

You don't even know what you're talkin' about.

What the hell's that s'pose to mean? It was all siiiimmmple simon, the whole damn thing. I 'ranged everything, arranged it myself. All you had to do was drop her an' go. You're just soft, the two a yous—yer *soft*! You can't do the simplest thing—I mean—

—Lay off, orders Harry. Before Florrie and I were through the kitchen door he was in the refrigerator. The bottle in his hand farts as he eases the cap.

That's the problem with you two—you never wan' the truth. I mean you dit'n even have to pay. I 'ranged it all so that any moron could a done it.

After setting her handbag on the table, Florrie pulls the freezer latch, conjuring an arctic landscape. Cold air crystalizes around her neck, shoulders, and breasts. She puts her hand there to feel the cloud, belches then yanks a box out with the image of an iceberg on it. When she relatches the door the veil of cold air vanishes. Harry tipples a bottle to his lips, rifles three sips, and sets it back on the formica.

What 'm I gonna do with the two a yous? Diana shakes her head. I don't know how you'd manage if it warn't for me.

Well, by some miracle. . . .

Florrie's hacking away at a block frozen solid, there on the surface of the kitchenette, though the payoff isn't great. I should wait, she comments, pushing the thing away. It's gotta soften some. But just as quickly she takes up her task. When she's finally scraped a small pile of shavings together she takes a bite—Oh, dear lord, that's good.

God knows you eat enough a it.

A'least it don' go t' waste.

It's true that nothin' don't go t' waste in this house. Not with you around.

Well there ain't no reason to be unkin'.

You're just so undisciplined—you n' Harry both. The two a you're just as bad.

Harry has killed one soldier and is about to rough up a second. He closes his eyes and vents the cap of the bottle while lifting the opener. It's like a peak moment, the sound of carbonated air set free. He tilts his head back and froth spills over his lip, chin, and onto his shirt. He sighs then rests his forehead on the back of his hand, his elbow on the table top.

Oh god, responds Diana.

Lordy, lordy, reflects Florrie. She's spooning out another bowl. She burps in the middle of querying, Where's Ruby? The spoon springs to her mouth and, always looking for for a slip, I gaze as it returns to the bowl. None for you, Precious, she comments, noticing me officially—I was starting to think I'd become invisible. Part of the furniture.

I'm gonna have t' put you on a diet.

Diet, schmiet, I reply, watching as a line of white rivers between her breasts. I move closer, wheeze and cry, but Florrie isn't paying me no mind.

Gosh darn it, she complains. It happens every time. And to think I just washed this blouse. She braces herself on the side of the table, steadies her grip on the pink formica, and when she's verticle she treads across the room and pulls a large bottle from the door of the fridge.

Where's Ruby?

Pour me a pop, too. While you're at it.

Gimme a minute.

No ice.

She's done this hundreds, maybe thousands of times, poured Diana a pop—what's one more? That's the look I read, the same one she pulls when Diana's thirst waits for Florrie to finally coax her body from the chair.

Here—she hands the pop. Carbonation rockets in the air. Where's Ruby?

Where d'you think? Diana takes a sip, clears her throat— *Tit-hmm!* She takes another sip, rests back in her chair, gathers a tangle of fluff near her neck to tame it, coils and recoils the ends.

Well, I thought she might a come in.

When're you gonna tell what happen? She's playing good cop now in an effort to prime the suspect, tease from her the real and not some edited tale, as though Florrie were capable of that. Tears well in Florrie's eyes.

After killing a third beer Harry swoons. He doesn't give a damn about Diana's questions, that's for sure—let Florrie spin the tale, relying on the right mix of bare-naked facts and a detour or two, enough to satisfy Diana's curiosity as to how, how long, and into what detail a story should be told. Florrie's taken care of more than a pint by now, the sharp edges of life having been filed down as a result, the burrs smoothed away. But rather than subject herself to further questioning, about me and Donald both, I assume, she calls my name and we pad into Ruby's room. I catch her smiling when she sees me, a mute wonder that says, What are you? Yet when I approach she reaches as though I were a known thing. Florrie extends me toward her so Ruby doesn't have to strain, but she seems to lose interest, retracts her hand, and points to something in the yard.

It's pigeons, Florrie explains. Pretty ain' they? The shiny colors.

Ruby's lip quakes like my joints at times when she tries to squeak out a word. I struggle to get down, think maybe it'll help if I'm nearer, but her face washes blank again. Two old gals, I think, we two. Two mutes.

Florrie finally gets a whiff of something I deemed obvious the minute we got home. She remarks, Oh my! We need a change.

We leave Ruby to stew in her rocker, the perch life has brought her to after so many years, except for a walk now and then to the living room to watch—I'm not sure. A bag of dime novels, a gift from Midge on a rare visit, rests in the corner, though I haven't seen her crack one in years.

How can you beat ten for a buck? Midge enthused. Never mind Ruby knew them by heart. Never mind too that most of them Leo dumped at the Catholic Charity that time, after Miss Glasby died and when Midge was in a cleaning mood, vacating the books and what was left of Ruby in the house. Now here they sit after a circuitous route from there to here.

I only read the dialogue, Ruby used to say, explaining when she had a voice, arguing that nothing is ever newsworthy other than what comes out of people's mouths. She used to underscore the point to Wren, who took an interest too in what people said, to a point, though she was equally keen on what wasn't spoken.

Grammie, I don't think you can always trust what people say.

These days no one bothers to read even the dialogue to Ruby, with Wren banished from home and Jake gone

MIA—she gazes at the books and her eyes veer away. I'm no genius, but maybe Wren's right, I mean what does dialogue reveal? Yet Wren used to accommodate Ruby, doing her best to animate the stories, dramatizing the tête-a-têtes, including the boring parts though, the descriptions with their eye toward endless detail, once you've made it through the exposition.

All those names! Ruby used to complain. What d' they all mean to me? No one could make them come alive—the entire kit-and-caboodle—like Wren.

It's ironic that when Ruby speaks now it's only with her eyes, and with her body too—don't kid yourself. She leans forward, reaches her porkchop hand in a language I comprehend, one that makes up for words she can no longer locate, like so many treats booted out of reach. We share a lingo of eyes and bodies both, as much as anything from a person's mouth, but for now Florrie and me return to the kitchen, she to solve the immediate Ruby problem and me to see what's going down, as in off the tabletop.

It turns out it's only words after all, straight from Harry's mouth—his tongue is surprisingly loose in his wife's absence. Diana towers over him.

What?! she exclaims. Whatwhat*what*?! How soon can you get a new one? I need to know when to make another 'pointment. I mean you can't just sashay in there any ol' time a day an' say, Here, get rid a her, will ya? You gotta schedule aleast a day in advance. You can't just drop her and leave. Not without a 'pointmint.

Why don't we just take her in your car?

In my car?! No way! I don' wan' her in there—it's bran' new!

Frustrated, Harry heads to the living room in his usual vanishing act, and Florrie halts, sits, then takes me in her lap, kisses me and pulls the hairs on my head as she massages it.

Jake and Wren'll be crushed—

Seriousbusiness music comes on the tube in the living room.

Then why don't *they* take 'er? Harry yells from the parlor. If they like 'er so much—

—We tried—but it din't work out.

Outside the pigeons jod and coo through the window. Florrie scattered crusts of bread and leftover rice so Ruby could watch from her perch. I leap on the chair by the window, witness the frenzy for a morsel or two on a patch of here-and-there green.

Even without the mess with the car, Diana analyzes, I doubt you could a gone through with it. I'll go next time. T' make sure.

We'll go. You gotta realize it ain't easy after all these years.

There ain't nothin to it. I can't take it nomore. The messes.

What would you know abou' that? I'm the one gotta clean 'em up.

Unemployment rate jumps to 10.1 percent, up 2.7 percent since the election—

Soviets carry out underground nuclear test—

No, I'm gonna do it. Period.

Wull see.

Harry divides his attentions between the tube, *The Plain Dealer,* and *Press*—I see him glance up from one or the other, towards us in the kitchen. He holds his fire.

Dollar gains strongly—price of gold rises—

Wull see, indeed! apes Diana. I mean—rully. I can't take it.

Praetoria moves to close school where Indians and coloreds mix—

Wull see, asserts Florrie yet again, in a battle of wull-sees.

You never wanted 'er in the first place. You're the one who said, Get that thing *outta* here! when Jake brought her home—I remember like it was yestaday. You said, It's the last

89

thing I need—havin' *that* aroun'! You said, Jake! What in the *world* were you thinkin'?! Don't *even* bring it in.

How could you think a such a thing? It's so unkind. You know how I feel about 'er. People change, you know. It ain't a sin.

There's somethin' dapraved about it, Diana argues. Like you had your head and you gone an' lost it.

Well what *can* y' do? Leastwise I'm happy in my doddering.

You sure do mope a lot for someone so content.

Leave 'er alone, carps Harry from the other room. We been through enough a'ready down in darkytown.

The comment causes Diana's lips to go taut. She swivels her head away from Florrie, in the direction of the living room. Yer a dinosaur! she bellows. Born a cent'ry too late!

SHY OF BLISS

JAKE *PFFFTS* as Leo doffs his shirt again, the table decorum having passed.

I'd give my right nut to hump Wren, he moans, man to man. Jake replies with a look—I can't b'lieve you just—

—She got me *goin'*. Check it out, Jake.

That's disgustin'! Jake bleats, pleading with Leo to stop, who in turn hands over a photo as if it were a resume.

I had all but one a 'em. Me an' Romeo both.

Jake takes the shot, flashes it toward me, and I peer at the blond in the Minnie Mouse tee, her and the others, then peer away, listening to the floorboards squeak as Diana nears. I glance back at the image—what am I supposed to say? I'm not sure of the point—it seems more about notching lines, adding to some kind of triumph. I spy Leo in the shot with six or seven young women arrayed before and behind him, the big-winning smiles, all except for too-cool-for-school Leo on one side and Romeo, king of the gridiron, on the other, his arm draped over the shoulder of the blond in a tee like Jake's, skin tight. The two men pose in shoulder and thigh pads, codpiece and girdle under their uniforms, probably the very girdle hanging on the door of Miss Glasby's oven, drying after an early scrimmage at St' Andrej's. Leo and Romeo with their pride of lionesses.

Romeo an' me, we share em.

You an' Rom—

—She's the one he's soft for. The one in the shirt same's yours, pal—I tol' you it's a girl's. They're gonna git hitched someday.

Hitched?

I glance at the blond, in a sense Jake's alter-ego, while Leo crows about the bond between him and Romeo, a kind of brotherhood, full of potential in what, he implies, might be called The Pursuit, a different kind of teamwork than the one on the field. We share a lot, him and me.

—Share what? asks Diana on entering.

None a yer business.

Who're they? Diana grabbed the shot from Jake's hand in order to study it.

Jus' some girls. Leo shoots a knowing look at Jake, a guy like himself, because only a guy would get it. Diana muses she knows the sisters of some of them.

They were in my class.

Who asked you?

A willow stands in the yard. Its branches shoot up then cascade down like fireworks in July. They spread from the center, explode, then drift back to earth where the property dips, where a brook runs, loosely marking the line where this and the adjacent property butt up against each another, where they part ways. The world beneath is sealed in a belljar of sickly green this time of day. The sound of voices shattering. Another month an'—Iss pizza time—Like glass—Oh, man—Mygod she's soooo, so— Man gonna be—Far out—Hot—Ground meat—The tits on tha' one—Man—Oh, god—Two jobs for it—Eww, god, that ass I can't—Lookn forward—I got my—Yeah those knockers!—Eye on a—God would I love to—GTX—Her so hard—Boss car—If it weren't so damn hot man—Is that a Mercury?—Niney-nine degrees I swear, and hunderd precen' humidity—Ohhh god—No, it's a Impala.

I belong to Jake but in a real sense he also belongs to me. Him and me under this immigrant tree, near where the Eries ran once. Free. Ran period. As in here and there, alive and upright. Through mossed forests without boundaries, without leaving a footstep to track them by, easily clearing the ribbon of water along the edge of the property, the only thread remaining after centuries, millenniums probably, running aslant and defining these deeded lots, laid in regular geometries that are held in hock for decades to come. The loud crack of voices and Jake's only beginning to come to.

O ma go', Mol'—whahavigo'?

What have you got yourself *into?* You threw your*self* into this mess.

Howmuchmorcan I—?

Jake hurls.

There he goes agin!

Yeah, kid can' take it.

You know 'im?

I belong to Jake and he to me. It's a tony idea, like a road stretching a long, long way. Where he goes I go, though truth be told I've learned not to ask where we're headed. I shadow him, and sometimes he shadows me. Molly! he said once when he spotted a gray hair on my chin, not long ago, How could you? As though it would be *me* one day that would fail *him.* I chronicle him, though I wonder if he appreciates the energy paid, to my once ballsy and now tentative boy, hanging back and leap-frogging forward, but toward what?

He belongs to this world about as much as I do. Under this weeping willow, heir to others in the days of the Eries, the Lost Nation as they're called today, under this tree where only a half an hour ago he and Romeo urinated side by side, making their acquaintance officially, by chance or design I'm not sure. Romeo ducked through the curtain of leaves once he spotted Jake heading here. Of all the forms of making a connection, that had to be the most fluid, in terms of glances. Their eyes floated, as if batted by a breeze. Which was before the firewater started to kick in, inside this bubble, outside of which oaks, ashes, and elms once braved the sky, lining the shoulder of the lake, the one the glacier left, birthing the liquid landscape on the edge of the Forest City—and Laurentine, which is perched on this Indian run to the east. Among all this duff, vines of ivy and grasses native to the southern shore, greening the understory. Or used to. It was this that the French *courreurs de bois* and the Brits duked it out for, the land of the Eries, scattered and subsumed by their conquerors, the Iroquois of the Five, the Six Nations, lost to the world as a unique identity by being hybridized, well before the Euros came on the scene. For whose good did they scrap with each other? Definitely not the Eries, the remaining fragments of *Le Nation du Chat,* the Bobcats, or Cougars, all names given to the people who thrived on this tract of the Western Reserve before the west became The West. Not the west you come from, Tommy, with its sunburned earth and skintones—the colonists came to what they called The West at the time, but for whose sake? Ask the passenger pigeon, eastern elk, and woodland bison. Ask any Erie you cross on the streets of the Forest City. Or ask Mister Franklin, the double, triple agent, part American but mostly Anglo or French if residence is any guide—he knew how to play the field. What was he? fifty? sixty? when he sharked up a band of farmers, anyone with a wagon, to make their way here, as though he had a clue about the western front, and all for one of the Georges. The land-hungry Pennsylvanians, Virginians, Connecticutonians were operating on a royal dream. Yeah, Big Ben came here, or not far off, he and another, homegrown George, to offer promises like so many other white guys, American and Brit, not the least of which was the general the royal George sent. He paid a price for his ignorance. I mean, what did he know? About tribes or tribal lands? Indian cultures? Warfare? The French? Nascent America, too? The only needed thing, he thought, was a supply of gin—if you want to possess an Injun all you need is firewater, then let it flow. That was his motto. I'm not talkin' revision—no saints, the Eries, the Lost Nation, whatever name you prefer, memorialized in street names and country clubs around these parts, the People of the Cat whose graves supply plenty of specimens that are fingerless, toeless, and even headless. No, no saints there, or anywhere really—there's no such thing as a good conscience among human animals. But that's not the point. At issue is a not-so-little matter of erasure, of a certain kind of truth now lost today—Jake puking, but on what? The midden heap of history. Dirt and roots to him—what would he know about this bit of turf we're on, what it was before the developers seized it? Did he or anyone gathered here put his ear to the ground and query, What happened? Does he know about the graveyard below, the lives human and non that were ended too soon, the history heavying the air? Or is he just pissing the night away, every night, day too, drunk as a Hollywood Injun, the firewater killing his brain?

My newly-rited teen pissing before and beside Romeo, under this canopy, force-drunk as an Iroquois primed to sign his soul away with an X, arms and legs splayed, birthed in a sense in the bower of the Eries, the vomit notwithstanding.

Not able to hold his liquor, my brave, heaving for the umpteenth time. Man, says Leo, parting the drape of green and poking his head through. I didn' know you was such a lightweight, Jake. As usual his shirt is removed, I assume in homage to the braves who once lived here—he and his pals have all gone native. Romeo kicked off the party earlier, offering endless chugs from an endless supply of bottles in an endless number of cases of Boone's Farm, which quickly took Jake from the guzzling to the upchucking phase as the others tom-tom around.

At fifteen Jake hadn't touched alcohol before, except for a sip of Harry's beer now and then, and for that reason held back, until the crowd took notice. What're you afraid a? Leo jibed, coaxing him to lose the shirt as well. Jus' like the guys.

I'm not afraid a nothin'! Jake insisted.

Wull see, says one.

*'Actin funny. . .*sings one of the revelers, along with the music. *Not sure why—*

Let's get 'im! jumps another, causing Leo to fall back. He was looking on as his cousin got a body makeover, losing his shirt and nearly his pants over the Cyclone fence had Romeo not stepped in and halted things, the shucking of trousers most of all, not being proper in this neck of the woods. He didn't stop, though, the forcing of an entire bottle down the boy's throat.

—*I wanna kiss the sky,* continues the crooner in the group, trying to keep up with the track from the loud speakers.

There you go! That's more like it, suggests one, pulling his hair back as Jake attempts to stand up, his shirt lost to the neighbors.

Looks like you could benchpress a ton!

Am I goin' up or comin' down?—

Laughter erupts, and the varsity blast that Leo came all this way for has finally taken off, now that the team has chosen a mascot. Later I'll learn straight from the horse's mouth that it was Romeo who ordered Leo to ask his cousin to join in the party, causing Leo not a little bit of confusion, causing him to bark, Why *him*?! Of all *people*! *He's a nerd!* And yet here he, we, are, moving with what was once a mass of random drifters but is now a group brewed in a full-blown party. Still Leo hangs back.

Are you a freak? someone asks.

Or a *girl?*

Too white trash t'afford a haircut.

Baby you're, blowin' me mind—

Cmmmon Mollll, slurs Jake.

Cmmmon Mollll circles around the group, the heads popping in and out of the green.

I wanna know, is it th' end a time?

I'm go—

And the crowd echoes *I'm go....*

It follows us as we pass, *im go im go im go*, through the sliding doors at the back of the house and into the kitchen. The crowd watches Jake stumble then turns its attentions elsewhere as he falls into yet another racist parody of a Hollywood Indian. He tags the marble counter with upchuck, then the shiny new stove, tipping this way then that. When the wall fails to give way he makes a ninety-degree turn and teeters down the hall toward the living room with its overstuffed sofa, lined with gold throws, the old-world finery, the front door beyond as thick as a castle's with writing *Geeeee.... Eeeeee.... Eyyyyeee.... Esssss.... Teeeeeeee....* Jake reads, squinting and slurring in slomo, his head reeling back, just about falling into the sunken space—he's nearly paralleling the carpeting, until a hand reaches out and saves him from landing a single step down.

Watch yourself, cowboy! remarks a disembodied voice. Jake tries to pull himself away.

I cn d't—

A course you can do'it. But two's better'n one. You ain'
goin' nowhere like this, cowboy—you need t' lie down. An
arm thick as an anaconda on the hunt lifts Jake, lugs him
now easily, now with difficulty up a flight of stairs with
footsteps hush-quiet due to the thick pile, like an Erie's on
airy moss. Noiseless they are, feet that know how to keep
a secret. When he finally gets him upstairs, he flies Jake
down the hallway.

Why not lay here awhile? Sober up a bit.

Mushoblige—

—Don' mention it.

I observe as Jake is laid palely across a bedspread, as though
being readied for a ritual, the ceiling falling diagonally on
either side of the mattress, the contour of the roof like a
suburban long house, resting on a rectangular base with
the streetlight's glow streaming dully in the window, just
enough to light things. Jake stares blankly at the plastered
ceiling as though studying it, that and the reason he's here,
before his eyes roll back. I lie to his left while the other butts
against his right.

D'you even know yer name?

—

D'you know mine? Romeo begins unzipping Jake's Levis.

More silence until Jake comes to temporarily—I kno
yu—

—No you don't. You don' know nothin'.

Jake's eyes slit closed like a lizard's as the other's hands
run over the torso that Jake's shirt once covered. They shinny
first the jeans then the briefs toward the ankles, yanking
them free. The hands set to work with the economy of
thieves, knowing and getting quickly down to business over
unmarked flesh—once a line's crossed there's no turning
back. Romeo, a patient tracker, whispers, You're a dainty
doe. I've had my eye on you. I knew you wouldn' disappoint.

He mutters other things about the halls of Saint Andrej's that I don't get, having never been there, the place where he and Leo cat around on the field, according to Leo, a turf Jake is only allowed to intrude on briefly, long enough for Leo not to appear rude in the presence of the Geist boy, cousins being cousins after all.

The spider-silk of blood, the hoots pouring through the window from outside, wafting in with the summer half-breeze, raising the shears up and down, but only occasionally. Slowly up. Then slowly down. Up and down. . .and up and down. . .the party below, once a handful and slow to get off the ground, now swollen it seems. In fact the crowd's about to go shooting in the street by the sound of things. Jake's oblivious to it, and at the same time electrified, his body on autopilot, a reaction to lips and tongue in strokes here and there across the stomach, thighs, and everything between. He throws himself on Jake and his tongue heaves past the lips now for an an eternity really, dipping shallow then deep as the hands busy—

—Whadr yu do-een? Jake inquires, coming to briefly. Then he drifts off, forgetting himself and the world around him. His eyes don't function well, having lost the fuel to operate. The lids slit open as liquid fire or saliva, it isn't clear which, run across his cheeks and chin, which unlike Romeo's is devoid of hair, then down the chest as he moves back to the bed, running his tongue down the stomach and below, in strokes that reflect the streetlight. Jake's skin twitches as he's wrapped in warmth, more humid than the air in the room, a friction that's bound to cause sparks. Despite that he just lays there, though not entirely a dud.

Romeo's dead set. His body generates a heat greater than the summer air in the room, a tinder box, causing both bodies next to me to run with sweat and me to pant. More than a spark ignites, never mind that for Jake his brain's been doused with water. Still Romeo persists. He takes a moment to shed his second self, the one required beyond the door that he's secured with a desk chair, leaving the three of us naked to the very skin.

Running with rivulets of orange, lustered by the light from outside, Romeo dominates the space, turning the air into an earthy mix though Jake is dead to it. His head spins, the world revolves, his body loses its orientation, which way is up, down, or sideways, the room spinning like his torso now, revolving like an arrow until it hard-lands, his nose piercing the pillow, taking it all, something, in, nodding off then coming up for air, enough to sense Romeo sweating bullets while sighing in his ear. He jars himself awake long enough to file a protest, but again just as quickly as before he forgets his complaint, and his name, the cause he's suing for or against.

He loses the reality of the scene, unlike Romeo who is massively present, riding a wave, a swell that lasts forever, until a storm erupts and he anchors Jake to the bed, flattening him. The two lie lifeless in different ways, pancaked as they are, Jake paled and paling, almost vanishing under the wooly darkness of Romeo's skin, blanching like the sheets in a divergence of tones, never mind perspective.

All along voices have been exploding from outside, penetrating the space, including Leo, the ringleader's, most of all, as the air around us turns feral. Romeo's become a ghost of himself all of a sudden, collapsed on Jake like a beached whale, sputtering and dying, while Jake slipped away some time ago. Sounds from the street continue to come in as if they're responsible for raising the shears away from the sill, then setting them down again, like Romeo's breathing as it slows, until he's able to move. I watch the shears sway in unison with the ribcage of the one lying on his back now, next to Jake, his hairy arm thrown over as though he were claiming him, his property.

Romeo studies his trophy darkly, the life washed out of it, breathing all the same next to me. After flipping Jake once again he ponders the belly as it rises and falls, his head resting on it.

Cackling streams through the sticky air, the hoots, the ones that Jake seems to register even as a stiff, twitching from time to time to the pulsating sound. Romeo glances toward the opening between the shears. Without moving his head from Jake's stomach the whites of his eyes shift, then the centers return to what's in front of him. He tracks his hand over a sandy patch then between the thighs. He takes Jake in as though he's discovered a toy, adopted a pet, or made a friend. He takes his time, patient in his task of breathing life into an inanimate thing, and, just when it appears he's succeeding, howls from outside kick up again, causing him to lift his head and turn his ear toward the window. It appears as though the party has indeed spilled across the lawn and into the street.

Ro-MAY-oh! Ro-MAY-oh! Ro-MAY-oh!—the name snakes in.

After having returned to his task, he's forced once again to stop. Lea' me be, he whispers.

Ro-MAY-oh! Ro-MAY-oh! Ro-MAY-oh!

Jolted to what's happening, a look steals across his face.

Ro-MAY-oh-Ro-MAY-oh-Ro-MAY-oh!

I'm comin! he blurts through the pane, after flying out of bed without rousing Jake. He's silhouetted by the frame of the window. He slides a pair of briefs past Jake's knees and over his privates, as though hiding something from a thief, one who might come through the window and cart his prize away. He leaves the feet bare as though planning on resuming his task, then covers his own body, removes the chair at the door, and stomps down the hall and stairs with me in tow.

Where the hell were you?

That kid needed help, he complains to the group, now swollen with crashers. Wha'd ya do to him? How much did you give 'im? You should all be ashame. He crosses the lawn with the grace of a steer as the group parts to let him pass. You know you can go to jail for that! Doin' that to a minor.

I follow to where the main crowd is congregated, and the rest flood after. Some guy bounds up to us, from the direction of the fuss we heard upstairs.

Leo's F'n doin' it! He's doin' it, man!

Romeo doesn't have to ask what *it* is. He complains, Jesus Christ! That guy's got no class. He leads with determined, even parental steps through the rubber-neckers, over the empties and discarded tees, the stray crusts and pizza boxes.

What the hell are you doin'? he demands, catching up with the streaker. I'm never gonna hear the end a this. Do that over in that ghetto where you live, but not here!

Jus' bust'n their balls, Leo pants, grinning from ear to ear. He's staggering, though unlike Jake he stays upright. When he speaks he points with his chin at the party on Romeo's perfectly shaven lawn. We're havin' fun! he pleads. He grabs his crotch and pumps his chest as though he's just rifled through fifty, sixty yards, evading the other team's line of defense, just in time to catch the game-saving pass.

Put your pants on, cowboy! orders Romeo, gazing at two heads next door, peeping through the curtain. He barks, What're *you* lookin' at? as though the oglers could hear through the thick plate, raised high off the ground. We shift around, array across the grass, which might be as close to the perfect idea of lawnness as lawnness gets. No one ever treads such a green confection like this in our neck of Laurentine, far from the lake. It's so unlike our crab-grass bit of turf on the south side of town where we hear not waves but cars, speeding down the freeway, there on the edge of town. Meanwhile the block association in this gated section has convened a watch to insure against events just like this, but Leo from the youknowwhat, the part of the Forest City not mentioned around here let alone visited, doesn't seem to give a hoot for Romeo's rules.

He tries to don his jeans, having been corrected, acculturated, or whatever. He's jackknifed at the waist as first one and then the other leg locates an opening. He shinnies the fabric over his thighs.

Zip up! snarls Romeo. Leo struggles in his condition to follow orders, to mollify his hero is more like it. Romeo follows him with his eyes as Leo backs away toward the throng that's shifting again toward the backyard, though Leo fails to unlock his gaze as he retreats.

Lks like you could use a zipup too, he slurs. An yer shirts insi-dout.

Well, we gotta go tomarra for a new one—we gotta find somethin'. What else we gonna do? remarks Harry who returns to the kitchen while the TV sings the praises of pearly whites. He's been tracking the conversation in the kitchen as much as the one in the box.

I don't got no money, objects Diana. If that's what yer after. Why don't you ask Jake or Wren?

Pffft. Jake or Wren.

That's not my pro'lem. Why d'you al'ays ask *me* for money?

When she storms out of the room Harry tells Florrie, Don' worry. I'll speak t' her. She must have more moolah than god.

That's not nice. She's earned it after all.

But she lives here scotfree. Where would she be if we warn't payin—

—Shsh! She might hear you!

Harry throws up his hands—I mean what the hell? Is it so much t' ask?

Diana jettisons the photo of Leo-and-Romeo's "girls" on the bed and exits the testosterone world here, except for yours truly, until Wren enters.

You like football?

What?

Foot-ball.

Well, I'm not—

—So you *liiiike* it—Leo breaks form with a smile. But who doesn'?

Jake flies up, as if looking down on a calamity about to happen, on Wren who seems in danger of a head-on collision, though with what he doesn't know.

Shouldn't we all keep Gramma Ruby comp'ny?

I see her evry day. What's left a the old bag. He glances again at the women in the photo, the busty ones with pom-poms, short-shorts, and knotted blouses, the ones Diana got a good look at who cheer on Leo as he heads across the field, snatching hail marys from Romeo.

Stay here.

But Wren, Jake advises, I think we should go.

You go 'head, Jake. Wren and me're gonna talk.

Leo puts his jersey back on, the number tenting over the pecs and abs, jeans pockets too.

Go 'head, Jake—. *Go!*

Wren—. *Wren!* Jake pleads and Leo replies, Run along, little boy. She's a big girl.

So we abandon a world that to Jake is entirely out of whack. He glances behind as we exit then pads along the dark hallway to the parlor at the front of the house, but he can't help peering back as if he's losing Wren, the floorboards moaning at every step, until we land in a gathering skirting an outdoor tree.

Leo picked out a *beaut*, didn' he Jake? enthuses Midge. He bought it this mornin'. In' it shape nice? In' it fresh?

Miss Glasby explains from across the room, pointing to the branches, All this'll drop after it sets upright some. It'll fill out, look more like a tree.

She says that every year, gripes Ruby.

Never you mind, missy, counters Miss Glasby, and Midge, sitting next to Jake, leans and whispers, Harry has managed to cart the thing in, Despite quote-unquote protests. I reply, Never mind! The countryside fills the parlor here, perfumes it, overpowering the smell of cigarettes and beer with the scent of virgin stands before the chainsaws went at them, on a hillside quilted with conifers, that diverse category of beings living happily side by side, far from the lump of humanity I'm enmeshed with whether I like it or not—the firs, kindred spirits, unblinking under feet of snow, under Orion with his legs splayed high in the sky. Every trace of green left from before the cutting, descendents of pine trees before the invasion of angiosperms, flowering trees and their fallen leaves, in a world before humans and indeed even mammals came on the scene. A truly pioneer species, the green First Nation that moves in in the wake of a casualty, whether from a meteorite or mile-thick ice, fire, or corporate clear-cutting. Nature's ambassadors, like me, the very essence of treeness that has ducked through the door like a god and into this threadbare space in the center of the Forest City, filling it out and gracing the gathering, not far as the crow flies from Liberty. I get up in there, give it a once- twice- three-times over, make an offering, and now I'm like Harry in a drunken state in a world all my own.

Come away from 'ere, Precious! warns Florrie. It don't look too stable.

Jake, honey, can you double check the screws on the stand? requests Midge, and despite Harry's assurance that The're as tite anscure as there evergonna b, Jake snakes under the lowest boughs and it's the two of us under here, with Florrie, unbidden but hopping to, steadying the top of the tree in order to correct what she's sure is its drunken posture.

Looks better'n ours, rattles Diana.

Never you mind missy, counters Florrie.

Nevr mnd, repeats Harry, pleading.

Jake looks at me, and I return the gaze. My Moll, he coos.

A lone voice on the TV croons about snow, then four voices harmonize about it.

That's better, observes Miss Glasby, and Florrie crows, That's because there was someone to hold it.

Bravo! cheers Midge. Florence Nightingale, you saved th' day, yet again. What'd we do 'thout you?

Florrie croons to herself now, along with the voices on the tube, *I think of snow*—

Meanwhile I want to linger down here forever, but Jake starts skinnying out, ordering me out too, and in the process snags his tee on one of the branches.

Dammit. My new shirt!

Things happen, muses Midge.

Language, chides Florrie. She eyes Jake sternly, then shifts her head toward Miss Glasby and comments, That was a Won. Der. Ful. Meal. Cooked to Per. Feck. Shun.

Too salty, complains Ruby. She's gone and lost her taste for salt.

Let it go, orders Midge. It ain't gonna kill you.

Jake and Wren hardly ate a thing.

It was just the meat—the rest though—

—All the more for me, cracks Diana. Including leftovers.

Wher r the light crds? inquires Harry, and Midge objects, I'll call Leo—he can do it.

Jake offers, I'll go get 'im, but Harry motions him away.

Sty rht there. Im gudaddit.

Rully, pleads Midge, Leo likes ta do it.

I goddit.

Midge fires the end of a cigarette, sucks the flame in, and Harry takes a sip from a bottle. He's got the lights laid out in a tangled mess. They trace a web soon to cocoon the tree—cage it is more like it. Midge expels a column of smoke as she observes Harry's movements. Jake watches too, his finger inscribing a C in the upholstery, a C and a backward C, the bottom tails relaxed.

I miss the place on the West Side, remarks Ruby. We use ta have such a *nice* Chrissmuss there. With all that room.

Yu cdn pay me ta liv ovr here.

Ohhh, it's not as bad as all 'at. It's jus' I miss that great big house, 'specially at Chriss—

—You think you're better'n us? carps Midge.

Well yoo shda mved b'fore the place went to *them*. U shda mved ages ago.

Easy for you to say—try sellin' a place 'round here.

Leo interrupts, clattering in with his usual grin erased, replaced by a red mark on his cheek, which he massages with his fingertips. Wren slips in behind him, meek as a martin. Wher've you been? complains Midge. We coulda use your help. Leo jackknifes his arms, grabs his jersey from his shoulders, quakes it loose from where it's bunched up at the midsection then palms it flat. I could see Jake spying Leo's armpits, the ones that vie with the nose of pine.

Wren and me was just talkin'.

What kinda grammar is that? D'you hear Jake talkin' like that?

I ain't never gonna be like Jake.

Thank god! declares Diana.

Get thee to a nunnery.

Stop it! orders Florrie, and Midge returns, They're jus' kids.

Not my kids. Not like that.

Midge takes another drag from her cigarette and holds it in, then blows it clear across the room.

Are we goin' t' Mass t'night? inquires Ruby.

If we get back in time, Florrie replies, peering at Harry then Ruby. With all the weather an' all. She glances again at Harry who's seated on the floor next to the tree, his chin resting on his chest. Wull see what time we get back.

I haven' missed mi'night Mass in years.

Leo leans his mouth not a little inconspicuously toward Jake's ear. Can I ask you sumpin'? He heads down the hall, looks back, motions with his hand, and Jake lifts himself grudgingly, padding after with me in tow. Lured to his cousin's room, his shirt draped again over the desk chair which is groaning under the weight of magazines, he puts his arm across the entrance—Stop, Jake. Let's talk.

I'm gonna go back 'n join the others.

What's the rush? I wanna ask you somethin'. Leo's a good deal taller than Jake, his torso a coliseum of animals. His father must've descended from giants, unlike Midge, Florrie, and their whole clan, who are short by contrast.

I ain't sayin' anything! repulses Jake upon hearing Leo's proposition. It don't work like that. If you wanna say that t' her, do it yerself.

Leo rubs his cheek then replies, I want you to do it—I'm talkin t' you man to man, but—he halts, erupts in a fit of laughter that echoes down the hall, rumbles like lightening in advance of a winter storm—You're too much, Jake! You and your Minnie-Mouse tee! He brings his hand away from the doorway, falls crashing on the mound of coats on the bed, overcome with laughter. I take in the men in jerseys on the wallpaper, running, tackling, and passing. The lot stumble, tip, and roll in a clash of helmets and chin guards, clacking and clutting on the walls as Leo cracks up.

You're first rate, Jake—first rate! There's rumors about your sister, you know, down at St. Andy's. Romeo tol' me. Who she's whorin' with. You don' wanna push Harry over the edge with no news like that. I tried to reason with 'er—

You should talk t' her, Jake. She'll do whatever you say, break up with that Donald guy in a minute. I mean, what is she *thinkin'*?

Leo parts and Jake and I sit alone. He takes in the wallpaper. Why don't they hit this with a coat a paint—it's so juvenile. He paces back and forth, then sits on the side of the bed, tracing a C in the bedspread with the nub of his finger, a C and backward C, the tails relaxed. Jake stands then paces, back and forth, studies the wallpaper, fit for a kid's room but not a junior's at Saint Andrej's, Jake blurts it out, referring to the place that keeps Harry working so many overtime hours, Midge too. Leo's forgotten his ring on the dresser, and Jake slips it on, the ring identical to Romeo's as Leo keeps saying. He feels his flesh against metal, the chill, then sets it aside as Wren appears in the doorway.

You wanna see me?

By this time the empties are lined along the armchair and Harry has slunked down, his behind slithered to the edge of the cushion, chin bobbled on his chest, while the TV pumps personality-plus. Gone is the sober, serious talk from when we arrived. Now broad smiles and perfect whites, the uniquely American kind, spill from the screen in giggles, guffaws, and double entendres, common at night, year after year, since I came here at least, and probably going back to the year Jake was born, pitched from a stage that's meticulously artificial, despite the fact that for all intents and purposes there's no audience to witness any of it here, save one. Harry and Florrie half-sit, half-lie, each in their armchairs, his thirst and her sweet tooth sated. Diana has flown to her roost above and Ruby to her, that is Jake's room, back in the day. So we sit, my memories and I, take a reprieve from a day in a house crowded with ghosts.

Overlooking the beach from the lip of the cliff it's cooler than on the boulevard, especially after sundown. Still the southern air fries any current coming from the north. Jake's hand planes the breeze as it passes our way. He's wearing his Doctor Feelgood suit, having downed half a beer, even as the guy behind the wheel has chucked four empties into the blackness beyond. As usual I've been rendered a third wheel to this party, as if I don't exist. I morph into the background, having been lost in negative space back here with the speed of heat lightening. The upholstery and I are one with my view between the seats—but of what? Peachfuzz Jake and his hairy companion resting like weapons poised to go off. But never mind, this is a sterling thrill, even for me in the back of the bus, so to speak, with the roof removed and all. It's retracted like the canopy of the sky, allowing me to observe the void in front of me.

It was such a hot day! A scorcher the weatherman called it, made worse by the dumping of carbon in the air of the metro region by the sheer number of cars on the freeways,

along with the steel and rubber mills downtown, icons
of modernism and the defeat of nature. The valley of
the Cuyahoga, slicing through the city, has been remade.
A winding depression once cradling a river, home to
trout and wading birds, it's now a chemical band that
leapt into flames last year, sending shock waves not just
through the city but the country as well, during a heat
wave not unlike this. The river sent plume after plume
into the already toxic air, visible from Plymouth-on-the-
Lake to Sandusky. Were it not not usual to be blind to
your neighbor's house, just across the street, on account
of the pollution, it might have caused an even bigger stir.

Here on this blacktop, cooled as it is by the northern
breezes and the boughs overhead, the air is more tolerable.
Those were the days, Tommy, when few people enjoyed
the luxury of air conditioning—humans had gotten
along without it for two hundred millenniums, and they
were still slow to adopt it. Only the wealthy turned to
it then, that and this air-conditioning-on-wheels, this
smooth-riding Mustang with top removed, the one that
Geist Senior gifted Junior the day he turned sixteen. On
the way here, after the roof was lowered, the topic was
heat.

Damn air's like a oven.

Having never been in a convertible, especially one
lined with white leather, Jake was too busy taking in
the experience. Yeah, hot as a rumor, he replied absent
mindedly.

Romeo glanced to the right repeatedly as he drove,
suggesting in one form or another, Well, cowboy, why
don' you do somethin' about it?

Like what?

Wha'do you think?

I dunno. What?

Except for stolen looks in the halls of St. Andrej's, the two've known each other exactly one week, thanks to Leo's match-making, never mind that Jake remembered almost nothing about the experience. For that reason the call the day before, asking if he wanted to go for a drive, and maybe a night swim, came out of the blue.

Why don' you do sumpin' about it?

No, rully—I dunno what you mean. Like what? It's cooler here on top the cliff, and you already got th' top down.

Y' know.

No. I don't.

I dare you.

T' do what?

Y' know.

No—

—Take your clothes off.

My clothes!

If you do it, I'll—

The events of the previous week notwithstanding, Jake would tell Wren later that he felt he'd be undressing in front of stranger. Beyond that, I think it wasn't so much the act of removing his tee, jeans, and whathaveyou so much as the thought of doing it with someone with so many strings attached, all pointing to Saint Andrej's, but especially at Rauch, "that bigmouth," and Leo for sure, not to mention god knows who else, circling back to Harry, Florrie and, god forbid, Diana, from whom he'd never hear the end of it. In sum, even at fifteen, Jake sussed what was what. Never mind he'd droned on about Romeo—how many times?—to Wren and me, in tones even sensitive ears could never have picked up on through the door.

Wouldn' it be cooler t' be naked? Romeo persisted. The cliff falls directly in front, beyond which looms a well of darkness, the stars having been clothed by clouds and gritty air, the great lake too, that expanse of once-fresh water left by the glacier which lies twenty meters down, a body that can be both whiffed and heard but not seen.

C'mon let's do it. You an' me.

I dunno—

Romeo being Romeo, showing all the confidence of his class, as Marks insists—Marks, who would return one day fired up after a spell in the Big Apple, having headed east while the rest of the graveyard crew went west, to Sandusky. For the moment Romeo pushes, prods, and cajoles to get his way, his bulk making an argument as powerful as his words, though Jake, he still isn't sure. So we sit, taking in the nonview of what's in front of us, the two trading glances back and forth, crickets sounding in the silence as Romeo drums his fingers on the steering column.

Jake a lamb all of a sudden—it was what? The fact that he was coming from a world always on guard, where a comment never served as a statement and a door never served as a barrier? If just the idea of them, sitting undressed and overlooking the lake—if it ever got back. I could see Jake calculating the cost of throwing caution to the wind, along with his outer skin, the heated air lifting his hair and at times flipping it in his face—

—T' be honest I'm not sure why people even bother with clothes, argues Romeo. Not in weather like this. Animals got it better—I mean, sometime clothes ain't pra'tical.

I caught Jake mulling the idea, but resisting it mostly, as the green, leafy air stilled around us. We peer again into the darkness. We've been in idle the whole time and Romeo revs the engine, breaking the silence. He eyes Jake, whirrs the engine again, and Jake warns, Cheese it! The fuzz!

Indeed, just at that moment a patrol car ambles toward us, and the boys glue themselves to their seats. They're now two teens out for air on a hot night, bottles hidden between their thighs, not thinking of anything but the firmament as the police pull up. The two glance in opposite directions. Romeo is old enough to drive, though only just, yet the two know how to ditch the beer and play possum. If Harry's impressed one thing on Jake—no, two bits of advice—they would have to be, A, Always keep an eye out for the fuzz, and, B, Never peach on a fellow, as Harry heard say. No matter what. Even if he's trying to get you to disrobe in public. Keep it to yourself.

Satisfied there's no mixed company here, which is to say anything suspicious going on, the spotlight on the side of the vehicle switches off and the cruiser flips into reverse before peeling away, leaving us alone with our thoughts sailing. Jake's hand traps a gust from Canada while Romeo's fingers continue to tap the steering column. He urges Jake, lifting his chin as he speaks, C'mon, drink up! The boy raises the bottle he's been nursing, tips it and wets his tongue. Romeo waits then kills the engine. He slides the key in and out of the ignition then tosses it in the air. He pockets it.

C'mon, you can do better'n 'at!

Outside the vehicle cicadas drone with some kind of news. Peepers sound an alert. Crickets and gnats, lightening bugs, moths, mockingbirds too, whisper, gossip, and tweet as the two in the front start to talk turkey, the 3.2 kind that Romeo copped from his brother.

When pressed, Jake hazards another sip from the same bottle Romeo offered after we slipped into these leather seats, before passing out of Laurentine. Growing impatient, Romeo reaches over, rips the bottle from Jake's hand, puts it to his own mouth and upends it. He extends his tongue to catch the last few drops and chucks the thing like a football over the windshield and hood and into the vacant air. After a pause we hear it split into shards below.

That's how it's done, cowboy! Not with a thousan' girly sips.

Romeo extends his arm to the back and rummages blindly through a sack below. He takes another—Here! he remarks. Lemme see you drain it in one go. He screws the cap free and thrusts the bottle toward Jake who studies it for a second, not having had much practice. Again the boy lifts the thing daintily, until Romeo grabs hold of it. He yanks it from Jake's hand and teeter-tauters the boy's head back, gripping his hair, and with his other hand jiggers the bottle to a headstand.

C'mon! he complains. What are you waitin' for!?

I hear the boy cough then snort, pinching his nose.

Look at what you're doin'! Yer makin' a mess!

Rivulets glimmer down Jake's neck when Romeo pulls the bottle away, launching it atop the concrete blocks below until again we hear the sound of glass shattering. Jake coughs repeatedly, and Romeo informs him, That's how you drink a beer, cowboy. Now lemme see you do it on your own.

My boy, meanwhile, slumps in his seat. He says it feels like pop in his veins, warm n' fizzy. He quips, I'm all tingly, and Romeo enthuses, That's th' *point*! It's what it's all about, what we've been waitin' for all this time, ain't we?—he glances at me as though I were in on the scheme, then rests his hand on Jake's thigh. C'mon. One more. Jus' for me. All on your own.

Gimme a minute.

No, do it now—it's better not t' wait.

Jake tries to jerk himself upright so he doesn't spill anything this time around. He flips up until he's kneeling on the seat, leaning toward me so close that his face is almost butt up against mine. He lurches in an effort to rip the bag open, staring upward, not noticing I'm there. The contents in the sack are sent rolling around as he nabs a bottle, prying the cap with his teeth, a trick Harry taught him ages ago, but just as he's about to down the contents he again goes timid, opening a rift between the two in the front, the disappointment on Romeo's face registering clearly. Betrayed again, his expression reads. Mutinied by a guy expert at stalling, despite the press of nature.

The two gaze at each other for an eternity until Romeo warns, If you're not gonna play ball, cowboy, then let's go back—why d'you think we're here? It's a warning Jake responds to by craning his neck, opening his mouth, and emptying the bottle in one go. When it's clear nothing remains, Romeo chides, Was that so hard?

Jake pours his body now into the seat. He complains the cicadas are deafening, the crickets too. He wonders why someone's gone and cranked up the volume as his right hand flops along the flank of the seat, his knuckles dragging willy-nilly, chimpanzee-like across the carpet, until Romeo nudges him some.

You ain't gonna fall asleep on me again, are you, cowboy? C'mon—I need you t' stay with me. He slaps Jake's face. Best thing t' do is keep drinkin'.

When Jake demurs yet again, Romeo insists that he down one and then another, assisting him when the boy comes close to wasting any more of his time. When he appears on the verge of lights-out, Romeo dares him to stand in front of the headlights and do a little dance. He pokes and jabs, his fingers stabbing Jake's ribs, until the boy starts, then stands on the soft leather in his bare feet, having lost his flip-flops in the abyss beneath the seat, after which he removes his tee-shirt, jeans, and everything else, tossing them on me.

Now we have a *party*! Romeo claps, running his hand along Jake's thigh, up to his behind.

Jake sidles around the windshield and onto the hood, ooching and ouching as though jumping on coals, then down he falls on the uncut grass, after which he manages to get himself erect again, tightrope-walking along the cliff's edge. As though he'd never given it a moment's thought. As though it were the most natural thing in the world to do. To be leaping in slomo in the headlights like a deer all of a sudden, showing tail. Moths circle around and crash into the lamps as he attempts a jig with his hands thrown up overhead, as though about to be shaken down. He giggles as his knees buckle then lengthen out, and out of the car Romeo slinks after having had his fun gazing, whistling, and catcalling, sounding the horn and flashing the beams. In no time he and I are stumbling along the edge of the precipice, trailing Jake in the darkness, overlooking the deadpan lake. I nose here and there in the grass under the moonlight, and Romeo sidles, then clops alongside Jake. C'mere, cowboy, he sighs, in a deep, practiced voice. But Jake shies away.

I said c'mere! he repeats, drawing off his tee and peeling his jeans and what's beneath, lickety split, as though they're aflame, while Jake absents himself, having gone questioning the pass of events again, even in his drunken state.

I said, c'mere, you!

Romeo tracks after Jake, who yanks himself away in earnest now, almost tumbling head over heals below. He darts off, but Romeo snags his hand, overpowers and reels it in, touching it to his chest, stomach, and beneath. With his bulk he easily skittles Jake nearer still, and the boy now, broken in a sense, is petting a bull. He touches Romeo's bicep reluctantly, as though it were feral, pets the fur on the chest, moves his hand over the rest of what's there, the rigidity of it, the softness too.

I like you best without clothes, Romeo murmurs. I ain't interested in you any other way. When my boy jerks to free himself the other advances, then tackles him to the ground.

Jake lies pressed beneath Romeo, against the grass and weeds, unable to budge or hightail it out of there if he wanted to, only to escape where-to, anyway? No matter where he went it'd be short of helpful. Should he make a break for it? Tear through the parking lot? Stumble toward Lake Shore? Sprint the length of the boulevard, or the beach, all the way back to Laurentine? How would that work with Jake separated from his other skin, the one culture requires at all times except in the privacy of one's own home, and even then? In the absence of any clear option he remains put, contemplating, Romeo atop him then dragging him back to the ledge in front of the car where the blacktop gives way to softer grass.

Again Jake breaks for it like a panicked deer, as though being captured spelled his demise, but again Romeo tracks him down, his size allowing him to outpace and outpower my boy, who's slight by comparison. When he has him in his grip he commands Jake not to speak, traps his hand against his skin again, moves it as though it had no mind of its own, then flips Jake face down. He straddles and immobilizes him, then drooling a rope of saliva in his hand gets down to work. He grumbles in Jake's ear, Why the big fuss, cowboy? Admit it—Romeo pants heavily as he speaks, his limbs visibly trembling for someone so cock sure. I seen you. All them times, in the halls at St. Andy's. Checkin' me out—you been wantin' this for a loooong, looooong time—

Bitten

I KNEW THIS GUY—

The other's fingers charm the fret board, make it sweat. Jake eyes him, though the other doesn't return his gaze because he's eyeing his fingers, the sound hole, or god above, breaking away from time to time to peer up, upupup, to eye—whatever—only to return his vision to earth, where he seems to be in a trance. His vision flies skyward, then descends again on the fallen, unsaved world as his ear tunes in to the sad music of humanity, long enough to say, Praise god! Then off he flies to the ether.

I'm telling you 'cause I wanna be honest.

But the other continues fingering the fret board, his eyes now closed, his mind and body too, tuning in—to what? To Jesus, of course, somewhere in the substanceless air.

There was a guy. Him an' me—.

But the silky, steely arpeggios silence Jake, string together tightly, coil like DNA coupling with nothing, travelling to no destination other than up, up-up, to the void or that place Jake doesn't, never did, believe existed—

He hazards, I like you, and the other replies, Praise god! It's all from him. Shall we give praise?

Everythin'?

For sure. That is, t' everyone which loveth the—

—Are we on the same *page*?

Again the other, his hands flying in a blur, ejaculates, Praise god!

Just t' be sure—

—Praise god!

Peacoat's fingers pummel the fret board now. Relatively-recently-dried-out-and-sober Peacoat, saved by a loving divine through Pastor Bradford's stewardship, though not the kind down at the plant. By stewardship of another kind he coaxed Peacoat from the brink.

So what you're tellin' me—

—What I'm sayin' is praise god! Peacoat's fingers are as nimble as a spider's tail, spinning a web. It's all all right with god. He loves ya as ya are. That's what Pastor Bradford says. But you don't have t' believe him—it's in the book. He stops, brings his fingers at long last to a rest, a hummingbird lighting on a branch. He swings his knees around next to Jake's on the side of the bed, rests his hand on Jake's knee, massages it in the lord, says, It's Ohhh Kay. You just give your life over an' ever'thing'll be OK.

Jake looks at me and I gaze back.

Welllll?

Well what?

The furnishings are placed just so, as though aligned on a grid, that or bolted down, unmoveable, with not a thing out of place, or even out of square. The carpet fluffs like fur, fleecy and white. Unlike the rugs at our house, there's not a stain or spot to mar it. It feels as though inches of padding lay beneath each step. Jake and I are walking on air—I mean, this place is heaven. And yet for all its refinements, so well appointed, Romeo's parents have left it for the night, as they have so often since Jake and I were here the first time, half a year ago.

They're at some BS function, Romeo mutters, as though

Jake or I were asking. It's in their absence that Romeo has brought us here, yet again, to this place where last summer you could catch the music of the waves curling from the beach, upstairs, if you were listening. Though not tonight. Romeo plugs in a plastic pie and an aluminum cone shocks to light. It turns a series of tones, cast on the giant cone that rotates too, shooting stars at the ceiling, walls, and floor, and at us as well. Jake and I marvel at the pyro-technic show after Romeo has shuttled us to the couch—OK, me to the floor nearby. Don't get me wrong—I'm not complaining. Like I say this place is heaven.

To kick off the festivities after settling Jake down, Romeo reaches under the cone and mutters, Here—for you. He pitches a floppy softball of sorts in our direction, and because I can outgame my boy any day I snatch it, as is my custom when things are airborn. But Romeo charges— Heyyyy! That's not for you! It's for Jake. He attempts to free the thing without tearing it, it being brand new and all.

What can I say? Despite the fuss on the way here I'm in a gaming mood. Let! *Go!* Jake orders curtly, and I relinquish it—what's the big deal? When Romeo tries once again to toss the thing directly to Jake, the way one might shy a whiffle ball at a toddler—when he tries again the object strikes him in the face, even after Romeo encouraged, C'mon now, catch!

Jake nabs the thing from the floor before I can grab it again.

What is it?

What is it?!—Wha'd'y' think?

Jake replies unironically, It's sweet. He comes out with that before he's managed to unravel it, a present without paper, ribbon, or bow. He assures Romeo, as though he were fishing for a compliment, You know how to pick it. I'll treasure it. Always. He blurts it out just the way Florrie does when she opens a gift, usually before she's figured what it is, no matter what the article or how long it'll hang around, in or out of the box, in the attic, basement, or out in the trash—she always says, I'll treasure it always.

I'll always treasure it, Jake repeats as though Romeo hadn't heard.

I on the other hand, understanding there's nothing here for me, glance around and marvel. Again to be here is such a treat—I can't say it enough. Need I reiterate how impressed I am? Much more than usual as I take in the Rococo touches—maybe it's the slowly-turning color wheel casting everything in a glow. The *putti* and *fleurs-de-lis*, the gilding throughout, to the point of becoming a theme. The Chinese vases resting on several surfaces, the *chinoiserie* generally, proto-Asian figures that live in the wallpaper, making a statement or telling a story while defining the space. The *toile* window treatments, valences ballooning with dynastic, if generic lives of the Ming, or is it the Meiji, Joseon period, or some mongrel mix—they're a melting pot of colonial tastes. There's the layers of architectural touches, crown moldings, finials, curlicues, and bows, creating interest on so many of the surfaces. There are animal motifs too, lions, eagles, bees, and bats assuming many gestures, despite the prohibition on living, breathing animals in this space—Romeo reminded Jake of that once again when we came in, proof that the star of the field doesn't win at every game.

The opulence isn't lost on me. Such a step up, maybe ten or a hundred, from our place with its mishmash of forties and fifties pieces, scuffed and chipped. This, on the other hand, defines a certain kind of modern, old in new. Jake seems to shrink in the setting, even though he's won a door prize, which he's still fiddling with, unknotting it for what seems an endless amount of time, so much so that Romeo whisks it away and takes care of it himself.

I love it! he exclaims, snatching it back and holding it in front of him, flipping it from side to side.

Put it on.

Now?

Yeah. Just that.

Only this?

When Jake dilly dallies, Romeo grows impatient. He gripes, What are you waitin' for?! He tugs and pulls to assist the process, shying jeans, socks, and whathaveyou across the room, until Jake stands naked, as undressed as me. Then he arrests Jake's hand as he grabs his present, about to put it on, loath after all for Jake to cover anything up. He hassles him to forego the fashion show, then rests back on the sofa while Jake stands and rotates slowly, at Romeo's bidding, like the tree. He gazes for some time, informing Jake, We've got all the time in the world, and Jake obliges his viewership of one, two depending on who's counting. He slouches, then shifts back to some version of attention, until feeling too awkward to carry on, at which point he tries to skinny the tee over his head, as though it's not right to be the only one in your skin suit.

I said leave it off.

Jake ignores the command, intent on doing his thing as they say these days, however accusstomed he's become at submitting to Romeo's will on the nights we've been here, since the weather turned frigid—whenever the house is clear of adults. Despite the fact that Jake has been champing at the bit for just this moment, to the point of wondering out loud to Wren as to when, and if, it might ever happen again, there's something checking his usual enthusiasm, caused by an irritation he can't dismiss, the kind that leads an oyster to produce a pearl, an irritant that came up on the way here and raised a demon that has trailed us in. In short Jake was unhappy with the lack of face time lately, his face and Romeo's, the long gap between last time and the present. It'd been over three weeks since we saw hide nor hair of Romeo, Jake complained, after months when three days was an age, that is after that night above the lake. He accuses Romeo of apathy and blatant disinterest. And worse—

—Well, I'm here now.

But look how long it took. Longer than a act a Congress.

Nothin' takes that long.

You care more for her than me.

I care—

—No you don't. She gets everything, an' I get the crumbs. It's a crummy situation.

You don' know what you're sayin'.

In fact, during the past three-weeks-plus, Wren and I sat through a fire storm of moping, as though the sky were crashing down. Even Harry couldn't help but notice, drilling him—What's gotten up your behind—you're too young t' be depressed. That's for *old* people!

Nothin's gotten—

As usual, only Wren and I knew what was up. She advised, Don' worry! He'll come 'round—he always does.

Why do I always gotta wait?

I'm sure he'll come again. You gotta be patien'.

When we first stomped in, shaking the winter from our feet, the vibe I got was not a moodiness on Jake's part alone but Romeo's too, irked on account of Jake's barbs.

I don't owe you nuttin, cowboy.

Well then I don't owe you nuttin either.

Jake whisks the tee on and launches into a tirade, blaming Romeo for a string of abuses, causing him to shake his head and raise a hand, two, in place of a verbal defense. He turns away, peers behind the sofa as though pleading with another self, until he rises suddenly and plants his hands on the boy's neck, pressing his thumbs together, levitating the boy from the floor. He holds Jake there, his toes barely grazing the carpet—It doesn't matter what you like or don' like! Romeo's face draws near, though Jake's head is tilted back, parallel with the ceiling and unable to see.

I couldn't help myself, I charged the scene, let Romeo know my view on what was happening all of a sudden, though his response was to shoe me away, ignore me as if he never heard, so tuned in to an inner voice he was, the sound of blood about to boil or turn to steam because of Jake's harping, counting days and weeks in a way that threw cold water on his plans for the night, which was not right in light of the offering he'd made.

Jake heaves then gags. He coughs five, six, a dozen times after Romeo loosens his grip. His face turns colors in the shifting light, from one hue to another. His torso falls away, his arms dangling limply. When his body meets the floor Romeo bends over him and serves first one then a second blow across the face—You got it, cowboy—you *got* it? I don' need no talk from you! He grabs the boy's wrist, dragging him, half-raising him up with an animal strength, then loosens it until the boy reels and falls back to the floor.

Look at what you made me do! Romeo huffs in frustration, sitting excitedly on the edge of the sofa, erect.

Meanwhile Jake struggles to draw air. He tries to lift himself, as though he'd give anything to be upright. He feels his throat, cheek, and wrist as Romeo's torso softens and reclines. He swings then lowers his foot between Jake's thighs, leaves the couch and angles toward him on his hands and knees, nuzzles his nose against Jake's cheek, whispering, Why d' you make me do it? Why do you push that way? He lifts himself, stands and undresses, towers like a sculpture, the very one Jake has tried to picture for Wren in hushed tones behind his bedroom door. Here it is, the very thing, imagined by Jake during the desert stretch, the two or three or however many weeks it's been since Romeo said boo. As though the weeks flashed by with the speed of a kick.

Romeo lowers then wraps himself around the boy as though he were a garment, a whole other kind of gift. He tries to shinny Jake up, support him as though he were a doll or dummy, then snakes after him when he tumbles down again. He comments, If I had a camera I'd take your pitcher, you look so amazin' right now. A guy like you, Jake, you're a gem—trus' me. He runs his hands up the back and across the nape of the neck. Your hair's like sand. Your skin's like snow. He turns Jake's head around, remarking, Your teeth are like pearls. You'll look so sexy in that shirt I got you. Skin tight.

He goes on about Jake's thighs wrists ankles soles palms and armpits, his neck hands and kneecaps, backridge, hips, down to what he could imagine he'd find if he could cut Jake open and eat him up. Make jerky outta you, cowboy. Snack on you all day. Then we'd never be apart.

You'd like that.

Romeo kisses Jake from head to toe more amorously than I'm used to seeing, as though he were a gift, more desirable than anything on earth. He wastes whatever time's needed to coax Jake back to life, then takes him in, working his lips and tongue as though sucking a nipple, until the milk starts to flow. How hard was that? he pleads, observing, scraping his lip with his thumb. It took awhile for words to come by way of reply, for time to notice finally the Minnie Mouse tee, allow the thought of it to work its magic. Long story short, it required all that and more to mollify the boy, at the moment and in situations like it more numerous than I can count, once Jake's recovered the in- and out-take of air.

Yu shda movd a lng timago, admonishes Harry, rousing from a microsleep, picking up the conversation where he left off.

Let it go, counsels Florrie.

I like it here, interjects Wren. It's better'n Laurentine.

Slly grl.

I don't wanna talk about it nomore, finalizes Midge, flaring the end of a cigarette and setting her lighter on the arm of the sofa. I'm gonna get a a pop. Anyone want one?

I do, pipes Florrie.

Me, too, orders Diana. No ice this time.

Miss Glasby lifts herself from her chair, stair-stepping her arm from the seat to the rungs of the splat. I'll get it for you, she groans, but Midge insists, I can do it. She moves her foot, swollen to the ankle, the edema she's been seeing her GP about. The linoleum thunders when she plops the leg down; her heel sets off a hollow boom. Miss Glasby, free of the clutches of the chair, pads in Midge's wake, and Diana too trails behind. I look around the room, feel a bit of apprehension. The only sound to break the silence is Harry's presnoring and Ruby's humming, her rocker tacking the linoleum up and down.

Ruby's idle drumming. What time're we gonna leave? she asks. I hope you're gonna drive. She's looking at Florrie, commenting in that stage whisper of hers that the interred could hear, though maybe not Harry. He's deader than dead in a fashion, in no condition to catch Ruby's version of low tones. Leo switches the channels on the TV, bypassing the movie about snow, cycling through the handful of channels—other than the black-and-white film it's either a rebroadcast of Mass from the Vatican, or worse, the nightly news.

I'm outta here. I'll be in my room, he quips, peering at Wren, and Jake looks away. Jake now with Ruby, Florrie, and quasi-Harry, Wren having trailed behind Leo after all. After she leaves it's clear Harry has joined the ranks of the furniture.

When's the oparation? blurts Ruby.

Three mor' days.

The chattering goes on awhile, and I too make my way along the wainscoting, over the rose-garden linoleum. I walk under the pansy and daisy wallpaper, nose the door open into Leo's room, cracking it ajar, eye what Jake's afraid to see. Wren approaches—Mollykins, she enthuses, but Leo grasps the door handle and slams it shut. I continue my odyssey along the hall, through the swinging door in the kitchen, welcome and warm when we arrived but now turned something cooler.

Wha' d' you mean, she just threw it out? Midge tugs at the handle of the ice tray as she speaks, waiting until she hears a crack then the sound of fracturing.

She threw it out—you know, *out*! Like. A. Crazywoman.

Oh my, my, comments Miss Glasby. It must be all the stress.

She's gone batty, observes Diana.

Sure makes y' wonder, don' it? agrees Midge. To go off th' deep end like that.

Jake enters. What deep end?

No one's talkin' t' you, complains Diana. This is a private meeting.

Oh, it ain't private, comments Miss Glasby. You're welcome t' stay, Jake honey, that is if you want. Diana's just jokin'.

I'm lookin' for Wren.

Well, who knows where that twirp's at. Why don' you get lost?

Diana, remarks Miss Glasby.

Who wants t' be aroun' you anyway? returns Jake. C'mon Molly!

I eye Jake, tell him I'll be there in a minute, that I'm busy at present. Miss Glasby's started piecing on the carcass, spooning stuffing, room temperature, from the cavity into a plastic bowl while Diana looks on. Midge has just finished pouring three pops, plopped several cubes in all but Diana's glass. I distinctly heard the fizz as the ice splashed in, witnessed the overflow all the way from down here.

Give this to your mamma, will you, dear? yells Midge as Jake's about to disappear down the hall. She limps over to him and returns, sets the empty tray in the sink under a faucet that taps away in unison with Jake's footsteps. Midge pulls the one free chair away from the table and the legs spread as she relaxes into it. I watch as she reaches forward too, tugs a few patches of skin free, with hanks of fat attached, follow as they disappear from hand to mouth, back and forth, until Miss Glasby finally takes notice and coos, Here you go, Molly dear, balling toward me a wad of stuffing.

Diana rattles, Thass gonna make 'er fart.

Not such a small amount. A little bit ain't gonna hurt—is it, Molly dear?

Diana, continya.

It was on the lawn.

The lawn!? *What* lawn?!

Th'*front* lawn! *Our* lawn!

Midge jerks her head back as Diana speaks, sucking on a filter.

It. Was. On. The. *Front.* Lawn—d'you b'lieve it? For all the world t' see.

Oh my, my. Th' poor thing. It must be th'anticipation.

Poor thing, my ass, whines Midge. Sounds like she's gone coocoo. Her eyes cross when she says coocoo, her head cocks to one side, and she erupts at her own joke. She coughs up a spot of phlegm, hacks again until it loosens, swallows then chokes, and Diana laughs too.

Surely she din't mean it. With everything she's got on 'er plate an' all.

Jake and Wren were bawlin' like babies. But they always start bawlin' when she gets like that.

She always did operate on a hair trigger.

Heavens! She did no such thing! She was always steady as a stone.

Was not. You just don't remember. Y' always did like her best.

It happens every year this time, Diana explains. She juss. Flips. *Out.*

Well, and it ain't a regular year after all, so it makes sense. She seems fine now.

Still, she don' know when she crossed a line, says Midge. I mean t' drag a chrissmuss tree, fully trimmed, with balls and lights and tinsel, out the door and deposit it in the snow and ice, in the middle a th' lawn, in broad daylight, for god an' the world t' see. I can only imagine th' spectacle.

What happened to it, Diana dear?

Jake an' Wren brought it back. Or tried to. She was screamin' like a banshee, Don' you touch it! Don' either a yous dare touch it! But they wouldn' listen. She goes, I said I wasn' gonna put up with another holiday like this and I mean' it. If he wants t' ruin it for the rest a us with that demon a his, then let it be on his conscien', not mine! Then Wren bawls, He ain't the one ruinin' it—*you* are! And that's when she haul off an' hit 'er.

Hit her?!

She. Hit. Her.

Wren?!

My poor Wrennie.

Like I say, she's gone coocoo. Again Midge crosses her eyes as she pronounces her diagnosis, and again Diana laughs, so much so that she chokes on her pop until some comes out her nose. Meanwhile, between intervals of laughing and dismay, when no one's paying any mind, Miss Glasby slips me a sizeable chunk of white meat, which I inhale.

Jake run up t' her and goes, Don' do that! Don' *ever* do that! He pulls Florrie away from Wren and tells her t' take one end and help 'im bring the thing back inside.

And all this this mornin', right in front a th' house.

Do. You. B'lieve. It.

Diana dear, I'm not sayin' I do. I'm not saying yer lyin' neither. But I swear she was never like that. Are you sure it happen jus' that way?

I swear on a stack a bibles.

Miss Glasby sits for a moment thinking. A great lake taps from the faucet before she speaks. You might not wanna go spreadin' that story around, Diana dear. You neither, Midge. It's a little shocking, don' y' think? You don't want that kind a thing to get outside the fam'ly?

Midge offers me a piece of skin and I do magic on it. She quips, Why should I give a crap? What in the world do I gotta hide?

I'm thinking about dinner, which was especially sweet.

I made this just for you, Precious, Florrie enthuses, she practically sings, setting the plate down in front of me. It's true—she didn't miss. She boiled an egg, and what's more she didn't go off and forget. She kept it soft the way I like it, mixed it with fowl in a heap—my favorite. Don' let Diana see you, she warns. But I was scarfing it down so fast I was sure she wouldn't have the chance.

Let's hope it don't cause a accident. Her nightgown juts at the chest, embracing a world. The topography looks unstable at the top with its usual support gone; it's as though things have become dislodged, fallen, like a crumbling pyramid, the loss of a civilization.

She vanishes, and I hear the shower run. When she returns she lowers herself. Did you enjoy it, Molly dear? Her hair, usually inflated, has collapsed like straw around her face—she takes me in her arms. The two of us head down the stairs to the landing and out the screen door toward the backyard. *Fwap!* the aluminum frame goes behind us. The air this time of year blows cool. Drifting colors have matted into a carpet, the leafrot setting in.

Oh, Jesus. Dear Jesus.

Florrie wipes beads of sweat with a damp dishcloth, the air mercifully cool though Florrie is mercurially hot, sweating profusely, as though in her own private micro climate. It's enough t' drive a woman to drink. And after all my life without a drop.

There are dependencies and dependencies, I learn—who knew a person could be addicted to such a tiny pill, the one she's been taking since the operation, a couple days after Christmas all those years ago? That is until lately. The desire to cave, end this torment with a swallow, halt this heat in a second or hour or day, a few weeks perhaps. The salty rivulets pour down Florrie's forehead, cheek, and neck. She dabs her face, blows short, delicate breaths.

It'll pass. . . . It'll all pass, Mollykins.

No doubt the heat and sweat, the whole kit-and-caboodle, this green we're on, carpeted with leaves, me and Florrie, our generation and beyond—it'll all pass, someday. But for now she, and by extension I, am fired like the sun in the lit black of the yard. She sets me on the grass. The October air, almost a month past the equinox, has chilled the lawn to the edge of freezing, with Florrie a walking firebox having the potential to burn up everything, the whole world I belong to. But when she speaks it isn't about thermodynamics or the failures of modern medicine to mimic nature, to mimic hormones. Not that, side effects, withdrawal, or anything— instead she laments, That girl.

She can' help it. It runs in th'blood. How can you fight it? I can't even blame myself nomore. If only Jake was here, my little Wren. But god has his ways.

Back inside, after the fire's abated until next time, Florrie latches the screen, snaps the lock on the door with the paralyzed handle, her slippers shuff, up the linoleum treads, and she pours a pop from the fridge, just for herself. She ambles to the kitchenette and steadies herself as her body lowers, groaning as she descends and lands. I stand there looking at her.

What, darlin'?

Her cheeks hang on her face for the first time I can remember. Always youthful Florrie, the one whose age people usally misguess, the one everyone wagers is younger than Midge instead of the other way around—look at her now.

What d'you want, love?

My mind strays even as my body remains glued to the spot. I've been warned, my name worn tissue thin with use— Molly! Get back here! Molly, don't wander off! Molly, what in the world are you doin' over there?! My name tethers me, the violence in a name, one I never chose and wasn't asking for, a sound so unlike my natural idiom, but one that defines me all the same the way names do, they limit you, all the while Jake and Romeo flap around like newly fledged birds, playing on a field of dunes, the frilly wave foam skirting the place, silhouetted by the morning sun, the two boys' bodies shade black from a distance—you'd never know they were trotting like horses without dressing. From an opposite perspective, when they stand in a different attitude toward the sun, the boys flash light, almost white—like I say it depends on your point of view, the slant from which you eye things. One thing's for sure and that is other than me no one but god is watching—or that's what these two are assuming. How closely or with what level of approbation, condemnation, or indifference the divine sees—who am I to judge? Not being a mind- or spirit-reader, the only thing I know is no bolt bears down from the heavens, though a thunder bumper or two threaten on the horizon, sailing in from Canada, positioned to arrive a little later in the afternoon. At the moment at least there's no worm to mar the apple—or the egg of an idea hatched in the mind of the pale one, never mind it was the darker of the two who planted the seed the way he always does, not being one to suggest things directly. It was Jake who piped up and said, as though it were his and only his idea, Let's get naked on th' beach.

Excellent idea, Jay.

Jaybird is more like it. Two. They were lying on Romeo's bed and the barometer at Romeo's core that never lies registered on the intense-interest end of the spectrum—and so here we are, though this is no gingham-and-lace picnic the way Jake and I are used to. There's no wicker basket or Tupperware burping the air of cold cuts, smoked fish, potato salad, or slaw. There are no relish plates, deviled eggs, or celery stalks, stuffed with cream cheese and topped with a shake of paprika. No radishes, cornichons, nor any other garnishes, no colorful plates shaped like roses, let alone silver-plastic utensils, paper napkins or otherwise—to sum up, there's none of the typical Florrian fare we usually enjoy when dining in nature. Instead, Romeo told his mother this morning, the Tirolean beauty he calls Suzie to her face, he informs her, I'm takin' this, then extracts a tray of potatoes and sausages with aluminum foil crumpled around the edges, leftovers from the night before.

Vell? Vare are you goink?

None a your bus'ness.

Don' talk t' your muzza like zat!

I'm goin' where I'm goin'.

I haff a *r-r-right* to know.

No, you don'. I'm eighteen.

Romeo rests one side of the pan on his hip, the other under his palm. See you, he gabbles. Sometime.

He's slipping his moccasins on as he zips past his mother who's trying to block him at the door. Jake and I stood looking on, aghast—I'll speak for him and me both, attest to the fact we were in a state of disbelief—to think of talking to Florrie that way. But we kept mum, afraid to upset the apple cart, which had been upended enough already.

D'you see how my son *tr-r-r-reat* me? Vare can you be goink at seffen-sirty in za mornink?

But we're already rolling, slinking down the driveway while eyeing Mrs. Geist, slump-shouldered in her nightgown and oversized slippers, smoke trailing from her hand. At each traffic light along Lake Shore, wheeling west toward the Forest City, the outer layers peel away. Romeo and Jake slide closer and closer to me in my native undress as we wait at each successive light until we finally arrive at the beach in what might be called a state of precivilization, a time before the second skin was adopted, mandated is more like it, in the safety and security of the Mustang, or is it a Trojan horse that threatens to overthrow society, or usher it back to its roots. In a manner of speaking we were closer to nature, to whatever degree there is such a thing, it and culture being one and the same—if there's a word for something it's lost. To humans. Custom. Whatever you want to call it, too knowing for its own good. Nevertheless, the state of the world shifted as we drove.

After toweling their lower halves to satisfy the sensibilities of passersby, the two naturists and I made our way to this patch of sand, a good deal distant from anywhere Harry and Florrie have ever been, historically or metaphorically, so far as I know, light years from where in their early years they paddled together, feet in unison as they propelled a boat around Rockefeller Lagoon, not long before it was christened with a name. That place is miles away, a most public of spaces compared to this stretch, private enough for us to prance around, the three of us naked to the very skin—derry, derry, derry, da. It doesn't look like the place has drawn the foot prints of humans for years—it's somehow escaped the usual stragglers and daytrippers on the public beach, there to the east, at the end of the horizon where the members of the night shift will gather someday. Once you venture far enough over the concrete blocks, bulwarks that have failed to slow the advance of the lake, you land on a smooth patch all your own, the homes set back, above the cliff. The three of us in an animal state skirting the waves, the sand between our toes and backsides.

Seagulls and swallows, loop-de-looping among the breakers, descend for a tidbit when Jake lifts one in the air. The two tag each other too, run keep-away from me when I try to land a bite, a minor morsel, registering my disapproval at the rigged game of hot potato, in which I always had to give over my quarry, even though I outperformed these two. Despite the look of things, pre-culture and pre-speech, Jake's tendency is to rely on words, especially when he fails at more primal skills like catch, complaining as he does about the stones dotting the sand, his slippery-watery hands, the strong winds, and so on, though Romeo pays him no mind. To his excuses, but even more his brazen ideas lately about Where all this is going.

Shut it! We're here! Enjoy it, an' button that lip a yours.

In the long and short of things, Jake morphs into Notjake, having been mummed. To put an even finer point on his sentiment Romeo adds, Really, Jake. Can it. Or wull go back.

So the two drop the chatter and instead fling the Frisbee back and forth, though as I say I outcatch Jake every time, snatching the thing from the air, a feather-light cousin of its metal forebear. Romeo with his upper body strength sails the thing toward the stratosphere, yelling, Grabbit, Jake! *Graaaab*bit! and then retreats behind the usual, Nevvvver *minnnnd* when the he flubs the catch a dozen more times than not, until finally the saucer hits him—*Fwhack!*— in the face—which, were it the antique thing, the boy wouldn't survive the day. So, thanks to the miracle of plastic in its usable form, before it ends in a pile across the land- or seascape, everywhere the eye can see—thanks to that a fourth-rate athlete like Jake, with his inability to coordinate a catch without a dose of luck, he'll walk away from the day with nothing more than a scratch, or a line, red and sore, written on the length of his face.

Truth be told he suffers these games for Romeo's sake, especially after the rift he caused last time that stretched months and maybe more than half a year, after Jake went and put his foot down, demanded better treatment than what he was getting, beyond the lack of face time, a tack that put Romeo in a pet to say the least, frightful to behold. It made him quit any further contact, the opposite of Jake's intention, during which time Romeo focused his energies on the woman in the sister-tee, shirt-twin to Jake's, the one that Leo pointed to at Midge's house that time. And yet—

wonder of wonders—Romeo turned out to be as pliable as plastic after all, unable to get by without a dose of Jake now and again. At least that's how Jake read things when he spotted the Mustang slink by the house then circle back, not long ago, holding off until finally pulling up the drive. Romeo didn't even have to open the door or beat a humble path to the stoop because Jake shot out the front first, made a beeline to the car and jumped in, bucket seat to bucket seat, telling Romeo, and Wren and me later that evening, that the guy couldn't live without him after all. It never occurred to him the reason might be trouble in paradise between Lover Boy and the Other Woman, who might be going through something akin to Jake's own troubles, because Jake viewed her as his nemesis, it never occurring to him that the two might have something in common were they ever to compare notes. That she might be a body to warm up to in another sense, as an ally, one unaware of Romeo's other life. Instead, Jake read Romeo's actions from a single perspective, a reader's no-no, namely as a way of saying yes to him alone, to their own, private idiom, mostly physical and devoid of words to label it by openly—god forbid—at least until a six pack had kicked in.

Their own private language, or so they flattered themselves.

It should be pointed out that the two didn't invent the idea of any of this here today. It was in a sense common, in the air back then, or the film reels. As though a good portion of America were shedding its skin in a trend moving inward from the coasts, a society of nudes that was condemned in the opinion pages of the *Press*, and *Your Sunday Visitor* most of all, cast as a movement from the devil. Herds of young people living buck naked in communes where morals and goods were checked at the door, along with the clothes of the country's sons and daughters, making the virgin cry, Florrie argued, what with marriage surrendered, chained like a mutt to a stake. Communists, the word was. Degenerates. An undoing. Of not just democracy but civilization itself.

As though you could ever return to that state.

Again it was in the air, the movie reels. Nudity extolled in a three-hour film of uncouth, ill-bred youths, as Florrie put it, despite the fact she'd never seen the film herself, a motion picture about hippies sliding in "nuttin' but filth an' mud." Romeo's brother turned over his and his wife's IDs so these two here could catch a glimpse of that world in the blackened theater. They sopped it up, the rain, mud, and flesh, the topsy-turvy array of bodies and body parts, normally verboten but now flouncing and flapping and jutting around. Tossing a Frisbee.

Cowboy, we can do that too, Romeo declared. It only required a bit of hybridizing because there was no nod to the kind of nakedness I'm seeing now at the bottom of this cliff here. In fact the film was all Adams and Eves, as Jake pointed out in Romeo's car later. To find anything similar to this you had to skulk around the theaters downtown. It was Jake who flashed an ad for one of those films a few minutes ago, advertised in *The Great Swamp Erie Da Da Boom,* a copy of which he picked up on a foray under the Terminal Tower—there's the picture in black and white, mostly black but not so dark you can't get what's going on.

That's disgusting!

I think it's sweet.

If that's what you're after, cowboy, you're barkin' up the wrong tree.

Don' say that.

That's def'nally not for me. I mean I could puke.

And yet there it was in a photo in the underground rag, though the image, a frame from some movie about youths in some kind of band, Romeo had turned face down, plopping the tray of food on top. Jake carried the *Great Swamp Erie* in his knapsack just to show Romeo what was possible, to suggest in some way that there were other options than their routinized fare, which had developed almost fascistically as most routines do, going back to the time above the lake and possibly before although, like all ur-moments, it was veiled in mist.

Jake wanted to switch things up now that he and Romeo are keeping company again, he said, and especially now that he's starting to realize he has some kind of power over Romeo, after thinking for so long that things were the reverse.

—I mean wha' do you want from me! Lemme see you guzzle this.

Jake swills until his lips curl, then Romeo takes his turn, though it requires a great deal more than Jake before he begins to feel the buzz. After that the sky's the limit.

Florrie wakes from her usual presleep on the davenport, switches off the light in the kitchen, and listens to the tick of the clock in the room. In the dim light she squeaks the floor boards beneath the indoor-outdoor carpeting. Sounds pipe like an organ at each step, groan under the threadbare pile as she mazes her way through bottles and newspapers near Harry's chair in front of the picture window.

Harry, she whispers, shaking his shoulder, but he fails to budge. His jaw hangs slack, almost serenely, his head tilts back.

Harry, she repeats.

Harry!

You can't sleep here all night. You're liable ta end up with a stiff neck. Catch your death a cold. After several more efforts she shifts her gaze. She looks at me as if to say, Well? Then she peers back.

Harry. She quakes his shoulder again—Harry. She asserts again, more loudly this time though not enough to stir Diana. It's chilly and you're gonna catch your death.

Still no response to the kind of budge that always works. As if startled awake herself now, by a line she's used a thousand times if she's used it once, a line that comes from Ruby, and no doubt from her mother Ruby, and from her mother, in a daisy chain of Rubys, stringing all the way back to the ur-Ruby on the green island—the Ruby Eve—You're gonna catch your death is what they always say, as though it were in the genes.

Florrie's moved now. Her posture alters. She leans in the low light, sidles closer to the man in the chair. Her face nears his chest—to see. She looks at me, What should I do? I eye her—What would I know? Still jackknifed at the hip, her breasts rocking down, she peers toward the ceiling in the direction where Diana sleeps, the bed-by-nine, up-by-eight type, with rare exceptions—she's already ascended to her perch and doesn't like interruptions. Night is her time—Best part of the day, she likes to say—god forbid Florrie should cast a cloud on it. Diana, the beauty-sleeper, the one who pronounced Florrie an it after the operation when Ruby came to live with us, a visit that started as a sojourn to lend Harry a hand and that morphed into an exile. From now on, said Diana on the evening of the operation, while Florrie lay in a Demerol haze in the hospital—Diana was cornering a piece of pork from the Chinese take-out that Harry splurged on, because Ruby wasn't really one to cook, chasing the bite of pork around with her fork, that and a piece of miniature corn, avoiding the pool of duck sauce on the low side of her plate—From now on, she said, she's gonna be an it. As in no longer gendered. Other gendered's more like it, I thought to myself at the time. Her and me. Not neutered or degendered no matter what they say, in the rush to reduce everything to two, granting a third, slush cagegory for everything else that doesn't fit. It was yet another massaging of the options A or B. X or Y. Florrie herself held to that algebra. Until the operation.

She taps Harry's shoulder with the nub of her finger. The metal tips of the silk bow at the neck of her nightie catch the forty-watt glimmer, enough to reflect toward me. She waits for a response but none comes. What should I do, Molly? she pleads. What should I *do*? I stir, repeat that her guess is as good as mine—I shoot her that look. Her face is adjacent to Harry's now, closer than I've seen it in years. Do you think I should call Wren and Do—? I mean they're close enough. But before she can finish, as though a portion of the name itself were enough to raise Harry from the underworld, he gasps, like a free diver who at long last, past the point possible to survive down there, has finally come up for air.

Florrie starts, breathes, Oh ma god, Molly. Just think—

Having resigned herself to the fact he won't be coming to bed, she leaves and returns. She drapes a blanket on what appears to be a heaving corpse. It falls over the torso and legs, chair and ottoman, that christian fantasy, Harry swagged in seagulls on a dark sea, his face rosy as a sailor's morning. His jaw drops, the back of his head props on the chairback. Florrie kisses the forehead, avoiding the lips, the portal to the stomach, the bowels, and the demands of the flesh, the blackened lungs too, the lips that part like gates.

Less go t' bed, Precious.

She lifts me with a groan, carries me to her room.

But that was earlier. I wake now from unsettling dreams while Florrie's dead to the world... *Khhhhh...Khh!...Khhhh...*

I nose her.

Florrie.

Florrie!

But now it's she who doesn't wake. I bring my nose close to hers, endeavor to kiss her awake, but does she budge?

The whole lot ringed around the parlor, the place for parleying that doubles as Midge's boudoir where she entertains gentleman callers, in hushed tones, after the house has bedded down. I've tramped here to the kitchen in the wake of Miss Glasby, to the place that Ruby, a once-upon-a-time-married lady, never warmed up to, to pots, pans, and plates, chopping, dicing, and mincing, or any of the things that devolved over time solely to her twin. Ruby never worried with her around, the sister who never went for getting hitched, that or offspring. What was she to do, having been born when she was, when suitable alternatives to Ruby's life didn't exist, when the gods of time hadn't dealt her an especially good hand, not in her position? That, at least, is the way Midge will one day relate the story to Wren and Donald, when Miss Glasby is no longer around to rebut her.

To me she seems content. As though she never hankered after Ruby's life, especially once Ruby's husband kicked the bucket, as Midge puts it, and had to parent alone. Miss Glasby hunched her way back to the kitchen with me in tow to retrieve the package Wren gave her when we first arrived. Ever spritely Wren, despite the comments of her sister.

Why's it always *you* th' boys pant after? complains Diana. You, with your four eyes and a blatant lack of interest in a mirror, except t' glance an' go? Diana read those leaves long before tonight perhaps, the evening on which it's become official, or semi-so, about her calling to a life Miss Glasby rejected, decidedly. Limiting her options further in some ways, Harry argued, as though she'd shut down the lottery on options. In fact I wonder if Miss Glasby didn't serve for Diana as a cautionary tale.

My hopes were scrapped when I realized the nature of Miss Glasby's mission—it was a letdown given what was still left on the carcass. I padded behind her at a turtle's pace, even though she switched on the light to brighten her path, the pansies daisies roses jumping to life.

I knew I'd find it, she announces after we joined the others. I just fergit where I set it, Wrennie dear. You could just about hear a pin drop in the room were it not for her footsteps creaking the linoleum. The whole group, aside from Jake and Wren, mummed in a tryptophan haze.

Open it! sings Wren, rising from her seat. Open it!

I will just as soon's I set down, dear.

But the untying takes awhile. It's bound with the strength of youth, and Miss Glasby's hands are knotted with age.

Wan' me t' help? offers Midge.

I can *git* it, insists Miss Glasby. Wren wen' through all the trouble. Least I can do—

—You can get mine, pleads Ruby. It's too much.

I'll do it, Leo remarks. He trailed Wren here several minutes ago, the bloom on his cheek doubled in intensity. He rubs the spot to soothe or erase it, though it colors forth, even in this light. I'll do it, he repeats, pulling his hand from his cheek and pilfering the package, jetting scraps of paper through the air. Ribbon uncoils with youthful energy, landing across the linoleum, and from that mess a pair of socks is birthed.

Ruby studies them.

Wren knitted 'em herself!

How nice, returns Ruby, setting them on the coffee table, then looking away.

Here—I'll do that! Leo reaches over and filches the bundle from Miss Glasby's lap where she'd generated a pile of paper pieces, until Leo grabs the bundle, leaving her nothing but air.

I could a got it if you woulda let me! she complains, as a pair of hot pads is tossed in her direction. She grunts forward, grabbing lamely toward the floor until the tips of her index and middle fingers pincer one and then another square. Did you make these too, Wrennie? she asks, forgetting to thank Leo for the help. How pretty they are. I use t' be able t' knit.

I wouldn' study 'em closely, cautions Diana. She ain' won no prizes at the couny fair.

Did you have t' say that? Florrie objects. She tried 'er best.

Wrennie—. Can you ever have enough pot'olders?

Thus the yearly opening of the birthday gifts progresses, coincidentally on the eve of another's birth, or so they say, during which time Diana gifts the sisters each a tube of lipstick, hot tomato like her own, that she bought in a two-for-one sale, meaning one for her and one for each of the Glasby sisters, which came from two separate coupons in two separate sales, meaning two visits to the store, limit two per customer; after Florrie bestowed them each a new rosary to add to their collections, the ones hanging on two rosary trees on two separate night stands, which Florrie gifted them on their birthday last year; after Midge handed over two greeting cards, each stuffed with ten singles; and after Jake presented his offering too, larger than any so far. Leo spots them on the table and, being the strongest, carries them into the bosom of the faithful. Standing in the center of the circle, in the eye of a storm of refuse from the gifting so far, he studies the packages before handing them over.

It's pitchers, he announces.

Oh boy, it's pitchers. Jake's pitchers, echoes Diana.

Don' tell what it is!—yull ruin the s'prise!

Yup, it's pitchers, Leo can attest with one-hundred-percent certainty. Nice gift, Jake. Wish I got that.

I'm *sure* you do, cracks Diana.

Miss Glasby takes one of the canvases from Leo after he's peeled away the paper, and Ruby, getting a good look at hers, sets it on the floor.

Ohhh Kaaaay.

Miss Glasby effuses, How sweet a you, Jake! It's got plenny a color. And, and—action—in spades. Tha's for sure.

What're they of? wonders Ruby.

He did it in school, informs Florrie.

You can tell, adds Diana.

It's a *kind* a copy. Of a famous pitcher at the museem.

Some copy, remarks Leo.

You always asked for Jake to paint you somethin', mama.

I was thinking more of a bowl a bananas or something. I guess I'll hafta watch what I ask for in the fu—

—Tuttut, interrupts Miss Glasby. It's the thought that counts, Jake dear. We'll hang these over our beds an' think a you each time.

They're *ugggg*ly! blurts Leo, falling on the floor and holding his stomach. Diana catches the giggles too, rolling into full-blown laughter, inspiring a smirk on Midge and Ruby's faces and even Florrie's, try as they may to suppress them.

Not just a pitcher! A copy! Of a famous pitcher! summarizes Leo. In a mus*eem*!

But a what? cracks Diana. She's leaning on her side and wiping the tears from under the false eyelashes, trying to avoid smudging the mascara.

Cat scratch!

Cat puke!

A copy!

Stop it, you two, insists Miss Glasby, who herself can't seem to stifle a grin. The colors 're pretty, Jake, she remarks, leveling her lips. And goodness knows there's plenny a action like I says.

Is that what you got t' show for all that time in th' artroom? implores Leo. Jake you gotta get out more. Hang with Romeo an' me for a day. Normal up—

—Leave your cousin alone, interjects Miss Glasby. Not everyone needs to be like the Geist boy.

It wouldn' hurt, counters Diana.

Hre, hre, seconds Harry, jarring himself awake.

The sun slanting across the sandhills, the shadows of nearby grasses growing as long as the forms trailing the breakers, the giant concrete blocks—they cast their darker selves on us. Jake stretches out, facing skyward while Romeo works his hands over Jake's body. The two shift to their sides. Usually fidgety Jake calmed to a stupor, not noticing the fly in his ear or shooing it away. He presses flat the hairs of Romeo's chest, whose jaw rests against Jake's cheek, the sand beneath. I was only half in their orbit, chained as I was a few feet away, after I'd been warned a thousand times off chasing the many airborne invaders, harboring so close to the cliff, in the folds of a long line of bluffs, resting on a mishmash of fallen trunks along the beach. I was kept from exploring, so what was the point of bothering? Don't blame me if I notice things these two miss, as though it's inborn. Don't blame me if I divine worlds while they lie in a bubble. I can't help if I eye things, the sand rat no more than twenty paces, the raccoon pups stowed in a toppled trunk nearby, never mind the chipmunks squirrels—the killdeer!— darting back and forth, they and a knot of snakes mating nearby. I let what passes pass, though I whiff them all.

I'm disappointed we're no longer playing games in that the world's a more tolerable place when humans are engaged that way. As for the day's fare, a bite of sausage was all I got, the one Jake passed on and Romeo was too stuffed to eat—I got that and a few bits and bobs of potato because these two hogged the rest, or humaned them. Jake and Romeo at least lie sated. What will they do for an encore? Move the conversation to Jake's pals at the factory, of course, as they've taken to doing now that they've gravitated there, one by one, after St. Andrej's, the only job they could find in these parts, including Cin and Diablo too, who were brought in by Rauch after they gave up the idea of a calling. Everything seemed to be going along fine until recently when Romeo began warning Jake about clouds on the horizon, including lay-offs, because of what looked like a major recession brewing, like the storm headed this way. Romeo repeats the principle of last in, first out, which he says his dad is considering.

Well, if we're all gonna lose our jobs cuz we were hired last then. . .what if?

What if what?

What if—in general. What if we could live like this forever? What if we never had to wear clothes ever again? What if you and me—what if we lived t'gether? Like married people. If we left Laurentine, you'n me. Moved to th' Big Apple.

Like *married* pee-ple. Are you insane?

Why not?

It don't exist for one. An' even if it did it'd be for freaks.

Not so.

This-here, Jake, is jus' for kicks.

I watch as the boy deflates. What's that spose t' mean?

It means what it mean. I'm gonna marry someday—you can bet on that. But def'nally not you, cowboy!

Well, what if we just moved t' the Big Apple then?

The Big *Apple*!?

Rauch said Marks and him are movin' there. Leavin' Laur'ntine f' good. Goin' where they can be—

—Rauch's gonna shack up with that trouble maker—that Jew?! Or half-Jew. Whatever the hell he is. Romeo blurts it out, weaponizing a perfectly good word.

That's not nice—

Half a man's more like it.

Don't say that!

—Everybody knows he's half kike, half nigger—great combo. I thought Rauch had a girlfrien', some spic. Is her name Cinthia?

She's now with Diab—

—That dyke? Are you kidding me?

Jake pulls away. What kinda talk is that?

The truth, that's what that is. That Marks guy, and Rauch too. The people you hang around with. What a group.

What a way t' talk. They're my—

—It's my right.

But it don' make it right.

—Ask my father, he'll tell you. The Marks type—they're all crooks.

Your father—

A few days later when Jake and I'll visit Wren, who had by then been eighty-sixed from home on account of Donald, and more specifically Billie, who hadn't arrived in the world yet, Wren will remind Jake of the rumors about Geist Senior, who was not just his but Harry's boss as well, although on different shifts. Rumors about the war not that long ago and how he came by his fortune, via ties to the north of where they lived at the time, across the ocean, a move that caused the family's wealth to mushroom while most everybody else struggled—rumors that not just Harry but most of Laurentine buzzed about.

Jake picks up his tee to slip it on.

Leave it, commands Romeo, ripping it from his hand and hurling it. We ain't done.

149

I am.

You're not.

The way you talk.

I'm an American—I can say what-ever I want. It's a free country.

Well with that attitude—

—You brought it up, cowboy. You're the one makin' a big deal.

If I were to query either of the two about what just happened, it wouldn't be Romeo but Jake. Why all the fuss now, after so many similar comments you've heard from the guy and even worse, comments I've gone out of my way to omit from my story, Tommy, if you don't mind, coming from not just Romeo but Harry especially, taking the liberty as I have to make more than a few changes for either the exact same words or ones along those lines, a whole language that Jake managed to look past. Since you come from a different world I've lifted the blanket just a bit so you can view it in its raw state, so to speak. And again if I had one question to ask Jake it would have to be, What about this time made you hear it, after so many times, and so long a time?

In fact Romeo's words landed Jake in the mud in a sense, beyond the simple problem of how he'd get home if he decided to split. I could tell he wanted to go—I know the body language well enough by now. The wheels cranking in his brain—what to do? How to get unstuck. To discover that you've been carrying on with—your own father—in another skin.

Romeo pulls away. He complains he's fallen not once but twice for Jake's con job, for something he'd always seen but tried to ignore. When Jake complains he doesn't know who Romeo is anymore, the latter gripes he missed the old Jake, that this one here was the worst kind a faggot.

As bad as a girl! he snorts, shaking his head. They're always tryin' t' remake you inta something you're not.

What to do, Tommy, in a moment when the two lie naked as me but have only now eyed each other, maybe for the first time? After years of keeping company. For the moment Jake takes the decision to stuff it, which he's learned to do in situations like this, fearful of what might happen if he rocked the boat too much, lest he find himself and me both stranded with the garter snakes here, all around, which neither of them would have noticed had it not been for me. He lets things pass, even as he murmurs to himself, Then in that case I'll go without you, by which he meant with Rauch and Marks. Which is to say he managed to mollify Romeo and in so doing avoided the usual consequences when he gets riled. He clothes his feelings even as he lies naked.

After a real and not metaphorical storm passed, unleashing a doozy of downpour in a relatively short order, the winds and rain, the two soaked to the bone—after that they slip into a 3D reanimation of the epic film they caught in the darkened theater, their bodies muddied like those in the film, limbs slimed, and in the process recharging Romeo's battery. For Jake, the scales having slid from his eyes, not all realizations being equal, much more is required. Still at Romeo's bidding and bred with an ultimatum, he winds the clock back to where the day began, only this time around, completely out of the blue, Romeo produces a concession. One which Jake had been jonesing for for so long he'd about plum given up. Yet there it is, however wooden or awkward, the noses nearing, pacifying Jake in the event as only Romeo can when he suspicions the boy might be about to bolt, leaving him short of an option. Initially it's more of a bite that morphs awkwardly into that thing that Romeo abhors doing with a man, as though it were against nature, that kind of affection, which he now offers fully and nakedly and I, Molly, swear, Tommy, passionately, though it comes from the lips of a bigot.

PART TWO

CIRCLING

OH MY GOODNESS, PRECIOUS—you inhaled that! It isn' very lady-like.

I ask Florrie what she expects given what a delicacy it was. I mean, don't we love a grade-A, farm-fresh egg with cheddar overtop! Don't we love bacon? Never mind Jake and Wren wouldn't give it a look.

To make something dematerialize so quickly, just like my Peacoat. Whom in a sense I've put off re-membering for you, Tommy, as much as I could, though he slipped in the door of my story as people do, as if an errant snowflake. I suppose I've left him out, or tried to, largely because some memories resist sowing out there in the world, or dredging up, as the case may be. How do you speak about someone who just vanished—*poof*? According to everyone but me, a mute, and a group of reticents. The vanishing act came as a mystery to Jake, discombobulating the order of things, especially when one considers the principle that nothing ever unexists; it only shifts into a different form, an embodied energy, to which I can add the transition doesn't come without shock waves: A body vanished alters everything, those left behind most of all.

Cracks appeared in Jake's armor, which after Romeo he'd set about creating. The turn of events seemed to render him defenseless, much more than the loss of Romeo-heaven. As unsettling as that was it paled against what was to come, the events vacating his spirit and rattling him to the core.

Reducing him to flesh-and-bone, as though he were trying to join Peacoat in the other world. Tommy, he claimed he'd have nothing to do with the idea of giving himself to anyone, ever again, as Peacoat had prodded him to do— You just give your life *over*. In that case to Jay-sus, a name he pronounced like Pastor Billy did, though they were both born and raised in spitting distance of Laurentine, there on the edge of the lake.

When Jake first parroted that line back to Florrie she replied, Well, it don't mean committin' ment'l soocide. You still got a head on your shoulders. A'least I think. By which I believe she intended to nudge—shame or shoulder—Jake back to seeing things her and Harry's, i.e. the Roman way.

What *are* these people, anyway? 'Piscopalian?! Loothrun?

Not quite.

Well then what? Where's the church?

They don' got a church, if you mean a buildin'.

They don't got no *church*?! What kinda religion's *that*? She sucks her teeth. You can't have a raligion without no church. Sounds 'spicious to me. Like it's a cult.

We're small, an' we don' got the money for a buildin'. Yet—

—*Pfff!*—

—But I'm sailing ahead of myself, Tommy, a storyteller's no-no, never mind it's all one to me, including diurnal, nocturnal or any kind of cycles—the world leashed to the mechanical universe. I mean clocks, wristwatches, and all other timepieces are flawed in that they fragment time into increments of twelve, arbitrarily, or twenty-four, divorcing you from the physical realm which is less bounded. A more accurate representation would be a series of turns in actual, concrete space. It would be a watch with a blank face and a single hand, or better yet a dot that projected from a pivotal point, mimicking your place on the planet as it tracks around its axis, mapping your spot in actual, 3D space, lifting you, however momentarily, from the quagmire of constructed time with its splitting of hairs—hours, minutes, seconds, and nanoseconds—instead of the more seamless movement that exists in space.

As for me I exist in a sphere both temporal and a-temporal, a storyteller caught between the collision of events, mashing together on a timeline like two vehicles on a tree-lined boulevard. It takes an effort to sort them out—do you follow me? I speak from below, from the storyteller's underworld or subterrain, this alternate, zombie universe of the talking dead, bare matter that springs to life whenever you split the fly-leaves, a category of existence that doesn't exist up there because, for the living, the only possibilities that exist are, A, pastness, like a body moving in a river, leaving you peering at a void when you try to say it's there—or no it's there—which is to say the present can never be tracked; and B, futurity. The world of a story toys with those realms, even as it resides in an eternal present.

In the saddle of experiential time, Peacoat was that to my boy, futurity, a something-to-come after the bankruptcy of his past with Romeo, going bust at the lake. To spell things more clearly, Jake took issue, however late as I said, with what got spewed on the beach that time, regarding Marks most of all, but Cin too, and that ended it. Beyond a belated smack on the lips he was gobsmacked, perhaps because Wren had just been forced out, leaving him to ponder the power of words and their link to bare life.

On the day Wren was evicted I thought my boy and his old man were going to come to blows if Florrie, and me too, didn't step in—and, like Romeo, Harry was a tough nut. Wren would pay the price for the sin of association.

Intermingling or interbreeding—like dumb animals without a clue, as Harry put it. And now here comes Romeo on the coattails of the event, spitting venom, sullying Jake's friends and painting a picture of things to come were Harry ever to discover what was really going down.

Enter Peacoat and Desperation. A mix that produced an openness, the flower of adversity. Diversity too. After all the talk about randomness and relativity up to that point, a measure of gray about the known—a posture not poohpoohed but actually fostered by the Brothers at St. Andrej's—what Peacoat peddled seemed black-and-white, at first, tolerable only because it came from his own mouth. His world view, or Pastor Billy's, became a bit more bearable over time, though only just. When Peacoat introduced Jake to the reverend, part-time shop steward at Geist and full-time steward of souls, Jake's objections deviled him, Pastor Billy that is, though not Peacoat. While the Pastor warned Jake he had to choke the demon, Doubt, wrestle and try to snuff him, Peacoat seemed to take things in stride. Jake's doubts, most of all, having been there. He granted they were a part of what it is to be human, a comment which raised doubts of my own, though I let it go.

The many questions Jake spouted initially at Reverend Bradford's bible studies were almost verbatim parodies, or parrot-ies, of comments made by the Brothers at Saint Andy's, the ones who instilled in the boys the idea that using your noggin is the best way to glorify the divine, who, like them it turned out, valued thinkers. As do I. Despite that training, we've seen how easy it is to falter when you're in the thick of things, in a malaise and not seeing a way out, circumstances flying at you from every quarter and causing a person to doubt her own thoughts, not to mention resorting to blind belief from sheer exhaustion.

Cry uncle is more like it.

But there I go again, getting a head of myself.

I can tell my boy's troubled. For the first time I remember
he's not pausing before jumping, at least at the moment, and
truth be told I'm amazed—I mean, Jake, you are not yourself.
He fidgets. Looks this way and that. Again, I know by his
body language that the only place he wants to be is here,
with Peacoat, who's tuned to another world than the one in
Jake's brain. This hand-to-knee thing, specifically Peacoat's
hand on Jake's knee, is stirring things up. Memories most
of all after the many months since Jake and Romeo flamed
out. Sitting there at cross-purposes, the chatter, never mind
the physical closeness, comes as a bit troubling to him. All
this optimism! Especially since Jake has been mulling, to
the point of scouting, a way to un-be. Now here comes
Peacoat throwing surety in the mix, and though Jake looks
more than interested, and even ready to say yes, doubt again
makes an appearance, tugged at him and not in a good-
feeling way. The strain between the two modes breaks him,
the floodgates too. It's a whole other kind of language for
Jake, unlike his twin, pointing up the failure of words at
certain times in a body's life, their wanton lack to capture
a complexity. He's lost in a watery blue hole, for reasons
too many to say despite my efforts, though I'm working at
it—Jake pulled and pushed—it makes me squirm, even in
my current state.

Just as the water works squeak on, the door smashes open
and Diana barges in. What're yous doin'? Is this a private
meetin'?

She has only just returned from a commitment she
couldn't keep—at least that's the line she's putting out there,
arguing it's a decision she herself had taken.

Beat it!

There's no excuse for rudeness, y' lurp.

I told you t' get lost!

What are you tryin' to hide?

Get the F out! Better yet, go back ta the nun'ry! We were happier then!

The door slams and now the tears pour out—Jake, what's come over you? It's as though he isn't thinking, or is he thinking too much? He frots his knee with his right hand as Peacoat frots the other. The latter slips his arm out from under his guitar and drapes it over Jake's shoulder. My boy wipes his face then rubs his hand on his thigh; he returns to moisten his hand and dry it again. Maybe it's—what? The lack of sleep? The monotony since he called it quits with Romeo? Tactile—scratch that—compulsively tactile Jake, on some brink because of the loss of so many pleasures, if ones that never came without a price.

Everything's Ohh Kaay, Peacoat reassures with a lamb's-ear softness that disarms Jake and puts him off his game. Peacoat's wearing jeans, a pillowy flannel, and delicate touch. If ever there was a buyer for a product, an entire package, one so imminently near, it would be Jake—that I can tell—and yet he holds to his reserve. So Peacoat simplifies things in a mix as alluring as vetiver and lavender.

The soporific nature of his words contrasts the space, cluttered with canvases covering almost every inch of floor. They're stacked several deep, layered with impasto, paint sloshed on in an effort to expand on a style a century old. Peacoat fails to notice any of that, canvases, brushstrokes, and textures, similar to Romeo when he was here, focused as he is on a more singular purpose.

Again the door clatters open and Diana announces in a voice full of metal filings, Phone's for you, you jerk.

Get! The! Hell! *Out*! Jake sounds, like the Prince of Darkness, the one that's been skulking around his bed at night, not to mention wherever he seems to go—leashed the two are as though Jake were his pet.

I'm gonna tell Florrie you swore. You know she can' stand bad manners.

Get! Out! Gedoutgedoutged*out*!

Diana warns Peacoat, eyeing the book next to him, See how he is? He's beyond hope—even god can't help.

Jake picks up the volume that Peacoat has only just taken from his knapsack, setting it next to them on the bed in a perfectly timed choreography. He assumes it's a book like any other and hurls it at Diana, who dodges it and laughs as she squeaks the door shut.

Missssed—you loser!

Peacoat retrieves the book from the foot of the door, smooths the crinkled edges and bent cover, touches his lips to it and explains, Jake, this is sacerd.

Trus' me, I like t' read too. It's just she was drivin' me—

—Peacoat with his hallelujah-chorus of optimism about the gnarliest of subjects, twisting so many strands into such an organized ply of yarn. He comforts Jake despite his fit of pique. And to think I always thought it was such a problem, Jake's expression seems to say. The way I am—I mean the way I AM. But Peacoat has spent the last hour singing, praying, and assuring him it's the opposite, namely that god loves him just as he is.

Me—I was raised Cath'lic, Jake explains. You took it all for granite. God was out there—maybe—but far above in th' ether.

He's as near as me. Even closer.

Peacoat counts the reasons for rejoicing, alters the semiotics of tears from sadness to a cleansing, argues an angel has come and is wrestling Jake's doubts at the bottom of a ladder that is anchored in this room but stretches to the divine. Jake but-but-buts Peacoat, wondering, Rully!? Are you sure? Love and only love? Jus' the way I am?

And Peacoat, with his single-eyed assurances, promises, Nothin' can go wrong for them that love the lord. Trus' me, Jake.

Truth be told, I did wonder, Tommy. Maybe something *was* underway in Jake. Never mind I couldn't relate to Peacoat's claim that he'd donned a new, immaculate body, and especially given what I know now, adopted another casing than the old one that masked the soul, a new self different from the one he wore in his past with Cin and Diabolo, Rauch and Marks—outside the hairy hierarchy of that world he'd been reborn. The thing he inhabits now is only a stand-in for the one he'll get in the next world, we learn, and all because Peacoat said the words. It was a language not without appeal for sure, especially for a person whose goal was to escape the past, end it all, himself, or start a whole new life.

In fact I never knew that words could be so powerful— that they could function as acts, that an "I do" served as a kind of *doing*—for Peacoat it came down to one and the same thing. To a marriage of sorts, as though he were wed to Jesus, a man like himself and Romeo too. All Jake had to do was read the text on the penny-tract, the one Peacoat holds in his hand that contains a mere snippet of the millions or billions of lines put out every year by the publishing industry, all around the world—read the lines, potent as a virus, and you achieve an orgasmic-yet-clean, pleasureable-yet-sanctified bliss, from this day forward. Demur and down you go—one day. Because, as Pastor Billy would later warn, Buddy, you had your chance—so don' blow it. That seems to be the gist of things. In time we'll learn it's only the Sparks-Notes version and that things are a tad more complicated, but even then it'll come down to the basic fact that you don't get many shots at this, and fortunately for Jake, sitting thigh to thigh in the midst of so many paintings, splattered thick, he's falling for it. In fact he ultimately folds, mouthing the words offset-printed on the tract, word for word, just as they're inscribed and repeated by Peacoat—*I give my life over. To Jay-zus.*

Ain' it great Molls? he enthuses. We're saved! You just give your life over and that's that!

To sweeten the deal Peacoat assures Jake that like the polio vaccine it's a one-shot deal. Once lisped it cannot be unlisped, though the offer isn't extended to all takers. Like me, if I were interested. Not me or anything in what Peacoat labels the natural world, of which, I'll discover, I'm a part, though not people like Jake or Peacoat. His divine is a whole other ball of wax in that regard—even if I were moved to follow in Jake's steps, it wouldn't matter. Peacoat will make that clear in time, though for now it's not a problem because Jake hasn't thought to question it before taking the oath. Indeed we'll discover it's more complicated still, that the deal Peacoat is peddling has never advertised itself as a capital-D democracy, especially in the current minting of the divine making the rounds across the country, a reaction to a decade of rank permissiveness, which is to say Pastor Billy's version of the CEO of Heaven Inc. We'll learn it's a trend sold in bookstores in the wake of all that free-lovery from Berkeley to the Bronx, Bar Harbor to Burbank, in the wake of the war, peddled in placards and graffiti, even on a dedicated channel on TV. And here's Jake, always on the cutting edge, purchasing stock in the company.

In a space not much larger than the walk-in closet in Romeo's room, this place where Jake crashed as a boy, the canvases having been swept out like dried insects, the three of us gaze out the window at the pigeons jodding for crumbs. They peck untiringly but not mindlessly. When they realize there's nothing to be had they fly off to try their luck elsewhere. Florrie remarks, They're pretty in a way. All diffren' an' yet the same.

It takes all kinds, I muse. At the time of Peacoat's disappearance, after weeks piling on weeks with no leads and with everyone in a stir, Pastor Billy and the faithful more than anyone, so publickly disconsolate as they were, to have lost their brother in the lord under such mysterious circumstances, the cops too in their methodical way—in the middle of that hooplah Florrie's approach was to suggest, Maybe it's time t' let it all go. Put things in god's hands. You can't do nothin' about it after all, Jake. Why go on about it so? I mean, is that what that raligion a yours taught you? That whatever happens ain't OKed by the good lord first? I mean, it's unseemly to question god like that.

Unseemly or not, I don' care. It don' fit. That he'd just up and go off like that—not after ever'thing—

—But don't y' think when Peacoat wants t' come back, 'e will?

Which from my perspective was a non-argument given Jake's angle on things, believing as he did that Peacoat would never just disappear—just because. Not after everything that went down and after so much time and, quite frankly, effort. He admitted to Florrie he'd heard of not a few believers going off to be with god in nature, as though it were some separate realm, and that some didn't make it back in their original state, which is to say their right minds. The experience changed them. He'd heard from Sister Pauline about a guy who was found, just in the knick a time, who's surviving nowadays on basic brain functions after six weeks fasting in the middle of Nowhere, as though that place existed too.

He'll be instatutionalized the rest a his life, Jake lamented. It's true it's a thing with that kind—but Peacoat weren't like that—Jake spoke in the past tense. T' just go off.

In god's outpost steam rattles pipes that fart, hiss, grunt, and spit, like the plumbing at Donald and Wren's on the east side of the Forest City, a good deal west of here. The workings sag the floor, shake the walls, upset the sills from their foundations, as though the whole kit-and-caboodle were possessed of some angry spirit. Yet the proprietor, the one Peacoat addresses as either Sister, Pauline, or both, despite the fact that she could pass for his great aunt, doesn't seem to notice. She's not the kind of sister I'm used to, not the familial or the conventual kind, as Diana was for a spell, shrouded in black, when she was both sister and Sister, until, as she insists, she was the one who decided to up and quit. No, this-here sister isn't either of those, and yet Peacoat addresses her that way still.

When we first arrived she stood there, studying me. She remarked, I ain't sure about this'n here. Whether I can let it in. But Peacoat, ever the diplomat, sussing the strength of the tether in Jake's and my connection, went to bat. He assured, She loves the lord too, trus' me. To which Sister Pauline replies, How can I know f' sure? I, meanwhile, stayed mum, because the least reliable source is the one you got your suspicions about, regarding my standing with youknowwho, whether him or her or something different altogether. In the end it was Jake, and to some degree Peacoat, who managed to convince the woman that I was no walking gate to the fallen realm that would compromise her store, saggy floor and all.

You never know, Sister Pauline concludes warily. Devils have a million faces. Even cute ones like this.

I accepted the compliment humbly, in my demeanor and in my heart—I much-obliged her for thinking I have hope beyond the way I look on the surface. I much-obliged Jake and Peacoat too for not relegating me to the bone-rattling cold outside, the thick flakes fluffing around the tires of what Peacoat referred to on the way as the lord's vehicle, his comfy, two-door coupe with the egg-crate grille, a perfect marriage of Power and Maneuverability, which is slowly but surely being buried in the parking lot, more and more like a swelling in the drive. Peacoat looks out the window, eyeing what was once referred to as his Pleasure Dome on Wheels. On the way here he characterized it once as a rolling motel in the days he was in the world, whatever that is, arguing that like him it had been washed in the blood.

Gazing out I marvel at the metaphor, wonder if it isn't a bit too literal given Jake's enthusiasm about its crimson color. I ponder if we'll ever make it out of such deep drifts. It's all to god's profit now, we've been told, referring to Peacoat and Pauline's divine, Jake's now too, having turned his life over just yesterday. Reaching for a volume among the towering stacks, Peacoat insists, Get this'n. There ain't no other.

Jake takes the book and turns it. He's never paid thirty clams for a volume before, genuine leather and gold leaf notwithstanding. He's never shelled out much more than a buck ninety-five, though his usual price is ten, twenty-five, maybe fifty cents, max. Used. At his favorite dealer on Coventry. He looks at me as if to say, Even the idea of it—the excess. But as he leafs through the pages, sounds curl, sending goosebumps down both our spines. I can see he wants it—the physical body of the thing excites him. He caresses the pages.

What d'you think, Moll? He sneaks me a whiff of the onion-skin pages and leather cover, pieced together from the back of some yearling, which Jake fails to notice. The crinkly paper, culled from virgin stands of pine and stretches of cotton, sounds like water tinkling from the urn in Rockefeller Lagoon, when Florrie and Harry were in their prime.

It's a li'l more'n I'm use t'.

But it's like gittin' dozens a books in one, Pauline hastens to reply. From that p'spective it's a real buy. It's the only book you'll ever need t' own.

Jake runs his fingers along the spine. Once more my meatless wonder whiffs the binding. He closes his eyes, distances a voice that nags from inside, back and forth and back and forth he hems and haws and haws and hems until at last he utters, Hmn. . . . Hmn!—his Hmns harmonize with the sounds of the pipes, spirits rattling from below, as if warning a book is a dangerous thing.

Ohhhhhhh Kaaaaaaaay—he peers probingly into Peacoat's eyes. Ohh Kaay—he gazes at me as well, then looks away. OK, he remarks to Pauline. I'll take it!

The spirits trapped in the heating system register their complaints, over which Sister Pauline croons, Praise god! Yull never be disappointed. Everything yo'll ever need in this world an' the next is written in this pray-cious volume. After which Jake begins the process of gathering together his thirty pieces, the ones he's fixing to betray Florrie and Harry with—them, Ruby and all the hibernian Rubies before her, an entire clan that would—never possibly could—dream, that Jake could be so perfidious, to purchase a Protestant bible.

There'll come a day for that, as we've seen *in ovo,* Tommy, though not today for sure. Could any news be traded in such a driving snow, assisted by plunging temperatures so severe? And yet, I intuit, even as Jake plunks the money down, the news will emerge, that and a fuss, though as I say we're safe from it today.

Jake gathers together the heap of coins and crinkled bills. Before pushing the pile toward Sister Pauline he looks again toward Peacoat. Is it th' same one you got?

It is.

The exac' same?

It is.

OK, so then—yep. It's the one.

Praise god! pipes Peacoat, glancing toward the driveway, emptied of cars save one.

Praise god, echoes Pauline, practically bowing as Jake forks over the cash. She gathers it up as though it were winnings in a lottery, a reward for her efforts in the cause. She too peers out at the drifting snow, half daydreaming, half mumbling thank you Jay-zus to herself—thank you, Jay-zus. She gazes back at the cramped world inside, packed to the gills with merchandise so shoe-horned in that we can hardly move. The mountain of bibles, notecards, chapbooks, and trinkets, wall hangings, records, cassettes, and keychains soars to the ceiling, waiting for people like us to happen by, and in the interim amassing a thick layer of dust. While she's making out the receipt she regales us with stories of miracles, though she clarifies her faith in no way depends on them. She delights us with wonders, womanly cures and manly transformations, epiphanies of the christian kind, her specialty, tracking a shift from A to B, because, unlike Peacoat, she knows god is particular. Her god prefers more than just the words Jake tripped out the day before, written on the tract.

In the Monte Carlo after, heading east from Plymouth-on-the-Lake to Laurentine, I look out at the bungalows squatting in a schlumpy array. The homes are small, dotting an otherwise giant landscape, if only we could see it. Snow threatens the structures, not to mention the trees and lawns, which are all sheeted in white. Far more than a blanketing, it threatens a downy suffocation, the weight of whiteness in these parts.

While heading slowly west we're told the area holds a special place in Peacoat's heart. It marks the spot where he experienced the divine call, scales leaping from his eyes, coming down as he was from a nasty trip. If Reverend Billy hadn't come at just the right moment, this past summer, tooling the paths of the park we just passed on his way home from Geist, working the brambles in order to check who needs a hand, so to speak—if he hadn't come just then there's no telling where Peacoat'd be. Belly up under the snow, most likely—

—Revren' Billy save my life, juss back there.

Over time we'd hear the same story a time or twenty, each time slightly different, though the narrative arc's the same, how the Pastor came to Peacoat where he was at, assuring him, I can take care of you, son. But you must put your faith in Jay-zus, who'll lift this burden from you. You must be willin' to give it over. Everythin'. Your life and loves.

It didn't seem to factor in, the way Peacoat tells it, that the two knew each other at the plant, that Billy may have heard a rumor or two about Peacoat and his penchant for visiting the park after a shift. Bradford was stripped of his work duds and seemed at home in the setting—Not the usual pain in the ass, as Marks put it when relating Peacoat's story on the beach that night, a version of the story that Peacoat related to him, perhaps in an effort to hook him too into the fold. Without success. Perhaps because he was juggling enough already, even more than enough. Anyway, strung-out Peacoat, stripped bare in a sense, from too much *carpe diem*, drawing the reverend's attention and ultimately bringing to a close the days that Peacoat witnesses about often, implicating members of Jake's circle—Cin, Diablo, Marks, and Rauch, unbeknownst to them—as though they were a compulsion back then, the gang the reverend rescued him from.

And as it turns out, Peacoat's alteration seems to be the Real McCoy. At least that's the tack he takes as we drive, granting credit where it's due, first and foremost to the father, head of a single-parent household in the sky, and next to his son, who lives in a domicile devoid of a woman's touch. At least, again, that's how Peacoat narrates the tale, based on what I've heard with my own ears, taking a few liberties to paint in the gaps, Tommy, as we negotiate the fallen flakes, drifting in heaps across the road, the devil locked out, weeping at his recent loss. I can practically spot the devil Danger peering in as we break the snow, while the saved ones, whose numbers equal two, total, glide through this inclemency, the dropping of thick, white splotches on the skin of the car, as if without a clue.

Ever'thin' that works for god is good, instructs Peacoat.

I reckon a set of studded tires don't hurt. I attune myself to their hum as they bite the pavement, aid us in making tracks in the thick, wet snow in ways our Falcon never could.

Their fears having been allayed, they're free to sink into more important matters than traction, including the parameters of eternity, starting with no small bombshell, namely that everything of this world is toast, marked for destruction, like several of the dwellings on Midge's— scratch that, Donald and Wren's—street. Everything people label nature is lost. Unsavable. Peacoat tells us it's a fallen realm, unredeemable.

Wha' does that mean? queries Jake. Does it include plants? Rocks? Rivers and lakes? Sycamores?—he's glancing at me. I mean what did they do?

Catching the gust of Jake's query, Peacoat suddenly demurs. I wonder if he doesn't want to make things look too hairy, out of consideration for Jake most of all, given he's so new in the life—too much truth too soon might dent his resolve, disfigure it. Which would be a tragedy on the first—shall we say maiden?—day since he's been revirgined. No, Peacoat doesn't want to go that far, trashing nature in the vulgar sense.

As if playing into his argument, the lake effect is unsettling the visual world out here completely, the road most of all. Peacoat applies the brakes, draws the vehicle to a crawl. It's not far now, he informs. Meanwhile I whiff what went on during days and nights past. I detect the olfactory mix of Cin's hairspray and Diablo's make-up. Rauch's cologne and stray hairs fallen from Marks's 'fro. Scents mingled with Peacoat's, though Jake doesn't have a clue. I raise my nose, take in the melange of testosterone and estrogen, hormones and sweat—what would Jake know of that kind of froth? This car saw a wholesome share back in the day when, we learn, Satan ruled it.

Peacoat's sights are now on the dimming road, the narrowing down of four lanes to two. Once an Indian trail, the asphalt ribbon wends along the rim of the great pond, from tiny Plymouth-on-the-Lake to East Shagaran, Laurentine, and further west, past downtown. It undulates horizontally, having given in to the whims of the water since the Eries pronounced a curse, not on the whites, whom they'd never met, but the Five, the Six Nation Iroquois, who decimated them and passed it on, the curse that is. Little did the Anglos and French know that their land-grabbing came with a time bomb in the form of a south-stealing lake, once the glacier lifted its thumb and the land began to spring back. Where the ice was heaviest, on the Canadian side, the land has been elevating the fastest, tipping the lake toward the south, causing it to chew up meter after meter and indeed entire homes along the rim, a pox for what they took. Once the miles-thick ice, the Laurentine

Lift, melted, is when the gnawing began, the chewing away of the beaches of the Forest City, chomping at a retreating cliff. In response, breakwalls went in, tons of concrete and granite, heavy as houses, dumped behind homes, municipal buildings, parks, and recreation sites, including the beach where Jake, Cin, Diablo, and Co. met that night, or will, and, coincidentally, where Romeo, Jake, and I also romped, a bit further west—Romeo, whom Jake hasn't laid eyes on in an age. With the southward march of Erie, miles and miles of smooth, sandy beaches were converted into a front line of defense, backing further and further inland, retaining only the odd band of sand where concrete breakers held.

It's taken an hour to come just shy of East Shagaran, a journey that usually takes ten, fifteen minutes. The footings of the guardrail beside us dangle in midair. The land behind it has been eaten up, causing a row of squat dwellings to succumb with it—the replacement for long houses centuries ago, they toppled in pieces, clunk-a-chunk, or whole, in a slo-mo swoop. At times it's a quick, unceremonious crash. One way or another they're history, replaced by air in the course of time.

Peacoat cranes his neck, pipes condensation from the windshield with his sleeve. Boy, it's really comin' down!

Should we stop an' wait?

Why would we do that? God'll take care.

Jake cocks his head and looks at me as if to say, Oh, yeah! God'll take care! It doesn't matter the Eries spouted a similar line, or that the divines have simply been switched. My faith is in the vehicle, the way it's been armored by so many engineering innovations over the past century, creating a car capable of handling a hundred road conditions just like this with its sturdy, reinforced frame and prickly tires. But whether a guiding hand or tried-and-true technology, something is protecting us and the vehicle, the one that

Peacoat bought and chose to keep, no matter how many memories it engenders.

It's her or me, Diana warns, slamming the door. She's only just started readying for work, and it appears as though the first order of the day was to discover the scene of my crime, committed in the wee hours of the morning. She insists, I've had enough!

She's no spring chicken, counters Florrie. You know she can't help it. Ruby has her accidints too, and you don't talk about gettin' rid a her.

It's diffren'.

I don' see how. They're both part a the fam'ly.

I swear she does it outta spite. Like she got it in for me.

How could you say such a thing? How can you even think it? What in the world could Molly possibly have agains' you? Against anyone? She ain't got a malicious bone in 'er body. Like she could ever even think a such a thing!

We crawl as the sky cracks. I'm not speaking tropes, Tommy—it's literally cracking. Winter thunder booms as we creep along the shore. The heavens rumble as if they were threatening to descend on us in frozen microbits, six-sided, each lacy but careening in a horde, an unstoppable army, inducing me to ponder the paradox of ferocity in fragility, sameness in difference. In this case we're talking hexagons, weak in the extreme, singular unto themselves, and yet potent in a heap. An airborn swarm or mute throng. The animal kingdom represented in ice, reeking its revenge on us.

Jake is in a whole other world, however, than this realm.

He seems to have set his mind on effacing the tableau of Jakeness up to this point, becoming Unjake, dissimilar to himself, miming Peacoat. If he lisps something, it's the gospel truth.

Why do I care? Because after seven days in his new life yours truly is finally implicated directly in this new creed, in high-contrast black and white, while we pass along the road to the Reverend's.

Not everyone has his name written in the book, informs Peacoat.

I accept the comment at face value initially, thinking, Great! Plenty of reason to take heart. Not everyone has his name—*in fine, his*—name written. I muse, So far so good. If it's just a guy thing, their names omitted, no need to talk til doomsday. If we mean men losing out, then it's about time—maybe the divine deck isn't as stacked as I thought.

But I see blank-face take hold of Jake, a stare that gets him into trouble—him and me both. He seems to be sketching a whole other set of conclusions than I. I watch his mien go, Huh!, all the while the lips pronounce, OK—Ohhhh Kay! Ohhh. Kaaay. Our newborn lamb shrinks a bit. He knows he's too unschooled to vie with Peacoat, who's got a secure *in* with the immortal.

Sooooo. . .what're y' sayin'?

Y' might not get t' see all the people you care about in the next world.

Not *see* 'em? You mean Wren? Donald? Billie? Romeo?—yes, he said that. Not—?—he glances back at me.

Not unless they're saved.

Well, who knew? I ponder. The first thought that struck me was that Florrie might consider the comment a bit rude, speaking iffily about someone in your direct, physical orbit—There's no excuse for that, she'd say. Indeed even I thought it marred Peacoat's practiced politeness up to that point, discussing who's in and out, when one in the latter category is sitting directly behind and kitty corner, in full earshot. But I leave it go—. Truth be told my feelings were a tad hurt, and they became all the more so when it sunk in what was really going down.

God's ways ain't our ways. His logic ain't man's.

Hallelujah! I say to myself. Ne'er a wiser word was spoken. To be honest I didn't know a man had it in him to say there's nothing godly about male logic—don't even get me started. I mean I have a story to tell, Tommy, and it would only cause me to stray from the straight and narrow, about the wilderness of male logic, where the world has gotten lost, and how. Especially given that my goal, as you can see, is to deviate as little as possible.

Peacoat continues, Only them who say the words'll be saved.

Jake replies, But if god's love is so great—

—At which point, for the first time since we've been keeping company, and by no means the last, Peacoat shoots Jake a look as if to say, Don't *even*. Take it an' swallow. After which Jake—him, me, and Peacoat too—mum awhile, leaving only the squish of tires in thick slush to break the silence.

What about animals?

Wha'd'you think?

After which comment I realize I'm riding in the back now more than literally. Me and my kind, a world that human animals have separated from themselves—is it a function of our apparent reticence? Their inability to read signs? What they take as our indifference since they penned us apart and rendered us prey? As sacrifice? And dinner most of all?—apart from the pet exception.

On the other hand I remind myself that on the subject of heaven's exclusionary rule god may go soft yet. I mean he's come a long, long way, tracking secular shifts remarkably closely. Women were property once and heaven the sole domain of war heroes—i.e. men. On some random spectrum those of a deeper hue were a mere fraction of themselves, that is to say three-fifths, or, worse, animals, that is to a paler population who pranced in their finery to church every Sunday; in the more recent version of God Inc. they now have a full-fledged shot at bliss. So I comfort myself with the idea that the jury may still be out on the divine's capacity for compassion in this or any life, no matter what Peacoat mutters at the moment. Jake and I may see each other down the road someday after all—he may follow me—because between me, you, and the lamp post that we just passed I can't help noticing that the gray-beard's heart is going a bit soft, although it's taken ages. I'd even venture to say he's morphing toward the feminine, though I reckon it'll take ages until he gets there fully. Which is to say there may be hope for the bearded lady in the back seat after all, though more importantly the bearded man in the sky in the basic humanity department. That story's always being retaled, or retailed as the case may be.

You won't hear that from Peacoat at the moment though—on the contrary. In all fairness those were the days before he got to know yours truly, and Jake too, truth be told, before we three became an item so to speak. That's crucial. Spend time with a person, anyone, get to know her past, beyond what's on the outside, and a world dawns. At the moment though, I find myself crack up against a brick wall of a certain kind of logic, against two firm truths: A) god is picky—it's as bald as that; the only thing that matters to him is a certain type of redeemed man; and B) for all the libertarian talk on the part of god's army in this world, how things should be run government-free, it ain't no democracy up in the sky. Even as many believers down here preach individualism, *carte-blanche* freedom in the civic meaning of the word, it's a monarchy up there, a pyramid something like a ponzi scheme. Everything top-down, at least in Reverend Billy's telling, filtered through Peacoat's lips as we drive. A chain of being determines everything, who's in and out, the big cheese sitting on top, then humans, followed by youknowwho down here.

To be honest, what I'm hearing causes no small amount of coherency discomforture, logically speaking, requiring a kind of mental back-bending, not to mention word-twisting, the same kind that has been going on for ages, since the idea was birthed in the middle of a civil war when that wrinkle in belief appeared for the first time, a tension between two visions—one of a flat world, an earthly democracy, and the other a heavenly dictatorship. They lopped off the head of a king for acting like a king while bowing to an authoritarian in the sky, never taking notice of the flaw in the logic.

The whiteout of reason, like the snow descending, not in individual flakes but *en masse*. When Peacoat finally breaks the silence that has reigned for some time, several miles really, we learn the way to get in the divine's good graces has nothing to do with charity or works of any kind but faith, pure and simple. In not just god but the evil nature of everything around, of which I'm part. We learn this entire earthly coil, anything with an actual—physical and not figural—body is doomed, if you don't say the words. Which returns us full circle. If you see something, including the most delicate flake, it's a goner, slated for distruction, already under erasure. A notion difficult to fathom on a day in which it appears the flakes are winning.

Praise god! Here we *are*!

Praise god, parrots Jake, recoiling in his seat as the vehicle comes apruptly to a stop. He studies the exterior of Pastor Billy's abode for the second time before he cracks his door, having failed to notice the last time, on Christmas Eve. He peers at the picture window with the fracture tape along the middle then turns toward me, waiting for Peacoat to get out. He glances forward and back then pulls me near and gives a kiss.

What in th' world could Molly possibly have agains' you? Florrie repeats. I appreciate the vote of confidence to the tips of my toes, and yet I'm troubled. I'm no simpleton—I can put two and two together. I keep thinking about last night, or morning as the case may be.

Again I wake from unsettling dreams.

What the hell are *you* doin' here, like you're the Queen a Sheba or somethin'? Like y' own the goddam place—ain't you got the life?

I'm not fully conscious. The last I saw Harry he was slinked in his chair, his body covered except for his head and feet sticking out from either end. He looked to be either levitating or palled.

Nex' time 'round I'm gonna come back as you. Live a pampered life. Eat an' shit, eat an' shit. Take an' take some more. No family t' bust yer butt for. No job t' break you. No wife or mother'n law t' suck' the life blood outta you. No litter a ungrateful kids. Jus' eat an' shit. You don' even gotta think.

A streetlight casts Harry in silhouette. His body crooks forward and to the side, old as Methuselah.

Just leech off everyone.

I peer at where Harry's eyes must be, though I can't see them.

The pressure—and for what? Wha'd I ever get? Another job, one after another, and sometimes three at one time. Since

I was thirteen. I been bustin' my ass ever since. 'Thout a day a rest. Unlike you, lying there like Cleapatra—*in my spot*! Ain' that a pisser.

I'm unable to reply because my brain is still shifting into gear. When later I'm able to actually ponder Harry's complaint I wanted to respond in an idiom he could understand. That we're not as different as he thinks. I mean when did I ever get a vote on things, one way or another, having been chained first to Jake and then this lopped-off family, their every whim, my life and future, pad-locked, control beyond reach always, the way what-they-call-nature is leashed to the whims of man. It's true that Jake and Wren had good intentions, but a lot of good it did me. In fairness Wren tried, which is more than I can say for youknowwho. Now here comes Harry, caviling about his condition as though he were the one in the dog house, a thing to contemplate coming from the head of the household.

And yet maybe that's the point—think for a second, Tommy—about the big man in the sky. It appears he had no control over his own house either, couldn't seem to keep it in order—at least the way Peacoat told the tale in the early days. He suffered rebellion in the ranks. But if you were to look up heaven in the dictionary, wouldn't the definition be: Heaven. *n. sing.* Heaven. And if the definition of heaven is heaven, then how could there be discontent, enough for not just a handful but legions to rise up in countless numbers? Which is at least the case in the modern, if not the original telling of the story, though it's taken by many as gospel. Which only goes to show the power of fiction. Doesn't it imply that heaven wasn't heaven after all, what it was cracked up to be, that the father's house must've been on the dystopic side, that there was some kind of lack up there, just like this domicile here, the turn of events that serves as the source of Harry's crabbing, inferring as he just did that his life's a kind of hell? Where's the fault, above and below? I mean what kind of operation was the big man running up there, such that it was so easy to sow discord, and on such a scale? And what about Harry's house? What were you expecting, sir? That's what I would have queried Harry had I the chance, had I not been booted from my post next to Florrie. Though I would have avoided asking whether the problems were systemic or the product of unruly subjects.

Outta my spot! demands Harry. He grabs my legs, yanking and dragging me from the mattress. Florrie's snoring halts the second I hit the floor, but once Harry's settled it resumes, and in no time the two are whistling a kind of tune.

WITNESS

THE TICK, TICK, TICK from the mantel, marker of mechanical time, the kind Jake and I observe as we wait on a Presence, Jake tuckering himself out, focusing on, attending some kind of immanence, however glacially slow in the coming. Worse than a bad high, he quipped to an unsmiling Peacoat as we watched the minutes beat by. Is it possible that The Spirit, unencumbered by a body, could be so sluggish?

It takes awhile, Peacoat replies in low tones. It comes subtle and not with a flash.

Hapless Jake, craver of a buzz, especially on this of all nights of the year, of fireworks of some kind. The boy hankers for a high, an experience at the upper elevations, blood coursing through the arteries, though at the moment everything appears leaden. He feels chained. Sister Marnie, on the other hand, is already keying in on the other realm through its portal between the lines of the book, the same one in everyone's lap—she leans over it with its center cracked, her hair writhing and face invisible. Sister Pauline's eavesdropping on that world too, her head also trained on the book, as are Sisters Cathaleen and Jeanette. And so on. We're arranged in a ring, including me, arced like a serpent eating its tail.

Sister Marnie commented earlier she'd never seen my kind in the pastor's house before. Jake replied, Then it's no longer a virgin. Though she failed to conjure a smile.

It's probly not the kind a thing we can make a habit a, Reverend Billy informed Jake the first time we were here, just last week, and he repeated the sentiment again this evening when we arrived.

Though we'll make a exception jus' this time.

Never one to intrude, I peer at Jake, eye to eye, say, I don' need to hang out here. I even make a move to shy away from the room, sparsely furnished and impeccably clean, including the linoleum, scuffed but not a hair on it, a room without a fraction of the clutter we're used to, Jake and me, who by the by replied to me *sotto voce*, Molly, you ain't goin' nowhere. No matter what. You ain't leavin' my sight.

We all got our thing, I assure him. If they don't wan' me—

But he arrests me, commands, You're stayin'—else I'm shaggin' too. At which point Peacoat, loath to lose his quarry, petitions the pastor, Can we leave it be, the whole subjec'? For awhile? The lord has 'is time.

To which the pastor reflected long and hard, as is his custom. After a time he replied, How true, Brother Peacoat—i'n it, Sisters? People new in the lord—it takes time.

Given that, how could I feel anything but grateful to my toes?

In all honesty, it wasn't easy, Tommy, the *persona-non-grata* thing. Jake insisting I stay, as though I were his shadow, leashed to him, or as though he'd cease to exist without me, given the way a shadow lends a thing substance—I mean how can you represent a world without it? Anyway, there I remained, Jake's double, despite our different prospects in the world to come. Bound to be severed someday and sooner than I ever thought. That it was Peacoat who served as my advocate, coming on the heels of such hard lessons in the car, touched me as much as Jake.

Truth be told, Bradford tended to elevate most of what Peacoat said. He eyes him uniquely. Rubs his shoulder. Runs his hand down his spine in his avuncular way. He adds, Brother Peacoat has brought Jake to the fold, Sisters, and we welcome him, as well as 'is little friend 'ere.

Meanwhile Jake perches on a folding chair with one knee crossed over the other, jeans torn, his behind peeking through the threads and causing not a few raised eyebrows. The women are dressed in A-line skirts that fall below the knee, attesting to the fact that the miniskirt hadn't made its way into every corner of the culture—when was it, yesterday for all intents and purposes? Bradford sports a pair of ironed corduroys, a dress shirt newly pressed, and bow tie. The many steps from Jake to him, with Peacoat hovering somewhere in the middle. Later I hear Bradford venture, as though I weren't even there, regarding Jake's look, Lots a youngsters dress like that nowadays, Sisters. I see it ever' day down at the plant. Torn dungrees an' all.

It's a the world, insists Sister Marnie. That kind a dress. She tips her eyes toward Jake then glances at Sisters Pauline and Nancy.

The road t' glory's a long one, Sister.

You don' hafta be strung out and wearin' torn dungarees, showin' whatnot, t'appreciate god's grace, opines Sister Cathaleen.

Well it don' hurt, Pastor Billy replies. He smiles, but the others don't follow suit.

He catechizes something about sons prodigal, a conversation that goes right past me, to which Sister Marnie shakes her hair, complaining, Well, in some ways it don't seem fair. You spend your life doin' th' right thing, and then comes these upstarts—

The reverend eyes her and she averts her gaze, then eyes Jake whose hands are quaking for a nicotine fix. He traces a

C with his thumb on the slatted surface of the folding chair, a C and a backward C, the tails relaxed. Reading his body language, I'm getting the vibe he wouldn't mind a drink as well as a smoke—after all, what night of the year says bottoms-up more than this? But here in this house, a dry state unto itself, this Tulsa on the Shagaran—out here, east of the Forest City and Laurentine but west of Plymouth-on-the-Lake, the juice isn't flowing. Or only juice is flowing. That or tea. No fizzy drinks, because they might prove a stumbling block, reminding *some people* of mixers and the wrong kind of spirits.

It's true Peacoat preceded Jake here by several months, but temptations are slow to go the way of the flesh. What matters, we're told, is that they've arrived at this banquet. To a meal which, Jake whispers, Couldn't hold a candle to one of Florrie's affairs. I return, Manners, boy. You were taught better'n 'at. Take what comes and shut up.

Glancing at the card table against the wall, its ends flipped up to accommodate a feast, I wonder what he's going on about given what lies waiting. Including a mound of Jell-O, trembling with shredded carrots inside; a casserole of green beans and onions, still steaming and topped with bits of bacon; a bowl of black olives, which Sister Cathaleen said reminded her of biblical times and climes. There are plates of crackers smeared with cheese and chopped ham. Two rice dishes, one topped with hunks of fish and the other chunks of chicken. There's a platter of lunch meats and a twin plate lined with slices of Wonder Bread. For dessert there's a tray of Rice-Crispy treats that Sister Pauline threw together—she's been enthusing about them since we arrived. They await the savory portion of the meal to be consumed, though I'd have no qualms going after them first. Peacoat has brought an angelfood cake which will also come in due time, after the cold cuts and other dishes have disappeared, in order to avoid waste, almost all of which—too bad Jake—you can't eat. Canned olives and Wonder Bread—it's not nothing.

Besides, why focus on it too much, even though they're calling it a feast, because it pales compared to the fact that you've had to go without a cigarette, cold turkey, in the space of week. In fact—manners, boy!—what have you brought to the table, other than stories from your life, pre-grace? You're going on about The Romeo Years, that period you obviously feel compelled to spill about, as if it were some Golden Age. As though all of a sudden you live to tell the story, interrupting the reading in progress. Sister Pauline glances at Sister Marnie, their sensibilities curdled as you speak, though they sit mute.

Oh my, my, Jake, the latter comments finally. Oh, my, my.

Which you take as a license to resume. Is it the juice of the apple, which you downed in lieu of a proper drink, rushing to your head, loosening your tongue—Just think, you muse. Las' year this time I was in the arms a another man.

Eyes around the circle flash wide, Sister Marnie's and Sister Pauline's especially. Sisters Cathaleen and Nancy's, Pastor Billy's too, glance toward the crack-taped window, a patch-up job as wide as the Mississippi, until they return their gaze to Jake. The pastor remarks, We needn't give witness ta all god's savin' ways. Though you continue still.

We were an item for five years. We started the summer after my sophomore year. Peacoat queries, Are y' sure y' wanna rehash all that?

But a story, once commenced, must work to completion, or so you think. You unburden yourself—witnesses is the term they're using—more aptly you confess as if this were a Roman congregation. In Jake's defense, I can attest that this generation relishes the notion of a confession—god knows you see it enough on the TV, when Florrie and I are alone in the house on an afternoon and Ruby's napping, when we steal a little time in front of the tube, before Harry returns and commandeers it. Accordingly Jake will spill everything, come hell or high water, start-to-finish in the order that things transpired, despite the fact that everyone is looking away. Or down. He'll divulge as many details as he can, enacting a Catholic custom for this Calvinist crowd, unaware it's not at all their thing. He proceeds until Jeanette stands up and approaches the piano at the end of the room, paraphrasing for the others when she remarks, Such a life you lived, Jake! And at such a young age! Thanks for sharing all that.

To which Sister Nancy, having bitten her lip for the latter part of the past half-hour, pipes, Amen! Let's sing!

Praise the lord! Pastor Billy enthuses, wiping his brow. God has steered you safely here, Brother Jake. Let's rejoice in that alone!

There's no need ta glorify the beast, adds Sister Cathaleen. The main thing is t' focus on the life the lord's brung you to.

It seems that was not quite the hook Jake was looking for though, out of his narrative—he's got a serious hankering to catalogue his life in the flesh.

I was with a man for years, he pleads among the squeaking of chair legs against the linoleum. From the time I turned fifteen. Though he never actually kiss me. For real, that is. I mean like he mean' it. Until a year ago tonight. After I dumped 'im he told me he wasn't gonna have nothin' t' do with me. Ever again—I mean his name was Romeo, of all things.

Sister Pauline's eyes are again cast wide, Sister Marnie's too. Actually were Jake to circle his gaze around he'd discover everyone looking away, everyone but Peacoat, whose eyes were wide as double moons cast on Jake. To think of all that was going on under his very nose.

He turn me out then I turn him out, with a *veng*ence, even though we work at the same place and I see his car in the lot every day. Reverend Billy's eyes have flown wide open now as well, rotating up. Jake continues, I didn't see 'im in a age, not until we end up at the same party, by accidint. I was drunk outta my gourd. Passed out on the floor. Then all a a sudden I feel these lips on mine and then a tongue—

—Jake! Peacoat interrupts, his face flush. Jake!

Let's sing! interjects Jeanette.

Yes, let's sing! lilts Sister Pauline, raising her head again, the tone of her voice celebrating a triumph. The group stows away bibles, the purpose of our coming here in the first place—

—The lord'll understand, remarks the pastor. If we don't finish our readin'.

Peacoat did you bring your axe?

He pulls himself from reverie, or is it a spell? An epiphany? As though eyeing something foreign and familiar at the same time. Slowly reaching behind his chair he remarks, Praise the lord! Got it!

Nancy is the keeper of the sheets. As Sister Jeanette takes up her position at the keyboard she passes well-fingered leaves around the room, with notes that boogie across the page, black on white—for musical notations, at least, it's OK to mix.

Praise...god...from....whom....all...blessings...flow.

Sister Marnie's tremolo ranges above the rest, more or less in keeping with the tune.

Sister Nancy is moved to assume a seat at the piano next to Jeanette. She waits for the second verse as Sister Jeanette's hands march across the keys. By the time the interlude begins the group's tongues move in sync. Sister Marnie's eyes glance around the circle and her face beams, as if to say, This is how it's gonna be in the nex' world, after th' rapture.

I try to picture it from Pastor Billie's living room, perched not far from the lake at the mouth of the Shagaran. The squat bungalow is some remove from Romeo's split-level affair with its three-car garage, the kind of place Florrie never tires of reminding Harry she dreams of moving to someday. The pastor's father's house, as he refers to it, exists far from the flood zone here, where most of the homes in East Shagaran lie situated. In the next world it'll be more like Romeo's part of Laurentine with one exception: the grass up there won't ever need mowing. It won't flood either the way these low dwellings do, sitting on a cursed terrain. Sister Marnie's, Pauline's, Nancy's, Jeanette's, Cathaleen's, and Pastor Billy's houses await to see, year after year, how high the river will rise as the lakes and rivers begin to crack their frozen skins, throwing open the flood gates. The water ascends. Ice moans like infernal souls just learning their fates. You see the flooding on the local news on TV, every Spring, a kind of inundation here on the Shagaran, the river the French named and the Brits changed, however imprecisely, and which some of the locals have dubbed the Grand Chagrin, referring to the whole Shagaran network, frozen stiff at the moment but pregnant with trouble.

Who knew, Jake whispers to me, That the lord likes piano an' guitar t'gether?

Sister Jeanette's hands twist over the keys, her knuckles tight, the tips of her fingers shooting out. Sanctioned or not her torso half-dances, swoons to the tempo that Peacoat, consciously or not, has picked up, rushed a jot, despite looks darting from the Sisters.

We'll make a merry, Sister Pauline had said about this New Years Eve event. She declared it in a voice as sweet as syrup only a week ago when Peacoat, Jake, and I were at her store. And now here we are, making a sound for sure, to which I add my own voice from time to time, though I get the sense Sister Pauline is trying to drown me out. She lilts between the verses, nodding toward Peacoat, A l'il bit slower, Brother—no need t' rush.

When the music halts, Sister Marnie's voice trails off slowly as if floating on air—I read the pleasure in her face. Meanwhile Sister Nancy—about whom I heard Sister Pauline comment, *sotto voce,* She's not at all invested with the greatest of musical gifts—she wonders, after the song has finally come to an end, Isn't it time to eat?

Sister Pauline pleads, Jus' one more!

Let's indulge our Sister, ventures Pastor Billy—Shall we?

Truth be told Sister Nancy has been ogling the table all evening, from the time we arrived up to and including the last three refrains. But Sister Pauline, the elder of the group apart from Sister Marnie, wants to sing, so damn it, we'll sing. Accepting her fate, Sister Nancy stands and backs away from the piano, after which Sister Jeanette pries open the lid of the bench, rummaging for another set of sheets, sending leaves tumbling in the process until she's landed on the hymn she's after. She begins to play.

I witness it all because Jake insisted I stay, despite my status. It would turn out to be the case not just on that but many other nights, and later as well when he and Peacoat began their forays around the Forest City. It was three of us for many months, during which time I witnessed a change, though it happened at a glacially slow, if unstoppable pace.

Intentional or not, she's gone an' done her business in my room again! complains Diana.

Florrie pours boiling water into a cup, steam still buzzing from the kettle. She peers up, toward where her god resides, toward where Diana's voice comes down as well.

Diana, Florrie stage-whispers. Don't get so upset. She's juggling. She has me in her arms while spooning crystals into scalding water, then halts, clinks the spoon on the counter and pads to the bottom of the stairs, muttering to herself, What a way t' start the day, eh Precious? G'mornin' t' you too. She looks up.

She can' help it—don' blame her! I'm sure she didn' do her business up there on purpose.

I hear Diana thump to the head of the stairs, stick her head through the door, her voice bursting like a fire-cracker. Well, why does she al'ays do 'er business in my room? Why don't she ever do it in yers?

Florrie steadies herself on the wrought-iron banister, supported by a filigree of vines, tendrils, and leaves that remind me of Harry's garden, the one he sows the second Sunday of every May, come hell or high water, though without help these days. When the twins were young he planted in them the idea of the soil's potential, even the clay around here, deposited by the glacier. Aside from *Jim Doney's Adventure Road,* the plot behind the house was the only turf where Wren and Jake met Harry one on one, or two on one, free from Florrie's filters. The iron flora that now supports Florrie reminds me of the tangle and gnarl the space has become without the twins' help. Florrie's legs jut from her nightie like the spindles of the sofa. She glances into the living room, toward the chair where Harry refused to budge the night before, until he roused himself, piling into bed next to Florrie and dislodging me in the process, after a few choice words. Florrie fingers the bow at her neck that knots the opening shut.

I don' know why she did her business in your room—shooting a glance at me. I'm sure it weren't nothin' personal—for pity sake. It ain't the end a the world, y' know.

Well, either she goes or I do—I mean it!

Florrie backs away from the stairwell and shuffles to the kitchen, then sets me down. I hobble around behind her, and she reaches down to kiss me.

Poor Mollykins. I know you couldn' help it, she comments in a way that infers, You an' me, girl. She straightens at the waist, returns to finish spooning granules in her cup, watches the tornado kick up as she stirs, browning the water—I've seen it many times. She looks toward the ceiling, exclaiming in a much louder voice, I had 'er in bed with me last night!

Well she got up 'ere somehow. I ain't gonna be the one t' clean it up, that's for sure!

No a course not, Florrie mutters to herself. Looking at me and in a whisper she assures, Don't worry, Precious—don' worry. Then, looking up again she yells, I said I'll get it!

Meanwhile with a little help I climb onto my perch with its view out the back, my own roost on the back of which Jake inscribed with magic marker that time, *This is molly's chair*—how many years ago? He got Florrie's Irish up something fierce, I recall. It was frothing, enough to break something, though not Jake's neck ultimately, the way she threatened. Years and use have effaced the characters some—time has done more to eradicate them than all Jake's soap-and-water efforts at the time, his and Florrie's both, attesting to the power of an inscription.

The shuffle of shoes where previously none were allowed, as though treading sacred territory. Adult feet clomp here and there as loudly as Leo in his stocking feet.

It's hard to b'lieve, remarks Florrie.

Hard to b'lieve, nothin'. I been lookin' forward t' this day.

Y' should a done it decades ago.

Easy for you t' say.

Leave it, the both a yous, directs Florrie. All water over the dam now. What you gonna do with the sofa? That side board?

I'm leavin' 'em for the kids.

Why you gonna do that? You can sell 'em. Make a prutty penny.

They need it more'n me. An' a whole lot more.

Let's not talk about it.

In fact the place appears schlumpier than I remember, especially given how long it's been since we were last here, once or twice since Ruby came to stay with us and not once since Miss Glasby passed away. Patterns mark the walls where dressers and armoires stood, leaving rectangles in the wallpaper where it never oxidized. Stains mark the floor where philodendrons, sansevierias, and other troopers in this light-deprived world once stood and were overwatered, rotting the wood beneath the linoleum. A burn mark blackens the wall where an outlet overloaded, where wires frayed and erupted in sparks. Everywhere you look you find evidence of life, departed.

It was OK while Leo was here. But what'm I gonna do here all by myself? Now that he's with that girl.

Well don' he come aroun' to visit? Don' 'e help out?

He's got 'is own life.

I make my way down the hall to the kitchen, my favorite room in any house. The fridge, suffering still from slumped shoulders as bad as Ruby's, seems to have given up the ghost, its motor no longer chatty like back in the day. It held many a gift, raw and cooked—if anyone was headed this way I could almost always count on a pay-off if I hung around long enough. My nails tap dance across the linoleum, dented and worn in more places than I remember. Every flaw is laid bare.

What're you doin' back here? remarks Florrie, studying me. It's somethin' else, ain't it, Precious? When Midge and Harry join us she asks, When do the next tenants move in?

You mean Donald an' Wren? They're gonn sleep here t'night.

Then we best skedaddle, returns Harry.

Yeah, we better scoot.

And yet we hang around. For all the times they claim they'd better go, as if Midge were keeping them—Let us go, remarks the one repeatedly and then the other—for all their talk the two shift here and there, rush in slow fashion, no doubt to take in the ramshackle look of the place, as am I.

It's hard t' believe someone'd ever wanna live here. I mean this is the pits.

Harry—

—You don' know what you're talkin' about. It's bigger'n your place in Laurntine. It's just it's all on one floor. A li'l paint's all it needs.

You need t' drop a bomb on the house, the whole goddam neighborhood—hell, this entire city. Start all over again.

Harry, stop.

A little love's all it need. If I could do it myself I would. But it's too much with my leg an' all.

Only a fool'd move here. Two fools. A'least when you moved in it was a real neighborhood, 'fore *they* ruined it.

Did the next tenants say what they gonna do with it?

What d'you think?

I mean will they actually live here?

Well they ain't gonna ren' it out—they're agains' that. They say that's the problem.

They really are idiots.

T' think about raisin' a child here—

—I did it—why can' they? There's two a them after all.

Two idiots with their heads up their asses.

They gimme five hunderd cash as a down paymen'. Ain't nothin' wrong with 'at.

Wull see if y' ever see another dime.

I ain't worried.

If it's such a good deal why din't Leo stay?

He wanted to live near the Geist boy and his wife. Somewhere out by you. If you ever run inta him you can ask 'im yourself.

Ye shall not eat it, nuther shall ye touch it, lest y' die.
   And the serpent said, ye shall not surely die:
   For god doth know that in the day y' eat there of,
   That your eyes shall be opened and y' shall be as gods....

Water cycles through the toilet down the hall. Otherwise silence trumpets itself in this supersanitary space. The spirit moves among the bowed heads.

Like I said, some a these verses is a burden, remarks Sister Pauline.

Bradford replies, God can make 'em light.

Women get blamed, complains Sister Marnie. It al'ays come down t' that.

They're th' weaker lot, asserts Sister Nancy.

The snake was male, returns Sister Marnie. It was him t' blame. I mean, if he hadn' come along—

—Well, an' what about Adam? lilts Sister Pauline in a voice sweet as licorice. He's a big wimp!

He merely follows her lead—
—As we saw.
He's passive!
Yet Eve gets th' blame.

But it was she who disabayed god's law, refutes the reverend. The woman tempted 'im t' gainsay it.

Pauline smiles. In a voice shaken by a tremor, she replies, I—may I quote again, Pastor? It says here, *When the woman saw that th' tree was good for food, an' that it was pleasant t' the eyes, and a tree t' be desired t' make one wise she took a the fruit there of, and did eat, and gave also unta her husbind wither; and he did eat. An' the eyes a them both were opened, and they knew that they were neck'ed now*—. Well, Paster. Not t' disagree with you in the slightest, but all it says is she gave unto her husbind. There's nothin' rully there about her temptin' him or nothin'. All it says is that she offer and he take it.

But how else *could it a* happen, other'n by tem'tation, since Adam knew god's law in 'is heart? How could he a ever transgressed had Eve not a entice 'im to it in some way, the way the Evil One tempted her? It ain't spelled out but it's implied in so many words.

Like Sister Pauline, I ain't at all here t' disagree, Paster, ventures Sister Marnie, her hair a nest of serpents. But it just ain't spelled out th' way you suggest.

Thank you for sharin', Sister Marnie, Sister Pauline, but let us actually listen ta the word a god. Clearly an' without prejudice. In verse three-eight it says, *An' they. . .they heard th' voice a the Lord God walkin' in the garden in the cool a the day an' Adam an' his wife hid themselfs from th' presence a th' Lord God amongst the trees a th' garden an'*—an'—let's see—*the Lord God call unto Adam an' said*—hmm hmm hmm—*unta him where art thou*—hmm hmm—let's see— and he says *I heard thy voice in the garden*—hmmm—*an'*

*I was afraid cuz I was neck'ed an' I hid myself an' he says
who told thee thou wast neck'ed hast thou eaten a th' tree—*
hmmmhmmmhmmm—Oh Kay, almost t' the part—OK
here!—*th' woman whom thou gavest t' be with me she gave
me a the tree an' I did eat an' the Lord God said unta the
woman what is this that thou has done and the woman says
the serpent beguiled me an' I did eat.* Now Sisters, Pastor
Billy reiterates, resting his glasses on the book, Doesn'
that spell it out rull clear? That th' serpent beguiled her
an' she in turn beguile her husbin—how else could it a
happen?

But Pastor, again, not t' disagree with you—I'm juss
tryin' t'—t' learn, explains Sister Pauline, smiling in her
tight way, the pitch of her voice lofting toward the rafters.
It doesn' say that quite. It says, *The woman whom thou
gavest t' be with me she gave me a th' tree an' I did eat*, which
is not at all t' say she didn' beguile him as you say, but
neither does it say very clearly that she did.

All it says is Adam took the apple, asserts Sister Marnie.
T' quote again it says—that is, Adam—*She gave me a th'
tree an' I did eat.*

Now Pastor Billy's voice bumps up an octave too—
Sisters, he declares, I appreciate your goodwill efforts t'
read god's word aright. But you must interpret not just
the parts that please you—you must read his word in its
entirety. Why would god punish Eve more severely than
Adam if he didn' feel she's the one ta blame?

It's a good *question*, Pastor, interjects Sister Jeanette.

Why would god say, Unta the woman, *I'll greatly
multiply thy sorra an' thy concepction in sorra thou shall
bring forth childern an' thy desire shall be t' thy husbind and
he shall rule over thee?* Clearly god wouln' a placed such a
burden on our Mother Eve had he not a considerd her t'
have committed the graver sin.

But doesn't he go on t' punish Adam too, though in a diffrent way? continues Sister Jeanette. It says here, it says, *An' unta Adam he said*—let's see—*has eaten a th' tree*—eccetera eccetera eccetera—*Cursed is the ground,* it says, *For thy sake in sorra thou shall eat a it all the days a thy life, thorns also an' thistles shall it bring forth t' thee.* Then it goes, *In th' sweat a thy face shall thou eat bread til thou return unta the ground.* Doesn't that not imply they each received a crushin' judgmen', that god considerd both t' be equally at fault?

Well your goin' agains' hunderds a years a exagesis by bulldozin' through such a line a argumentation, informs Bradford, running his finger along the bridge of his nose, his voice strained. Far greater minds than ours have viewed it just as I—

—Were they women 'r men?! Sister Jeanette interrupts, drawing her hand to her mouth as though something slipped out. Glances dart around the room. Pastor Billy adjusts himself upright in his chair, as though Satan himself had slipped in and taken a seat.

Tell me, Sister Jeanette, How d'you interpret the words, *An' thy desire shall be t' thy husbind an' he shall rule over thee?* Doesn' that spell everything out?

Well, says Pauline.

Well, repeats Marnie.

I told you, capitulates Nancy. Could it be more clear?

Bradford sits back, then slumps in his chair. Now I ask you—Is there anythin' ambiguous about a passage like that? God gave Eve the lesser part, and in so doin' all women. What say you, Brother Peacoat? Brother Jake?

I dunno, responds Peacoat. I see both sides a the argumin'.

What about you, Brother Jake?

He peers at Peacoat, then at me, trapping his hands between his thighs. He clears his throat, then ventures, How can y' believe in a story with a talkin' animal?

The others start and Peacoat shoots a look, different from the others.

Satan has his disguises, remarks the pastor, massaging the bridge of his nose. Includin' a snake.

Jake, mutters Peacoat softly. He seemed more concerned than anything. It's probly best t' jus' listen.

SHADOWED

I can't thank you enough, Auntie.

Hell, you're doin' me the favor. I was just gonna walk. Throw 'way the key an' not look back, same as everyone else aroun' here. I din't think I'd ever get a dime, so I should be thankin' you.

But it's such a great place. Really spacious. An' full a mem'ries.

You can't find details like this anywhere in the city. There's definally a lot t' work with.

The place is got its problems, for sure. I wish you two the best. Your father always thought I was crazy for stayin', but t' be honest I liked it here. It's juss it's too much for one person.

As for me, my feelings are mixed. How can I express the thrill of seeing Wren and Donald again, after what feels like forever? It must be since I saw them on the banks of the Shagaran—how long ago was that? I wasn't at my best then, to say the least—me and Jake both. And now here we are again, just like that.

I try to make Billie's acquaintance given I've seen her so few times, but when I approach she shies away. I tap my way in her direction but she takes refuge behind Donald, who lowers himself, extends his hand and remarks, See? Ain't nothin' t' be afraid a. Yet the child eyes me with suspicion still. She sneezes and I back away.

To be plain I have no idea what's happening. Why I'm here at all, without Florrie or Harry, who simply brought and left me behind. Little did I know when Florrie said, C'mon, Precious, we're goin' for a ride, what it implied. Again, it's not that I'm not happy to see everyone, my Wren most of all, but a body gets used to her routine, one that isn't so easy to shake at my age, just like that. I mean will I stay an hour or a day? A week or month? Or is this my new home now, for good? Have I come here the way Ruby landed at our house, first as a visitor then as part of the furniture? Separating the sisters like that, like me from Florrie, who's become a kind of sibling? Who's to say that wasn't what did her and Miss Glasby both in, albeit in different ways. I have no idea where I'll sleep—not curled up beside Florrie, that's for sure. And while I'm at it, will someone fix me an egg in the morning, or did I enjoy my last this very day?

Meanwhile Billie tugs Wren's hand and asks to see her room. Donald rests his behind against the side of the sink then folds his arms, while Midge pulls up the chair that didn't make it onto the van. Out of the blue she remarks, You know you remin' me a Leo's father.

Donald's head pulls back, his eyebrows elevate then lower. He remarks, Ohhh Kay. That can mean a lotta things.

It means what you think. You know, I never told that t' no one b'fore? My sister most a all.

Well, you didn't need t' tell m—

—Unlike you he wasn't gonna be no journalist someday, tha's for sure.

Water drips from the faucet just as in the old days, one of the few things that's survived from the past. Donald turns around and tries to tighten the spigot but a stream continues. I think it's gonna need a washer.

I never even tol' my son.

It's a shame, ta waste all this water. Donald turns his back to Midge, squats, then draws the curtain below the sink. D'you know where the shut-off is?

You gotta go in th' basemen' for that.

You think you should a told 'im? Donald continues to peer under the sink while he speaks.

I mean, wha's the point? It ain't never gonna change nothin'. I can go on from now t' Doomsday about this, that, an' th'other thing, but what does it matter? I ain't seen the guy in decades.

Donald draws the curtain sides together. He groans involuntarily as he stands and pivots.

I met 'im at Tia Juanna's, back in the day—gosh! That was decades now. We kept comp'ny for awhile—we were a couple a cool cats back then. Nice anough guy. Though like I say I ain't spotted 'im in ages. Unlike Wrennie's mama, I weren't no choir girl.

You went to Tia Juanna's?! *The* Tia Juanna's?

I went t' all the clubs.

What a gas! Does the father even know?

Know what?

That he got a kid?

Midge flames the tip of her cigarette and sets the lighter on the linoleum beside her. She turns and blows a trail of smoke to her side. T' be hones', I dunno. It wasn't no long, drawn-out affair—after all I had three people t' support, not includin' me. So I didn' have time for none a that.

I can't believe you went to Tia Juanna's. Where else you go? Maybe he woulda liked t' know.

Wren pads in with Billie in tow. Know what?

Billie dear, how d'you like your new room?

The girl hides her face behind Wren's arm.

I think she'll like it more after the wallpaper comes down. It scares 'er.

Y' know, I always like that name. Billlllllie. Like the good witch.

Tell Auntie your middle name, Wren coaxes. Instead of speaking though, the girl puts her face behind her hands. She curls them then lowers her forehead into her fists, peeps over the top of her knuckles.

Go 'head. Tell 'er.

Midge too encourages the girl to speak up. She rests her arm on her shoulder as if to nudge her. The air goes silent for some time as all of the adults in the room, including me, train our gaze on the child.

Can you tell Auntie who you're named after?

Again we wait for some time with only the tap of the faucet to fill the void.

Midge remarks, I was just tellin' Donald that he reminds me a Leo's father.

Donald and Wren peer at each other.

D'you know she was part a th' Glenville scene?

You?! One of the Hundred-and-Fifth-street cool cats?

Why not? I got around.

Billie sneezes then repeats a little louder this time, not at all in the soft, velveteen voice from before. She asserts what she's been trying, finally, to interject into the adult conversation. She chortles, then grows indignant, until she finally has the attention of the adults present.

In reply Midge responds, Aha! Oh! I see! Well that's a pretty name. She exhales a cloud into the room. The sink continues to drip drip drip. Midge sips her can of pop and clears her throat. Let's see. . .who doesn't remember? *Southern trees bear a strange fruit, Blood on the leaves and blood at the root*—Lemme see—I heard 'er sing it myself.

No way.

Wha'd'you mean, no way? Gimme a minute. . . . She tilts her head from side to side as though trying to shake something free—*Strange fruit hanging from the poplar trees. . .Pastoral scene. . . .*

When she's finished Donald proclaims, I don' really b'lieve it.

Why not? I was there. In the flesh.

You messin' with me—

—Am not. I heard 'er several times. Like I say, in the flesh.

You just made his day. Did my mom ever hear 'er?

Are you kidding?! Your mama? She was too much of a goody two-shoes for that scene—with all the stuff that went on in them places? Tia Juanna's, Moe's, Lindsay's—the list's a mile long. They were somethin' else. The people I knew and hung with—you didn' need t' go runnin' off t' the Big Apple or Chicago cuz it was all right here, jus' blocks away.

We got stuff t' talk about.

But Tia's was one a th' only clubs me and Leo's daddy could go t'gether.

Y' know, this guy spends all his time listenin' to that stuff when he should be writin.'

It's another reasons I stayed here, though how could I explain that t' your mama and daddy? I was here 'cause I wanted t' be. For Leo's sake as much as mine. I always thought he needed t' know, even if he didn' know, if y' know what I mean.

Hard to b'lieve you an her mom—

Ain't all families like that?

A stub tracks across the surface, tattoos the page with lines. Fields of conviction, set to question by a thumb bent on mixing things up. The skin pushes across the grain, causing the tones to soften—Jake grays things. His hand caresses the charcoal.

Meanwhile stiff-as-a-post Peacoat observes Jake's hand moving here and there, like the three of us earlier as we entered the railyard. He follows as Jake works the composition, attitude, and gesture, positive and negative space, then tilts the paper to shake away the excess. His head pulls back and his gaze hovers over the surface until he returns to his subject. Blowing on his fingers to warm them, he sighs at the page, as though it needed enlivening, like the divine's breath in clay. He sprays a torrent of fixative and waits, holds the drawing upright then faces it toward Peacoat.

Wha'd'ya think?

It's OK I s'pose. He leans closer. But it don't look like me.

Jake launches into a jig, attempting to loosen the cold in his legs, feet, and toes.

Well a likeness ain't th' point—an' it come with time.

Then what is the point, pray tell?

The goal's to capture a essense. If you want a mirror view have someone take your pitcher. Though even that won' be you.

A pitcher will definally be me! It can' help itself.

No, it wouldn' either. It'd depend on th' lens. The light. Paper. Exposure—on lotsa things. But it won't be you. There's only one a them.

Still, pitchers come closer than drawings.

Well again that ain't th' point. Jake has been peering downward, thinking, and now he lifts his head and glances straight ahead.

Peacoat returns the gaze with a vitreous eye, having squinted the other shut. That's goofy, Jake. A copout.

No it ain't.

If nothin' succeeds at capturin' things—

Jake rips away the top leaf on his pad and exposes a blank surface. Again he assumes his seat atop the rail. Large, wet flakes start to descend. He orders Peacoat, sitting two meters away, to hush.

No more talkin'! The side of his charcoal moves across the page. No pitcher's what it tries t' be.

Then why bother tryin'?

Shhhhh! He's chosen to work in reverse, establishing a field of dark on the page from which he lifts lines with the corner of an eraser.

It's what's revealed in th' effort.

When earlier in the day we found ourselves near Collinwood Yard, it was the endless crisscrossing of tracks and switches that drew us here, the parallels and perpendiculars created by signal bridges and lights, semaphore signals and upper quadrant signals in iron, steel, and glass that, when taken as a whole, appeared like a 3D drawing. Jake proclaimed the scene a Mondrian we could walk through, here on the east side of the Forest City. Double rails intersect over dozens of acres as locomotives and boxcars graze in place.

An hour before that the two of them, accompanied by Pastor Billy, polished off their last round of pancakes and refills of tea—I managed a taste, though not from Jake. It was Peacoat who indulged me, noticed me, as though I were a thing more than an animate machine. It's become a Saturday-morning ritual, Pastor Billy joining us, kicking off the day with prayer as he monitors his flock. Even though Peacoat's been intimating for some time that the reverend need not worry quite so much, assuring him we're in good hands—In fact, the Lord's!—the Pastor insists on being here nonetheless, like clockwork, every Saturday morning. When Peacoat came right out finally and averred that he and Jake had places they wanted to go, that it would be best if they came in two separate cars, what could he say? Billy queried about what kinds of things they had in mind.

I dunno—stuff.

Jus' drivin' around.

Never mind they entertained more specific plans. Jake wanted to go back to drawing, and maybe someday even pick up a brush again, both of which he gave up when he met Jay-sus. In the same way Peacoat found himself unable to cut the cord with his Monte Carlo, Jake's yen for a part of his past also proved too much to fight. Much as he'd done with Romeo he wanted to capture Peacoat, who when he broached the subject said he'd have to talk to the pastor, who ultimately couldn't come up with an argument, let alone a biblical passage against it, a brother drawing a brother, though it wasn't as though he didn't try. Unsupported by the book, a line that said, Thou shalt not sketch thy friend, he had to let it go.

To a point. When we parted from the Euclid Diner this morning I witnessed the pastor's jalopy out the rear window, tracking us, never so far back that he couldn't maintain a visual. As for the two in the front seat, outta-sight was outta-mind. Yet what was there for the pastor to take in anyway? A couple shivering forms jumping between flatbeds. Panting, shaking, and calling out to the sky, My goodness its *cold*!

Jake works while Peacoat inquires, speaking of tracks, Do they ever meet? I mean I know hypothetically they don't, but in some practical way? Far on the horizon—do they hook up?

I look west in the direction of Hough. The lines appear to head smack toward each other and even appear to touch, in the distance, obfuscated by thickening flakes that cascade in earnest from low-hanging clouds.

Peacoat tires of sitting so he ascends the ladder of a
boxcar. He rummages around inside then reëmerges.
After hopping from the bottom rung he heads toward
the switchyard, in the direction of a field of levers and a
collision of tracks. Left without a subject, Jake gives up
and gathers his things. We join Peacoat, and the three of
us pass under a coal silo that must have been here for over
a century.

In the distance I spy the diminutive form of Pastor
Billy, moving like a scent hound. Tall stacks above the
steel factory not far away emit flames that sere the clouds.
They shoot sparks and rain debris that mixes with snow,
the tyranny of whiteness starting to obliterate everything,
the rails in the distance most of all.

I'm sorry things didn' work out, Auntie.

It was worth a try.

Who could a ever predicted she'd be allergic?

We'd take her back t' Laurentine ourselves but I don'
think they'd appreciate that.

No problem—I'm long overdue for a visit.

Midge peers around. She crows, Place looks night an'
day diffren'! She runs her gaze along the walls, floor, and
ceiling, notices the bare plaster above the wainscoting in
the hallway that runs the length of the house, straight as
gunshot. No more pansy, daisy, and rose paper, the entire
space is a flat gray. No flowered linoleum, revealing oak
planks throughout the residence. She pokes her head in
what was once Leo's room, where the clack of helmets
and shoulder pads, the Whitmanian grass, and cobalt sky
have all vanished, the wall stripped bare and covered over
with a layer of paint. Several. In the room next to Leo's,

forget-me-nots no longer leap from the crown molding. Everything there too has been altered, erased by a couple coats.

What a change! Midge casts her gaze in the corner where Miss Glasby once slept, where Donald has set up a card table for a desk, directly in front of a wall-length shelf of records and cassettes. He's stacked books alongside the desk, there on the floor, not far from the mattress that's been plopped in the middle of the space.

It's gonna take awhile t' get the place the way we wan' it.

Too bad Florrie ain't here t' see. T' be honest she'd love it—she always did like settin' up house. Drove me nuts when you first moved t' Laur'ntine.

We got my mom t' make up for it. She's got more ideas than we know what t' do with, though with Wren it goes in one ear and out the other. She knows what she wants.

Th' apple don't fall far—

—Be nice.

Midge and Donald look toward Wren. No one's ever gonna accuse any one a that clan a bein' wishy-washy.

Once they get a notion—

We're in the kitchen and the oven is cheering the place. Wren has slipped a casserole inside and I whiff the bubbling sauce. The three of them are on folding chairs around a card table, identical to Donald's desk. A cake of cheese, rolled in ash, has been brought on a plate, placed next to a basket of bread, not far from me. Or maybe I settled not far from it.

Do y' mind if I give 'er some? queries Midge.

Knock yourself out, replies Donald. Though it ain't like we haven't been spoilin' th' crap out a her. At her age, why not?

What's one more then?

I much oblige both after inhaling the ort, querying, Encore?

Would you two be OK if I—?

—If you what?

Midge pulls out a hand-rolled cigarette. You know—it's the only thing ease the pain. Lemme close Billie's door—

—No need t' do that.

—Wanna join me—?

—Not me, Auntie. I'm guessing he wouldn' mind though.

Here's my girl.

Wren takes Billie by the hand and leads her to what was once Leo's room, where she settles to read a story. She returns to the scent of autumn leaves, piled high and burning at the end of a season.

No, you definitely didn' need to go galavanting t' Chicago or New York in them days. We had our own scene. The Count, Duke, the Prez—they all come through here. It was first class.

Think that can ever happen again?

They're sayin' that scene's dead, not juss here but everywhere.

If so, so's the country.

Gracious lord, prays Pastor Billy. Cleanse our hearts and souls of appetite. Make us clean, lord.

Clean, repeats Peacoat.

Clean, adds Jake. Dishes shatter in the background, and the wait staff freezes as the sound bounces off the tin ceilings. The hubbub and din everywhere around percolates then dies. The clash of metal cutlery falling on the floor, the opaque white world outside the window, all while the heads of the three near me bow in unison, or orison as the case may be.

Remove from our minds everythin' that's unmanly. Make us men in thy image.

Make us men, echoes Peacoat.

Men, parrots Jake.

Buckles of unlatched galoshes jingle as they pass. The white-white world outside is obfuscated and magnified by thick condensation on the plate glass at the front of the establishment, rippling with sweat. Only outlines of the world outside appear through it, forms of cars and pedestrians, white shading black shading white with an endless array of grays in between.

Free us from anything feminine and weak. Make us true soldiers in thy holy army.

Yes lord, intones Peacoat. Make us soldiers.

Soldiers, echoes Jake. He's caressing me unconsciously, his head bent low, his eyes partially closed, unlike Peacoat's and Pastor Billy's which are sealed hermetically shut. The pastor's hands fall from their prayer posture. His right reaches toward Peacoat's which in turn takes Jake's hand, creating a slapdash ring, the three in a daisy chain not unlike the kind hippies in the three-hour movie wore around their heads. Peacoat releases Pastor Billy's hand who relinquishes Jake's who again strokes the nape of my neck and upper back. I tilt my head, tune in to the island of silence in a sea of clatter.

Amen, punctuates Jake, breaking the spell.

Amen, repeats Peacoat, and Pastor Billy, unfurling his wrinkled brows, whispers, In thy holy name we pray, our precious lord.

Jake's fork jumps to hand—Oh, god, this looks good, he remarks, and Peacoat shoots a look.

So tell me again th' purpose a these quote-unquote outings you two undertake? How will they glorify th' lord?

Even after a month of Saturdays neither Peacoat nor Jake holds a handy answer to the question. Just for fun simply won't cut it, that they know.

It's a time a fellowship, ventures Peacoat.

To which Pastor Billy replies, Nothing pleases the lord more'n 'at. The wholesome fellowship a men. Brothers in god's army. It causes the angels t' rejoice a thousand-fold. How would you describe the nature a your fellaship?—I been meaning to ask for some time. I mean you two spend a *awful* lotta time together. Not all fellaship's equal in god's sight.

In response Jake tells it how it should be told, from the beginning, working to a middle and an end, even though Pastor Billy knows the tale perfectly well by now, how he and Peacoat met down at Geist, months after the break-up with Romeo, and etc, etc, etc. I got lost in all the drugs an' alcohol hangin' around with Rauch an' them guys.

Ditto, adds Peacoat, even though his and Jake's time with the group didn't overlap.

Jake has me next to him on the banquette. I watch as Pastor Billy cuts and recuts a wedge of pancake. He suggests god had granted Peacoat and Jake something special, a holy fellowship.

Beware th' devil, though. He's al'ays looking for a inroad in order t' ruin it.

Pastor Billy's words throw water on Peacoat's chance of witnessing. About how he met Marks and Company when Jake was preoccupied with Romeo. How their dealings only encouraged his addictions, which hastened his coming to the lord, and so on, all of which went unrelated, never mind that everyone present had heard it before.

Well, again, the importin' thing is t' keep the devil out. Not let 'im in. Your souls've been knit in heaven. The devil an' his minsters've been rebuked by a wrathful god, and you're protected by a host a angels. It's more sacerd than a marriage in a way, two men in clean, manly fellowship.

While the reverend speaks his hand massages Peacoat's shoulder in avuncular fashion. He moves his arm back and forth, nearly yanking Peacoat off kilter, causing him to miss his mouth with his fork. The reverend squeezes Peacoat's shoulder harder still, causing him to flinch.

The perversions a the flesh are legion.

The spirit is willing, assures Peacoat.

It's the flesh you gotta scrut'nize. Having pronounced on the subject, the pastor breathes in deeply. He exhales then sits back, causing the cushion of the banquette to fart, unsettling the women on the other side, startling them a bit, to the point that they each in turn glance over their shoulders at the pastor, who rests now, having made as strong a case as he knows how, his eyes downcast. He slouches in the seat, and again the leatherette farts.

A welter of dishes covers the table. The plates have been made clean by punctilious eaters because the lord abhors waste. A teenager moseys up and begins bussing the industrial-strength china, which has seen decades of service and is still not much the worse for wear. The same can be said for the diner itself, not to mention the banquettes and tables, all from another age but still trooping on. The number of buttocks sliding back and forth across the worn oilcloth, dozens, probably hundreds of times a day, through three services, going back—how long? Seventy? Eighty? A hundred years? I can tell it's been ages by the build-up of grease and soot that velvetizes the walls. And yet *Murray's* is a magnet for Forest Citiers. They've flocked here in droves, one of the oldest eating establishments downtown, long before its owner relocated to Miami Beach.

Well we best get a move-on, suggests Jake.

Yep. . .best be goin'.

Don't forget what I said. As he speaks, Pastor Billy pinches Peacoat's arm.

We'll pray on it for sure.

We'll be on it.

In the nearly vacant, free lot across the street Pastor Billy returns to the rusty Bel Air that followed us here, while the three of us repair to the lap of luxury, Peacoat's baby, the one the lord blessed him with when he was in the world and he decided to keep. The two sedans take off along Superior Avenue toward Thirtieth—I hear Pastor Billy's engine complaining. He settles it down then maneuvers it into gear. The thing submits, and we're all on our own now, with a white world to contemplate to our left, the broad, frozen lake, perpendiculared by a row of slushy streets—an entire, blank world lies beyond them. A field of ice straining toward Canada, pocked with divots and jagged with spikes of ice but only up close—sharp, glassy plates unseen from these streets bisecting Superior. I can't help but think what it must've been like on equally frigid mornings when the Eries huddled here, before all this. The brick and glass, pavement and lights, factories not far off, docks and unloaders, soot too, replacing trees, soil, and fauna. As Pastor Bradford has just a short time ago reminded us in such pointed terms, the terrain is possessed by a different landlord now, a fiery force overlording this fairy-story world, sandwiched over the one we see.

We scan the road. Stop at yet another light. The three of us on alert for something, but what? We motor some more. Jake fiddles with his sketchbook, jotting something down. The soft seats, the smell of animal hides, lives born of a mother just like me, sacrificed for this comfy glide, the binding of Jake's book, the heifers and bulls that traded their existence.

After turning south on Thirtieth I scope Billy again out the rear window, piggybacking cars behind, his head searching this way and that in the same way he's been shadowing us for ages—though again, do Peacoat and Jake have a clue? Jake rubbernecks as the vehicle slows and then accelerates, turning left on Chester and advancing until he announces, Here it is!

We wheel into the parking lot and Peacoat brings the Monte Carlo to a halt, crunching the snow under the tires. We pile out into deep drifts. Jake clutches his sketchbook, swinging it back and forth as he maneuvers through the thick accumulation of white all around. He jots something in his sketchbook, morphs into a documentarian, of whiteness I suppose. He scratches in pencil as I leap around, contours Peacoat with his darker skin as he bends over the trunk and extracts a knapsack. With the two preoccupied I alone monitor Pastor Billy as he glides by. He pauses, wheels down the passenger-side window, and assesses the situation, never mind the line of cars behind him impatient to move on. Before the two have the time to notice he windmills up the glass and pulls away, a string of cars tortoising behind him.

I turn to the brick-and-aluminum affair in front of us, realize there's not a tree in sight, despite the city's moniker. A song seems to be playing in Peacoat's brain, one that mimics the funereal pace of the traffic, slowed to two lanes instead of four. In truth Peacoat doesn't seem himself now, despite the fact he's moving with purpose after all the planning, not to mention the months-long discussion that preceded this day. Once inside, safely sequestered in our room, it's as though a death were imminent. The two stiffs glance around, avoiding each other's gaze, eyeing the torn curtains and worn carpet, the burn marks and stains on the bedspread.

Praise the lord, initiates Jake.

Yeah. Praise.

Shall we read?

Read what?

Jake pries a volume from his backpack, the pages intercollated with slips of pink and yellow paper, then flaps it open willy-nilly.

An' it came t' pass.

Well.

When he had made an end a speaking unto Saul that the soul a Jonathan was knit with th' soul a David. Peacoat sniffs, clears his throat, and wipes the end of his nose with his sleeve. Jake and I listen to the tick of flakes that have recommenced falling on the windowsill outside.

An' Jonathan loved 'im as 'is own soul and Saul took 'im that day and would not let 'im go no more home to his Father's house.

Peacoat's hands are shaking. He trembles as Jake reads, the first time I've ever seen him so discomposed. Jake's finger peruses the lines as slowly as the cars wheeling down Chester, heading in the direction where first Midge and Leo, and for over a year now Billie, Wren, and Donald have lived—*Then Jonathan an' David made a covenent because he loved 'im as 'is own soul and Jonathan stripped himself a the mantle that was upon 'im.*

Peacoat shuts the volume in Jake's lap.

What?

He reaches across, grasps, and folds the book, then when it's on his lap slides his finger from the spot Jake had been reading then cracks it slowly, as if afraid to look—. *An' gave it t' David and his garmints even to his sword an' to 'is bow an' to 'is girdle.*

Praise god, mumbles Jake.

—

Melting snow taps the aluminum ledge outside, as though it were raining. Beyond that, on the south side of the next avenue, smog-colored clouds frame a sycamore, invisible from the entrance to the building. Flakes of bark litter the ledge.

I draw my gaze inside and note that the proprietors have taken pains to avoid any superfluous frills, though they've primped the room in another way, providing amenities appropriate for a specific clientele, including complimentary soaps, tissues, towels, and whathaveyou. Everything about this place hints at the most ephemeral of stays given the lack of a tallboy to store your things, the absence of a bar in the closet for a coat, substituted by two hooks on the back of the door.

The place feels more like a way station than a place to stay—I mean who could live in a room like this? A stream of humanity has clearly passed through, ground it down not a little since it was constructed, mid-century. It feels like a home for the harried, like these two here who found it difficult to land upon a more suitable place. So here we sit, we three, though they appear to be on pins and needles, the clunky tome now resting on the spread.

In some sense it feels like a waiting room in a railway junction in the middle of Nowhere. We made it all this way, finally, but plans were not considered as to what comes next, never mind where we, or they, go after. The three of us sit peering along the rails so to speak. Waiting—but for what? For chance to take its course? For the god, Nature, to intervene? Show us—show them—what comes next? To enter into a territory so completely foreign, even for Jake, truth be told, who's behaving like a novice all of a sudden, having arrived at the ultimate station, and after so many stops over the past months, only to discover there's so much farther to go.

A knock at the door shatters the silence, and Peacoat leaps from Jake's side at the edge of the bed. His face flushes scarlet as though he were caught in some kind of act. The proprietor with his gruff voice pokes a head in, the man who after a protracted tussle at the front desk granted I could stay. How can I turn it away? he asked after Jake floated the idea of us moseying down the avenue, to another place, and after the guy upped the price for the night, afternoon, or however long, shifting the occupancy to three.

Here's some more towels, he barks. Don' make a mess—I'm the one that gotta clean it!

We're tired and wanna take a nap, replies Peacoat, never mind it's eleven-thirty in the morning.

The guy slams the door so hard a reproduction of a painting by Jake's favorite artist jolts from the wall. He jumps and collects the image and frame both, which were separated in the fall, then marries the two again and places them back on the nail. After a period of quiet it's Jake who again leads the choir.

Praise god!

But again Peacoat doesn't respond, at least for a time.

Then finally: Wha' d'you think Pastor Billy would say about this, Jake?

About what?

About—y'know.

About what?

About David an' Jonathan. You'n me.

It's as though he and Jake have switched seats. His nose started running the moment we arrived, which I initially attributed to the cold, but we've been here long enough now it should have stopped. He doesn't seem to have a cold or flu—he was fine at breakfast. So it's curious that his nose has become so active all of a sudden, not only running but quite frankly gushing. Oozing snot. He keeps nabbing tissues from the slot under the bathroom sink and dabbing it away. Liquid fills his eyes as though they're active springs. His irises, normally as dark as the lake at dusk, appear glassy, blacker than usual—again I don't get it. One thing I know is if he thought for a second there was something untoward, he'd have been history, from the get-go—he would've never allowed himself to come this far. Yet here he sits, or reclines, if reluctantly, splayed across the bedspread. He brushes the pile of tissues onto the floor, retaining one to catch the flow from his nose. For the first time since we've been here he peers directly, purposely at Jake, pulls him close, and Jake responds equally tentatively.

Jake queries, What *would* Billy—th' lot a them—think about you an' me here? Jonathan an' David?

How can they argue with th' word a god?

BIRTH

WHEN JAKE SHOULD HAVE BEEN IN SCHOOL, Tommy, he used
to skip out and drive me to this circle, lured by a tableau.
He'd shake the contents of his knapsack on the stairs, just
over there, scattering pencils, charcoals, erasers, and pads,
and after settling me below the pondering one he'd darken
sheet after sheet, each posing a series of riddles about the
nature of black, white, and mostly gray, while I took in the
new-day sun. He racked his brain, solving problems that
were apparently watermarked in each page, the trouble
with blank whiteness, the way it both warns off and begs
for a darkening, a mark, until at some point he gave up,
let his pad be, left it and me in order to pass again before
the image inside the beaux-arts structure. He studied it
for an interminable amount of time, the tableau he used
to coo about to Wren. Until viewers, who generally paid
it no mind, spotted him glued to it and thus grew curious,
shouldering him into the background. Their urge to avoid
missing Something, a work most considered unremarkable
because it wasn't reproduced on cards or keychains, posters
or coffee mugs—once they spotted someone fixated there it
induced them to blow in, around it. As they looked or half-
looked, they spoke less about the work than the painter,
Jake used to complain, about whom they seemed incapable
of speaking without going on about an ear.

It was the rows of sycamores that attracted him most
of all, similar to the ones along Liberty—the way they

gestured to him, they and the fairy lumps around their feet that looked like snow, never mind the place was too far south for that. He was drawn to them and the passersby, the workers mending *la rue*, a snapshot of reality rectangled and framed, an exploration of the mundane, as though the ordinary were enough for a work of art. Nothing out of the ordinary happened in the scene, and for Jake that was the point. A flurry of brushstrokes—Such a riot! Jake used to crow, long before sharing his experience with Wren in the car on the way to Ruby's. He said it was a scene that vivified the unremarkable, the day-to-day, what one docent referred to as "The little lives of little people like yourselves." That is, a bunch of zeroes, at least as far as anyone is concerned today, reduced to an economy amid an excess of strokes, the only witness to the fact the place, people, and moment ever existed.

And yet that's more than most get in life, he lamented.

He couldn't shake his pensive mood. Said it jarred him, his memory—the painting of common life did—burped up a passage he'd all but forgotten in a book by the great one, that irascible Russian who practically laments and even apologizes for his unsung brood of characters after parading them, many oddballs, across his literary stage, having turned to everyday types, and this apology comes after four hundred and sixty-some odd pages. He defends the shift to commoners by averring that to ignore them is not just inadvisable but impossible, arguing they're necessary in everyday life, as though they begged defending, and that overlooking them strains credulity. To focus only on the weird and unusual—and this from the master of crazy—is not just uninteresting: the commoner's lure is their indomitable blandness. Which according to Jake was another way of saying it was its own kind of bizarre, in any medium.

Meanwhile, while he was inside, I lapped the sun outside in the shadow of the dark-skinned one, that brazen nude like me. It was only after an eternity passed that I became unsettled, worried somehow that Jake had ditched me. I stamped my feet, vocalized, and in so doing incited the attentions of strangers, which in turn got them to alert the authorities. Jake and I were on the verge of splitsville more than a few times, though in each case he would come shambling down the staircase, OK tearing it up, charging past *Le penseur* on his way to me, barely in the nick of time. I can see him still, starting then skedaddling, gesticulating and crying, What in th' world are you *do*-ing?! Leave 'er a*lone*! She's *miiiine*!! Only after a flat-out sprint over a considerable distance, almost to the light on Euclid, was he able to forestall a rift between us. In any case, after the brouhaha passed we reconvened on the stairs, just below that guy, the one whose legs had already been blown out from under him by then, by someone who must have harbored a grudge against reflection. Of the dark-skinned sort most of all. There we sat, me and my boy, leafing through a new pad of sketches, studies of brushstrokes he'd jotted down, lines transposing a world.

Tommy, imagine my terror! That he'd gone and hightailed it out of there, exiling me to an island of questions about what had gone down. In fact, he interred me, unbeknownst to Wren, not too far from where he used to claim me, a jot away from where we parted, where the authorities idled their vehicle, filling out forms on the verge of carting me away. I can't shake the memories of Jake's forgetfulness, his lack of focus. Irresponsibility—call it what you want. No matter how you gloss it it comes down to a kind of delinquency, the type behind any crime—disconcern about how things will play out. Who is affected and how. The line between A and B. It's a hard pill to swallow, Tommy, even as I recall these events for you now.

On the other hand, that kind of thinking was in the air, silkscreened on posters and tee shirts, graffittied on walls, one that quite frankly I questioned at the time—I mean how could the world operate if everything came down to *Do Your Own Thing*? Isn't it, in fact, the opposite? Aren't a person's responsibilties what connect her to a life of meaning? But as I say, navel-gazing was in the air at the time. It had been glorified in Westerns on TV, personified in the lone cowboy, the manly individualist with a devil-may-care attitude that Americans idolize still, figures they lionize in black-and-white whose general attitude is *Numero Uno, Baby*. No doubt it goes further back than rustlers tramping herds across a virgin landscape, to the pilgrims' first steps on the continent, nicking Native terrain and crowding it with livestock from one coast to the other, in order to supply the new individualists an endless supply of Beef, the new-world's true religion, as Jake had often argued. By the time Harry and Florrie white-flighted it to Laurentine the country had gone drunk on it, though not my boy, his twin.

In some sense Jake's running from me started long before his final exit when he stormed his Valiant, threw it in reverse and never looked back. He'd been sending smoke signals that not even his god was capable of answering, it seemed, so he flared out, initially to the banks of the Shagaran, with me in tow. As if practicing for the real thing, I realize in retrospect, he up and quit Geist, Laurentine too, and in doing so induced a tirade from the CEO's son, both him and Harry who harangued, I been canned a thousan' times, buddy boy! Against my will!—he bellowed it as Jake was tossing all his belongings in the back seat. But you, you up 'n can yerself!

Jake snatched me last of all, tossed me in the passenger seat, pushed R on the transmission and we rolled backward, down the drive.

D'you think I could go runnin' off just cuz things got hairy? I had a famly t' feed, whether I liked it or not! Yeah, you, buddy boy—*yoouu!* I did it all for *you!*

Harry's on the verge of tears—or murder. As we roll to the street his hands continue gripping the window next to me. He's practically carted off with us when the wheels began to move forward and pick up speed.

D'you think runnin's gonna solve anything?!

Wha' d' *you* know? returns Jake, speaking to himself, braking for a moment after Harry's finally wrenched himself free. He was standing in the middle of the street behind us, snot hanging from his nose.

You'll be runnin' yer whole life! Harry harrangues, forgetting the neighbors. Himself as well.

Shards the size of dinner plates peel off. Jake fractures one from the side of the bank that crumbles in his hand. *K'plop!* *K'plopplop! K'plop!* again. The pieces drop like peas into a ragout, rock-crumble spilling from his hand as though the world were deconstructing before his eyes. Steamed Jake. Jake cooked. What are you after, my boy? I hazard that question delicately given the state he's in, but he pays me no mind. He hunches over his task, busy-busy. The water roils in his wake as he cleaves slice after slice of shale from the hip of land he's intent on dismantling. Water creeps up his jeans, darkens them gangrenously to the knee—the stain works its way as though someone were staking claim to him—is it the land or an irate spirit?

Shoes and socks he foreswore a fortnight ago. The sun beats hard on this unseasonably warm day in March—I remind Jake yet again it's two o'clock and we haven't had a lick to eat. Not this morning, all day yesterday, the day before, and the day before that. How long can we keep this up? Any other time I'd call this place heaven with its wondering-why of a river, questioning its way through the Shagaran Valley. The depression it has etched in the land stretches for miles, arriving ultimately at the great lake many miles from here as the crow flies. The sun bakes us and the river both, moves it along after having frozen it in a ribbon all winter long. The air swells during this bump in the weather, addling my boy's brains. I puzzle again, What is he trying to prove? Day after day it's the same old thing. He leads me down here, insists I keep to his side.

Stay with me, Moll, he orders. Durin' this, my night.

Your night! I counter. Son, it's broad day!

I nose as far as he'll let me but find nothing. As I say, I'm sure I'd like it here under normal circumstances—so bucolic and all—but, Jake, honey, I'd rather be home eating one of Florrie's delicacies. It's such a different life out here, one that suits neither you nor me, judging by the look of us. With you on a mission to alter the landscape, sediment of a thousand, million, maybe even billion years, resulting in inert rock, unalterable by a single agent. And yet there you are, attempting to undo it, shard by shard, single-handedly, as though it could be done by art, design, or even your god, though humans on the whole seem to imagine that kind of control. True, who'm I to say?—but simple logic dictates, Jake honey, that it takes time, that and a movement. An age. One that no romantic figure, no matter how hyped, can pull off, solo, in a towering stack of years. And, what's more, Jake dear, you seem just a shave too pressed. You're forging ahead to the point of distraction on some mission—for what? The landscape remains as we found it. Accept the fact that it'd require a machine just to make a dent. Try to abide by things as they are, my love, rather than bash your skull against the rock, consider that alterations of any kind come slowly. It's true they start with a refusal, an I'd-rather-not, but that's only the start. Disobedience, my boy, the civil kind, is a trek of generations, an enfolding of the democratic not back into the hierarchic or the hieratic but an altogether other kind of radicality. And look how far we've come.

Those were my words to Jake at the time. Though did he pay me any mind, admit I had a point, a brain? A connection to the earth as great as his?

He pressed on. It'll happen. By god, I'll make it. That's the vibe I got. God in me will make it come about, with god as my witness, so help me god. The riddle of an invisible divine buoying him up in this, his new life's work, the one he's cock-sure about in his heart as most believers tend to be, the practiced way they refuse to give doubt an airing. After all Jake was schooled in cock-suredness by Reverend Billy, which he copped to only lately, adopting the no-doubt attitude that's causing him to perspire so profusely, hair shot out, long and flat as the baptist's, matt-framing a face that has grown gaunt. The beard shaggy. Jake is surviving on god's love alone now, me too for that matter, whether I'm in or out of his graces. Circumstances caused me to suspicion it, interrogate Jake's resolve in dispensing with pecuniary work, not to mention everything he'd learned from the Brothers at St. Andrej's, the schooling Harry paid for with a job he hates.

The Brother-inspired doubts that Jake came armed with when he first met Peacoat gave Pastor Billy a dickens of a time, forcing him into not just ad-libbing but inventing biblical rebuttals, just to save face. In fact he had the whole fellowship on defense, inducing them to get creative with the book, a measure of Jake's, or the devil's, power at the time. The group predicted his queries would land him in hot water someday, meaning a burning lake, if he didn't throttle his reservations, because the lord doesn' give a fig about logic. Science. I heard the pastor declare it myself a thousand times, that prayer and fasting are required by anyone who in his heart of hearts knows he's displeased the man upstairs.

It chastens the body of its weaker, feminine tendencies, he remarked often.

There are not fingers or toes enough to count the times he chewed out Jake and Peacoat in that way, admonishing them to fast in the lord. To starve the flesh because it pleaseth the lord. Always *him*, I used to think to myself, a great big him in the sky, the one whose normal idiom has been reworded countlessly, though according to Pastor Billy only once correctly. Any efforts to rebrand his words not issuing from the king, the one replacing the longstanding queen, were all wrong, queer in some way, not unlike the king. Among the imposter versions of his word was purportedly the tome on the lower shelf of Florrie's coffee table, the one with Wren's name still inscribed, against Harry's will. That version, and others like it, we learned from the reverend, issue from the devil, a fusion of angel and animal—a hybrid—which is to say a monster.

Pastor Billy's ministry staked its claim on the authenticity of only one version of god's word. I found it amazing not just that he knew the one true god but the language he preferred as well. He said it was the first English edition, the one named after the guy who lisped his words the way Rauch does at times, Jake too when the wind blows a certain way, though never Romeo—Peacoat either for that matter. James the Firtht, the homothapian king, the namethake of the version Pastor Billy swears by. When someone sports such cock-sure conviction and never entertains a *soupçon* of doubt—how can you argue with that?

Jake's head screws on that way now, similar to the pastor's, who paradoxically wouldn't have a thing to do with Jake after

Peacoat's disappearance. Like Romeo after that time at the lake, he wouldn't look Jake in the eye, let alone allow him back in the fellowship. For all that he's made a purchase of the reverend's mindset, paying full price, and after so much hemming and hawing. After Peacoat disappeared—*poof!*— Jake found himself with too much time on his hands, having burned his bridges not just with Romeo but with Marks & Co. as well, after not just leaving them high and dry but apprising them, one by one, that they were all dead in a way, including dead to him now. Remnants of his old life in the world. After Peacoat disappeared, he discovered his back against the wall with only the pastor's cock-suredness to console him, even though he'd become toast to him.

I could go for Rauch and Marks's japes at the moment, a bit of irreverence, anything to lighten the mood. I could go for a bite of Florrie's chicken and boiled eggs even more, any of her castoffs actually, the bits she nudged to the side of her plate when on a diet, the ones she saved for me and only me. I've tried my hand at tufts of grass, even a bite or two of mud, just to take the edge off. Hayseed I tried, more than ample bread for sparrows dotting the grass, sated, chattering as if to mock me, a soulless wonder like them who unlike me seem to be thriving.

Unlike this human animal I'm chained to, who's rejected the security of home. Florrie spoiled me with her delicacies, salmon from a can and boxed mac and cheese. I guess I got a little comfy-cozy, stop-eyed in terms of what was right in front of me, but, Jake honey, I see clearly now. I'll never turn my nose up at another freezeburned chop, despite the fact that our earthly needs are what-now, as Pastor Billy liked to say.

I become them. Here at the final stop to Nowhere, the other reaches his hand out and I take it. I feel dizzy, about to fall, but he steadies me. He comforts me by a touch in the middle of this nonnative landscape, a place so completely foreign—I may have heard of it, but god knows it was never featured on *Jim Doney's Adventure Road*. If it were, Harry would have ditched the show, ceased dreaming of places he could never afford to visit beyond the Forest City, that pond of familiarity, and more practically Laurentine. It wasn't that he had no interest; it was the lack of means that kept him glued there, trapped in a sense, kept from touring two counties over let alone the next state, or, god forbid, another country. Still he dreamed. And now I find myself on foreign turf right in the center of the Forest City.

A hand remains extended, and in taking it I'm angled from where I've been sitting, perched on the side and invited to recline on a different kind of bedding. The gesture is deliberate, unrushed. The invitational aspect is clear, for reasons I can't articulate to myself let alone anyone else, caught as I am in a novel kind of incitement, a whole other kind of lure. Alien to a forcing.

The hand outstretched, Peacoat lies back, the neck of his sweater riding up near the scruff below his beard as he nests his head in the pillow. Red flannel peeks through where the hem of his sweater has inched from his belt.

Come 'ere.

We're two insects, burdened by arms and legs, the awkwardness of them flailing on the mattress, my boots pushing the spread here and there as I attempt to get traction, grunting while landing in inappropriate places, drawing a series of Ooofs! from the other, flat-out under me until finally I settle, limbs disappearing but not the lips—for Peacoat this is where the tale begins. A simple math of four divided, melting into two then one then zero. It all commences more slowly than I'm used to as well, like an Inuit kiss, nose to nose, a soft, gestural warming, igniting something below. Only after an eternity do things progress, as though everything so far were by way of invitation. A noodling for consent.

Two by two beneath the stubble on the upper and lower lips, deputized as hands all of a sudden, imbued with nerve endings more sensitive than fingertips, cheek sliding against cheek like two toms whisker to whisker, the impossibility of the pairing now leaping to bare life amid this queer landscape, one that's been rendered familiar lightening fast, like the winter thunder sounding from the windowsill. Lips, noses, and tongues mix—

—It's hot in here, i'n it?

You're hot? I'm wearin' four layers. Not includin' you.

I tumble off and we remove our sweaters, the two of us upright on the side of the bed. I slip off his flannel, turtleneck and undershirt, then the rest. With his body exposed he helps me skinny off the layers that cold and culture require, then slips himself around me like another type of garment, allows his tongue to run free, not with words but some animal idiom, until it becomes clear we two are naked to the very skin, more shocking than the vulgar use implies.

I can hear the cackling in Wren's yard as the hens kick up dust, causing a ruckus, a storm on account of the hawk overhead, the one that took up residence once she introduced the brood. The birds are threatened by a high-flier not dissimilar to the vulture Jake and I spy, far above the Shagaran, auguring something, the death of a body or Jake's wits. I mean I've never been technically aloft—I've made a point of keeping my feet planted on solid earth, considering it and I are one. But I can imagine all the same what it's like to soar up there, assessing things from a mobile vantage point, one that in some ways usurps god's position, or at least approximates it. In fact it's interesting that an animal with a noggin smaller than my own can suss out so many things related not just to heat and humidity, speed and visibility, altitude and lift, but energy and body mass, and gesture, indicating the overall health of a body down below, its odds of surviving, indicators that Jake with his private schooling seems incapable of—a vulture starts circling before you've breathed your last. She works the math, tots up the number of ribs jutting from the torso, not to mention the speed of the gait. She dissects the situation, far more than my boy.

To think of the paths he and Wren have traced up to this point, she with her eye for the domestic and local, municipal kind. It didn't take long until Jake's twin, as unidentical in some ways as a biological match can be, set up house with Donald, one that Harry complained should be demolished, along with the neighborhood and indeed the entire city. She did it in the interest of creating not just a life but a world, for herself, Donald, and Billie—for sure—but an expanding circle as well. While Jake starved himself and me to the bone, Wren was harvesting greens, planted initially in a cold frame, a sign that she was thinking futurity, despite the deep drifts outside. She laid out beds in anticipation of the last frost, where in time she'd sow beans, okra, and eggplant; brussel sprouts, broccoli, and cauliflower. She plotted out the largest rows for tomatoes, tomatillos, and peppers, enough to feed the neighborhood.

She and Donald spent months taming the undergrowth around Midge's house, only to discover a strata of earth beneath the trash and debris, black and rich and suitable for growing just about anything, far more than the clay in Harry's garden, nearer as it is to the lake. In the backyard of the long-neglected house on a long-neglected street in a long-neglected neighborhood they notched the soil, motioning the hens away, all the while Jake and I sat ambered in a past that could never change.

The hens joined in the planting, imposing their beaks near Wren's fingers, Donald's and Billie's too, fertilizing the soil as they scratched. Billie insisted they be named, a ritual that lifted them from the status of egg-making machines to something more complicated, and in the process short-circuited Donald's plans, which he kept private because quite frankly they didn't square with Wren's. Billie's either for that matter. That is in terms of why they were there in the first place and their place in the family. Paradoxically it was Donald who prompted Billie, What you gonna call 'em l'il girl?

I ain' a little girl.

When she hesitated, unsure, he offered a suggestion or twelve, assigning each a moniker, starting with Art B and Art T. Lester Y and Sonny R. Duke E and Dizzy G. And so on, up to Clifford B and Charlie P, who brought up the rear, all twelve having been branded with christian names, ones that got Wren's Irish up when Billie, having worked so long to get them straight, made a show of who was who.

They're all male names! Wren complained. But hens are female!—pointing to the brood. A man can' lay no egg.

Think they care?

Well I do! She was nodding at Billie while she spoke. Y' mean t' tell me in that other world you inhabit there ain't one woman?

Back and forth the two went about the semiotics of naming, Wren insisting that men couldn't help themselves, claiming the birth, or the egg-laying, function the way they did—I mean look a' the christian god, the way he claims female powers, though it's women who give life—to which Donald replied, thinking of his audience, Well they people now, not just animals. Ain't that enough?

You don' got no female names up your sleeve?

That set Donald in a silence, after which he conceded, The light one—that's Melba L. The black an' white one, Sarah V. And so on through the flock until at least half had been renamed, though none was Billie H.

We already got one a them, little girl.

I'm not—

Which only underscored the thinking about futurity, the world Billie would inherit, never mind that the male names stuck as Billie announced them initially, the genders crossed in some binary understanding of things, even as Wren refused to capitulate to a world in which they were set in stone. When Wren complained that *all* the hens should have female names, Billie remarked, I liked their names b'fore, mommy! Frustrated, Wren kicked dust with her shoe, claimed, It's hopeless. She yakked about the way you always have to settle for half—You never get the whole loaf! To which Billie, quoting Wren herself in many a conversation with Donald, replied, Baby steps, mommy.

Praise god, repeats Jake as a clod slips from his hand, scraping his ankle. Praise god. He's hobbling around, not bothering to brush aside splats of mud from his cheek. He focuses on his task, wedges the tablets of shale apart with his knife blade, splits the halves like the pages of a book cracked for the first time.

What *in the world* are you doing?!

Jake squints. Leave me alone.

No, we won'.

I don' wan' you here.

You're a mess. Jus' look't you!

I said go 'way.

I don't give a crap. We're stayin'. You got us both worried. We had t' come an' see for ourselves what was goin' on out here.

I'm gonna kill Wren.

Not a very nice thing t' say for a person a your faith. But never min'. We spoke t' Diana who told us t' tell you, "Th' old lady won' stop cryin'"—there. We said it.

Who cares. She's not my concern. Her or anyone.

Wren too?

I'm not goin' back. Jake shakes a rock free with his knife, the lone tool with which he means to reshape the terrain south of the lake, from here to Tarnation, or, barring that, to make some kind of dent, though into what configuration I'm not sure.

Well, you're ours.

I'm not.

What're you gonna do? Starve t' death?

God'll take care.

He's doing a pretty crappy job so far, Jake—sorry to inform you. Jus' look't you!

Cin and Diablo, no lovers of light, not so much protectors of paleness like Harry and Florrie as unused to the sun given their working hours—the two plead with Jake to come back.

Diana said it'd be a mistake, comin' all th' way out here. Useless—she said you're impossible. Bull-headed as a mule. She said you'd say, Who invited *yooooo*? But we have faith in you, Jake.

Don't.

We brought you somethin' t' eat.

B'hind me, Satan!

Even a little?

Diablo grabs the sack from Cin's hand and paces toward the side of the river. C'mon. Take it.

I ain't hungry. Even if I were I'd rather die—

—Well you're on your way if that's your goal, remarks Cin, advancing and taking up position next to Diablo. I half think they're going to rush my boy, charge through the water and overpower him, drag him kicking and screaming into Cin's vehicle and leave everything here, no questions asked. But they remain put, relying on the power of words and not a sand-bagging to persuade him. Meanwhile I try to beg a bite or two—I mean, it's been awhile.

Molly, baby! cries Diablo. Jus' look at you! You're skin 'n bones—an' filthy!

Jake! pleads Cin. She din't ask for this. I can see 'er ribs!

Cin stomps back and forth, so close to the water that her jeans begin to darken like Jake's. Forward and back she paces while Diablo remains rooted to her spot on the bank. It's as though something's dawned on Cin. She enters the water fully now—Jake, this ain' right!

He backs away, bends over and lifts one of the rocks that's broken free, holds it high—Back off! I said I ain't goin', an' I mean it!

But Molly—

—It's b'tween th' two a us.

Easy for you t' say.

The two, and ultimately three, gavel on for some time, with Cin and Diablo acting as public defenders for me while Jake assumed the role of DA, prosecuting my case, a trial of the fallen, the doomed. In that way the seed that Peacoat planted in his ear in the car that time has come to fruit.

An eternity passes in a duel waged in silence. The sun moves some distance in the sky before anyone speaks, all the while Jake sticks to his task. Crestfallen, my advocates give in, cry uncle.

Your sister's right. You are stubborn as a mule.

There're worse things.

Attempts to embrace Jake are dashed. The women's jeans are all darkened to the knees now. Once they've piled in their car they draw a circle in the grass; once on the road they roll away slowly, peering back at Jake and me both, so unlike the way Jake drives, jamming the accelerator and whipping up a soufflé of dust as he peels away.

Once they're gone Jake relaxes some, beckons me to return to the Valiant, our home on wheels which, like us, is starting to look the worse for wear. He assumes a place in the back where he sleeps. He takes up the book, gazes to heaven and cracks it. He reads. From my seat in the front I peruse the pages, try to glean whether they say anything about the practicality of giving into a wild hair but not a normal appetite. Maybe there's something in there about the importance of three squares—though even if there were, would it matter given that Jake isn't biting?

The problem is that his body and mine too aren't outfitted for such an angelic fare as air. What's more, I wonder what Reverend Billy's admonitions about fasting have to do with unredeemable me? God will pervide, Jake likes to say— he's imbibed the principle, clearly—though I suspicion that neither Pastor Billy nor Peacoat, if he were here, would last a fraction as long as we have because, I'm here to tell you, this ain't no picnic.

Jake minus Peacoat, his guru on matters of belief. He might have informed Jake that no one said you had to hold out the full forty days, that twenty-four hours, hell an afternoon, will do. That all that's required is a gesture for a divine

who's apparently keen on gestures, especially in the wake
of the fleshiness that transpired in the hotel on Chester.
And after, many times. Since Peacoat's disappearance
Jake's been shopping a catalog of prohibitions, a thousand
and one thou-shalt-nots, including thou-shalt-not-eat—
it's never a positive. Like: Be happy! Live life fully but
ethically! Do what pleases you, so long as no one's hurt!
On the contrary it's a laundry list of no's. And now Jake,
in the absence of physical pleasures, is choosing to slice
off any pleasure he can in order to tame the body, skin it
like pork back or fat blankets from a whale, strip it in an
effort to thin it, maybe expose the soul, as if it were a site
you could locate, an aura, dimension, or a different animal
altogether—you tell me, because I wouldn't have a clue.
What would I know about such things, me, an animate
machine as the philosopher called me, ever more a mere
text, an artifact of what went before—unlike you, Jake,
who's opting for pure spirit, the dualist kind, the one that
haunts the body so persistently.

We've been here for almost forty days, or is it forty
years? And yet you're bashing your head against the side
of a cliff, the sky, in a series of mental flights. But for all
your cock-sure talk it appears you're finding only silence
up there, that and clouds, empty air. The mission of Cin
and Diablo having ended without success, it appears our
only hope is the divine, and he remains mute. Or is he
mouthing in his way, Leave me the hell alone!

And while your're at it, get a life!

I'm in their heads, their bodies. The fever of flesh against
flesh, even in this unheated space with its lazy register,
its fifties-style windows with aluminum frames that let

in the winds. Encouraging the press of our bodies, my skin against the skin of my brave here, he and I on a search party of some kind.

Trembling and vulnerable in the chilly air, I tug the sheet from between the mattress and box springs and slip under, tenting it and inviting Peacoat in. He wastes no time, and the world is reversed, him on top of me. The mix of tongues in two registers, mouthing words and gestures both, the arms restless, legs jigging, the forwardness of the language, languages plural, a physical polyglossia, two babbling, babeling, at the same time but understanding somehow, the novelty of it, the push and pull, the dosey doe your partner around the dance floor, around this train station on Mars, do-si-do-ing around the place on a horizontal plane, two novices learning the steps.

Two virgins, truth be told. Two races. Invoking the jocular and not-so-jocular jibes to Peacoat's face from the others at the plant. The derision that escaped Romeo's lips behind his back once he learned the meaning of the dark eyes. And now the two of us, the bedding in a mess completely—could anything cool this heat under the sheets?

Some dance more slowly than others, I'm learning. Having said that, some are better equipped to pull it off, between the ears, at the core, and outer limbs. Character too, like this character penetrating me, the talk turned guttural. Swatch of velvet and blade of titanium. Easy glide and hard friction. Sere and slippery. Shaggy and sleek. Pink and blue.

One thing the Shagaran taught me, Tommy, as clichéd as it sounds, is nothing lasts forever. Neither cock-sure belief nor even an identity given the way things shift. Being on the river taught me that. That there's no sense dreaming about a stable me when the flow of life alters it so much. I mean a person's got to swim to keep up. Anything or anyone you point to as the finished thing is just yesterday's news, like a body bobbing on a river, shy of the point it went in. There's a plenitude of Jakes out there, Mollies too. In all my life I've never known Jake to be the way he is out here, and I'm sure you'll discover different ones as well, not just from year to year or decade to decade but day to day. You'll have to make allowances. And when you see each other morphing into something unrecognizeable, figure out a way to go with it. Truth be told I sense myself shifting even as I relate the story—the tale wags the dog—which is a koan to contemplate when you consider I'm history. The role I was relegated to was that of sound-board, and now here I am, sounding off. For these and other reasons I feel you, you and all of us who've been slotted, subject to a name, limited to a singularity. I've heard people say it's inevitable, that kind of reduction, though I doubt it—

—Oh god, cries Jake, looking toward the roof of the Valiant. Take this burden, or a leas' help me t' accept it as a sign a thy will. Worn fabric hangs down from above. Donuts of rust usher in light, dappling the interior here and there in the shifting shade of the trees above, forming another kind of ceiling, conferring on the space here a sense of tongues dancing, in the middle of which Jake and I sit mute for some time.

He cracks open the volume in his lap and runs his fingertip over the surface, as though dowsing for water. He scans the pages, runs his finger tip down one column and up the next, down then crack over to the facing page. *It repenteth me that I've set up Saul t' be king for he hath turn-ed back from followin' me an' hath not perform-ed my commandmints an' it greev-ed Samuel an' he cry-eth unta th' lord all night* fifteen twelve *an' when Samuel rose early t' meet Saul in th' mornin',*

*it was told Samuel sayin' Saul came-eth t' Carmel an' behold
he setteth him up a place an' is gone about an' passed on and
gone down to Gilgal* fifteen thirteen *and Samuel came t' Saul
and Saul say-eth unta him bless-ed be thou a th' lord I have
perform-ed th' commandmint a th' lord* fifteen fourteen *and
Samuel said what meaneth then this bleatin' a th' sheep in mine
ears, and th' lowin' a the oxen which I hear* fifteen fifteen *an'
Saul say-eth they've brought them from th' Amalekite for the
people spared th' best a th' sheep and a th' oxen t' sacrifice unta
the lord thy god and th' rest we have utterly d'stroyed.*

My boy claps the book shut.

What does this mean? The bleatin' a the sheep in mine
ears the sheep in mine ears, the lord, he forsaketh me not,
Jake repeats, adopting the Baroque speech, it and the good
pastor's, he cometh to them that wait. Jake pleads, Take
this burden from me or—and again he cleaves the volume,
he reads, *and th' lord spak-eth unta Moses and unta Aaron
sayin'* two two *every man a the children a Israel shall pitch
by his own standard with th' ensign a their Father's house far
off about the tabernacle a th' congregation shall they pitch,*
and Huh? remarks Jake. Again he slams the book shut.
Do I not please thee? Why did thou take him from me?
Again he's trying to get the idiom right as best he can in
an appeal to a Baroque god whose English, for all intents
and purposes, stopped evolving centuries ago. Sometime,
around 1610 or '20, maybe '30, I reckon. I mum, because,
well, who'm I to say, companion to woman, and man, but
not god? Unsavable. I'm outside for sure and yet too inside
is the problem, not to mention a disembodied voice, or too
embodied, which makes two of us out here in this terrain
that crumbles when you touch it, gives under your toes,
gets on your nerves when you walk on it and it washes your
tracks away with the flood toward the still-frozen lake, a
fair ways north and a good deal down river.

It's as though Jake were branded with the letter Q, as in too many questions. There was a time he would have snatched it by his own volition, owned and worn it proudly, especially with Peacoat. But now? The letter burns so hotly into his chest, turning his brain among the flames of light in the car, cast through the nylon webbing from the roof, lying on his back, staring through the windows, trying to figure out what the H is going on.

Again I'm inside them. He's inside me—or am I in him? Two bodies latched, ovipositors extended. So this is what it's about, is this the real thing? A new, animal arithmetic. Not a totting up—a division is more like it. A fractioning. Thawing, melting in a liquid, dark and woolen—the way it coats—I mean all the hubbub over such a simple form of math at the level of bodies, shading chesnut—anything but black and white. Two races—that's BS. There's only one, a multitude. So long as we're here, in this room. The aesthetics of burning snow trapped on umber earth— gathering—the slick curds melting into a lake, a lengthy, lacustrine landscape as far as the eye can see—the soggy, sloppy fluidity keeps on flowing, a moment stretched until the cows come home—the mooing. Mooning. The voyage from human to beast—Moll, I see you there! Seeing us with that knowing slit of an eye, pretending you're zonked out. One plus one equals one. Or is it an O? A lake.

Whaaaat a beauuuut! sings Florrie, craning her head through the screen door. Will you look't that?

Nice, huh? returns Harry, easing up the driveway, his head poking out the driver-side window. Nice, huh? he repeats. Florrie tramples the pinwheels in the bed between the car and house, and as she treads bumble bees scatter from lavender blooms.

How much did it cos'?

Don' ask. Main thing's we got it.

Diana heaves the screen door open, pushes past Florrie— OK. Not bad. How's she drive?

Better'n that old piece a crap.

How old is it?

Sixty-Eight.

'T's in great shape considerin'. But how in the world did you affor—?

—I said forgit it, remarks Harry, glancing at Diana—he shoots her a wink.

Well it ain't so easy when—

—Let's jus' say god pervides.

God or someone. The appointment's for four-fourty-five so we better scoot.

Ohhh. Florrie's face falls.

Oh, nothin'.

Oh, t' have your problems, bro.

C'mon, chides Wren. Cut 'im some slack.

Seriously bro, you should try wearin' it.

Wren trods over to Jake, attempts to embrace him but he shies away. You smell like crap. An' you're skin'n bones.

When she finally nabs him she remarks she can trace his shoulder blades under her fingers, the angular corners of his scapulas distinct. Why don' you come back an' live with us?

What good'd that do? Nothin' ain't ever change what's happen.

Well, you're th' only family I got.

Have there been any developments?

Just a bunch a interrogations, but nothin' more. We're talkin' East Shagaran PD after all. A "mere" fact'ry worker lost—Wren crooks her fingers in the air.

I expect them t' come an' cart me away.

Well if you keep this act up, bro, they'll def'ly be comin' for you.

Is that why you're here? Because you're scared a bein' arrested?

I ain't got nothin' t' be scared about.

Bradford did point the finger at you, bro.

I know you din't do nothin'. By the by, Cin said she an' Diablo're trying t' get Romeo's old man to take you back, an' he said it's up to his son. She said she's glad you're not involved with that cult no more. But she thinks you're a gonner anyway. Are you?

It ain' a cult.

All religion's a—

You don' know what yer talkin' about.

I got an idea.

Cin an' Diablo are pushin' for it, Jake. Even Marks an' Rauch. For you t' get your job back.

Rauch. The one who started badmouthin' me the minute I left.

Never mind—

—Yeah they wan' me back. Pre-Peacoat an' Pastor Billy.

Well, we all want—

—Donald! Jake, they want you back. Period. Just th' way you are. Why not come and stay with us? Billie can sleep on th' sofa.

Jake returns to his task. Truth be told, and quite to my surprise, he's managed to remove an impressive amount of rock and dirt in the weeks we've been here, much more than I figured him capable, working single-handedly and resting only on the sabbath.

Bro, this ain't logical. Never mind sane. I mean it's some crazy *shit*!

What's any a that mean? I mean, you tell me. The world ain't rational. You oughta know.

Ther're other ways—

The things I know—

The things you ain't never gonna know—trus' me, bro. I can tell you one thing, this ain't helpin'.

Me, I focus on not adding fuel to the fire. I ponder how far removed we are from the top of the Sandusky bridge that time, workers wading in the water below, barely eking out a living, lowering their traps, just visible above the water. Do they contemplate such things? And while I'm at it, did Jake blot from his memory his stammering on the bridge up there, all those lung-swelling yeps—yep, yep, yep—the self-affirmations, the deliberate, conscious recognitions of an I, directly related to the eye that sketched the low-lying world from above, the lake stretching toward Canada, invisible and to the north, sketching the fishermen and crabbers on an ordinary day, the shore near us lined with bungalows clustering along the edge where godknowswhat transpired inside, from the ebbing tide there to this shapeshifting world out here in the valley of the Shagaran—how far we've come, Jake, you and I, to this questioning stream as lazily serpentine as Liberty Boulevard, down the hill from Wren and Donald's where the sycamores shed their skin—the river sheds the winter here as well, the hills sloping northward and steep in places, with Jake doing his part to alter the direction. Soft-minded Jake with a hard-nosed resolve. He won't stop harping about the problem of sedimentation, the entrenched lay of the land.

Jake, you smell. Your clothes're literally peelin' off.

Bro, we brought you somethin' t' eat.

I'm not hungry.

All this time I was lying to the side, minding my own business while overhearing the conversation. To be honest I was feeling a great deal more than just a little weak, but how can I not respond when I hear food? I hazard, I'll have a bite of his, and when I front myself, out of the shade and into the sun, Wren blurts, Oh. My. God, Jake! How *could* you?

What?

Just look't her! This is immoral—you're killing her! We're takin' her with us, for sure!

Over my dead body.

No seriously, Jake, this is the worst kind of abuse. Really an' truly, it's fucked up—I mean, we had a pact. We said she was like you an' me an' not some dum-dum thing, her and everyone like 'er. Makin' it wrong t' eat meat. You were the one who said, Once ya know a thing you can't unknow it. An' now look at you, starving her t' death, like you forgot all that! Like none a it matters! Starve yourself if you wanna—*do it!*—but she never ask for this.

My boy listens while working at his task. He splits a tablet of shale as thick as the good book, studies the two halves, reads the folds on the face of it.

She's *fiiiine*. We been together all these years an' together we're gonna stay. I can't live without my Moll.

Best be goin', Diana advises, clawing Harry's keys. We don' wanna be late.

Oh lord, erupts Florrie. Lordy, lordy.

Enough a'ready. We'll all be better off.

Let's definally take that baby for a spin—but I'm gonna drive. Harry's dragging a cigarette that appears epoxied to his lip as he takes the keys from Diana. Let's see how she do on th' freeway.

Kill two birds with one stone.

Don' talk like that! I can't bear it.

That's why you're stayin'.

You'n me can go for a ride tomorra, offers Harry. You'll like that. A long drive in the country.

I don' care about going for no ride.

Ruby floats into the kitchen in her nightie, steadies herself against the back of a chair as though about to make a prognostication, or maybe nab someone, drag her to the other world. She steadies herself with her other hand on the formica as she staggers toward the sink.

What can I get you, mama?

But Ruby peers ahead. She seems on the verge of outing something, though her jaw merely palsies and shakes. Still I can't help but feel she's come all this way for a purpose, especially since she's been lost to a hard-fast muteness these past years.

What would you like, mama? repeats Florrie while the other two, and most of all I, focus our attention on Ruby as she peers voicelessly back. Like the rest I'm convinced she has something to say.

What is it mama?

When'll Wren be home?

As I say I haven't heard her mutter a word in years, and I'm unsure what to make of it.

Wren?! jumps Harry. Wren?! There's no Wren here! There never was!

She's gone away, Florrie explains in a voice loud enough to rouse Ruby's twin from the grave. Why don't you go back t' your room and rest? Ruby's lips tremble like plates in a seismic event.

Is Midge never gonna take her back? complains Diana.

It was s'pose to be just a few months t'get you through th' operation, but now we're talkin' how many years?

What am I s'pose t'do? Put 'er on the street?

Well she ain't even there, like she's a zombie or somethin'. Why can't Wren bring her t' live with them—?

—Stoppit! The two a yous!

We're forced to put up with her. Wren likes 'er, so why can't they—?

God knows it ain' easy, remarks Harry.

I would like to say that a work bred with good intentions lasts forever, though experience tells otherwise. Voices fail as people do. Any graveyard larger than this plot they planted me in gives witness to the hordes who've been silenced, never to speak again, leaving what in their place? Marble, granite, sandstone, or wood. Sometimes bare earth. I sense myself moving in that direction, feel my tell-tale wits giving in to the stone here, the one that continues to usurp my position, shouldering me from myself. It's nothing new to suggest— thinkers have been saying it for some time—namely that in spinning my tale for you, Tommy, I'm spinning my own death, the real kind and not the demise of the body, shifting me into another kind of body, as though this web of words were my undoing. And yet although everything I say mortifies me, sets me in a sense in stone, I live still. Which is to say that if you or Jake or anyone fancies exuming me, simply take to digging, unearthing where my heart once was until you track down this rock here, the one I leave behind, a mass of lines—just breath into it and I'll spring to life. It'll be me and not-me, me as you fashion me most of all.

Along Route Two the ticky-tacky houses roll by, bungalows that severed the remaining breast of land, the plot of earth that nursed Jake and Wren in their youth, lone remnant of the Western Reserve. The squat structures troop along. Whites marched to them rather than mingle in some impure mix, as they saw it. Rows and rows of boxes fly past this turf that rested under milethick ice, first the visible then the unseen kind. Miles and miles of domiciles lined up in a kind of battle array, uniformly, the blocks of houses frozen, policed by a force invisible to the naked eye. By an attitude—or is it a fear? Past Two-Sixtieth Street, then Two-Twenty-Two—I belong to Jake and he belongs to me. Memories tool past, each a house unto itself with its own furnishings, decor, not to mention its own ghost, raced, a dreadful haint, that rankles people even though they almost never mention it, like it doesn't exist. My where-in-the-world Jake whoring for life, the schoolboy games he included me in now come to an end.

When it dawned on you—

—When it dawned on you.

When it dawned on you, Jake. After so many years. To have gone off like that, black-sheeping me, black in the empirical sense, that reduction of a range to a simple, brutal binarism. You split, without a glance back—the fear of gazing in reverse—of glancing into the rear-view mirror to get a peek at what you were shaking from your feet, the dust cloud over the Forest City, in fear of turning into salty tears—you were miles, with whole states at your back the way Wren tells Donald, before you would even consider looking east. You refused to glance toward the morning sun, as though it would destroy you, turn you into a cow pie, or buffalo chip as they say out there, the dust following you, lofting in the air. Fallen on Laurentine, on Harry and Florrie, on the Forest City as a whole, on these homes, these clones—and me. Never mind Peacoat and Romeo, the ones you died for. And never mind Donald and Wren most of all. Billie, your chestnut kin.

You just kept going, peering out the increasingly-pitted windshield of the Valiant, that rattletrap, into a terrain people mislabel empty. Running is what Harry labeled it—Once y' start, buddy boy, y' never stop! And indeed the miles, days, the further you advanced, adding onto years— they passed by. For what? Only Wren seems to have the slightest clue, and she stays mum. I have an inkling—I'm no simpleton. I think of you jingling coins into baskets along the turnpike, lighting out to the territories. Who-what was freed by your exit, Jake, only some demon could tell. You're not given to returning to the land of thrall to reclaim your people, let alone your freedom, despite any ties you may have had. You're more into hucking around, here, there, and godknowswhere—you're all hucked up. Having said that, who knows what one would find were a sequel to your leaving ever written, whether you'll remain there or move on, or up as the case may be, from south to north like the six million souls in the great migration, that shift from thrall to liberty that turned out to be another form of thrall. What did they encounter? An army of Harrys, persons less than enthused to meet their new neighbors let alone bring a tray of cookiess as a welcome. Instead they were thrown back on their earlier woes, occasioning a migration of another kind, or a return flight as the case may be given how things have gone down.

I never thought for a minute that your going would be for keeps. It's true you vented your spleen about Laurentine, and the Forest City most of all, any chance you got. I realize now the writing was always on the wall. At the time though it never occured to me the brute was at the door, that you'd fly the way you did, without me, before my time was up.

Worse'n a death it is, Florrie has taken to saying. To think it's intentional. Did you ever, for a nanosecond, consider that this place—did you ever consider the problem wasn't us?

From newer to older, lighter-to-darker, nicer-to-shabbier, the houses pass in a kind of domestic regress. The glories of the American dream, shading black and ramshackle, and all and sundry kept safely separated, the danger of a mutting. To dedicate so much energy to fight a mongreling, the price you pay. If you didn't know at the point you left that I never gave a pip for the way you rolled, then you never knew me, not for all your talk. One thing's for sure and that is it isn't like me or my race to pass judgment.

Unlike you, Wren and Donald know perfectly well that nothing is solved by ceding territory—the best thing to do, Wren argues almost daily, is to stake a claim. Own it. Everything. The entire kit-and-caboodle. What other option is there? Unlike you, she and Donald sank roots, but not my Jake. You were—plunk!—over the side and into a current that quickly floated you away. But to where? Toward what other kind of hell? Only Diana remains in the fold with Harry and Florrie now, with me the black sheep—that's the world you left me to, hell bent as you were on absconding.

It rides like a dream, ventures Diana, breaking the silence. Florrie don't know't she's missin'.

She'll get' er chance soon anough. It's better like 'is.

You would a thought she was gonna die on the spot, the way she carry on.

She do get dizzy.

Well, when I get old I hope someone just shoot me if I get like that. Put me out a my mis'ry. I don't wan' no goings on like that.

It happens t'everyone. Like it's a fact a life.

The two a us takin care a things is best.

Well past One-Eighty-Fifth and One-Fifty-Sixth, we're

coming on One-Fortieth Street, past Collinwood Yard, somewhere to the south but not far, the parallel tracks there that will never meet, streets without streetlights—You did your bit for justice, Wren said. Never mind that Pastor Billy implicated you, labeling you the one last seen with him, less than mildly insinuating something ungodly. An unnatural affection. It was a hard nut to swallow, but truth be told it went in and out of Harry and Florrie's ears, the accusations, as though they were Teflon. They swore to god on a stack a bibles it were all lies, the shameless innuendos, about you and Peacoat—and from some crackpot of all people, a so-called man a god, whose sole intention was to blacken the reputation a their son—Best son two parents could a ever ask for, Harry argued in the most vehement terms possible, and in such a public way. He dismissed Bradford's allegations as the worst kind of character assassination, such awful, terrible untruths about his flesh and blood, insisting he had not a lick a proof. It all boiled down to he-said-he-said, Donald argued. Why in the world was that crazy nut following them two in th' first place, in that cruddy car a his?

I mean how sick is that?

It's twisted.

He must be twice their age, a'least.

Plus 'e never actually saw nothin'—

—The lawyer forced him t' admit that—

Had anyone asked me I could've given witness to the many times Bradford trailed our bumper closely. No matter where we went, there he was in the rear view.

Even if the guy did see somethin' with his own eyes, Wren argued, What would it prove? How would it matter? How would sleepin' with Peacoat in some cheap hotel downtown add up to a motive to kill?

Along the lake to the north, mansions perch on a brief patch of moneyed land, an island of wealth. The factory neighborhoods commence in earnest after that, all along the freeway.

American Classic Signage
Ace Tool & Die
Forest City Metalworks
Schmidt Pipe Fittings
Watley Steel Turnings
National Pipe Company

The machine-shops stretch as far as the eye can see. As I said at the time, Jake, it wasn't your fault if the church ladies chose to keep mum. And furthermore the finger never pointed officially at you, despite all the talk, so why did you care? It was just a chorus of low-mumbling and, quite frankly, bumbling busy-bodies, as human animals are wont to be. Trash-talkers. A bit of raucous chatter from house to house, though most of it was in your head, until you announced finally, never officially to me but to Florrie and Harry, you said, Yeah—I think I'll be movin' on.

Movin' on?

Wha' does that mean?

Movin' on.

Movin' on, deadpans Harry. Jus' like that. Yer movin' on.

Where to!? worries Florrie, at a pitch high enough to shatter the sun.

Not sure. West. I'm goin' west.

Well bully for you, boy.

Can you tell us where—west? You mean the West Side?

No, west. Wester'n 'at.

Well, west is a big idea—

—Like I said—

Back and forth the conversation went, as though once again it was you and the detectives. Once Donald came on the scene in that series of interrogations he took it all in, scratched notes for his article while you and the reverend were locked in a battle of wills that grew more and more vitriolic, the more you distanced yourself from him finally. Of course, Harry was AWOL at that point. He refused to breathe the same air as Donald, who sat where Harry should have been had Harry not been so concerned about a sullying, even as he was sullying himself, in Florrie's eyes most of all.

Along Liberty the sycamores spider by, leaves brown, brittle like old news. Bark-rot rains on everything, it discloses a world, a more earthly version of what it means to be born again. I can't help myself, I put my head out, take it all in. I'm no simpleton, I know the drill, caught as I am in a predicament, having crossed some god, or goddess as the case may be, for whom man is the measure of all things, some garden-variety homo-sap, against which everything else fails to measure. For that I'll pay. I know where I am and where I'm going, as all spinners do. The sticky silk that I cast may or may not exonerate, as was the case with my Jake—the three of us crawling now along the boulevard. I try to limn the sky but the branches, slimming to nothing, add up to a mess. We turn onto Chester, toward the place Ruby and Miss Glasby once lived, Midge and Leo too, where Donald and Wren absent themselves from me lately with their busy lives, the chickens pecking in the yard just a stone's throw away. We turn again. I know this place, this squat, midcentury affair, the white bricks blackened like the lungs of the Forest City. We pull in and all our eyes are trained on the parking lot. A smattering of unloved junipers. Yes, I know this place, how could I forget, having been regendered here at an early age—I remember.

Up the sandstone treads we go, past the gilded lettering F-E-H-E-R, wearing off the glass.

It doesn' take long, announces the lady at the desk.

Jus' wanna get it over with, pleads Diana.

I'll wait in th' car, announces Harry. You take 'er.

If you could jus' hold 'er for me.

Me and Diana in a tussle. The stranger muzzles as Diana manhandles me. Adrenaline surges from somewhere inside, the pale fire pumping, coursing in the blood, the quaking of the earth and my heart. Like I say, it don' take long, I hear a voice repeat. The shiny, stainless-steel surface, worn though still reflective, my feet frantically tapping a message, slip-sliding on it, I bolt for the door, that and my life with its earthly pleasures, Florrie's softboiled eggs, her warm body at night, we two old gals. When I attempt to make a getaway, back to the hum-drumery I enjoyed only an hour ago, Diana checks me on the stainless top, the cruelest metal on earth, the invention of some twisted mind, firing the body—could anything be more pernicious than a sheet of steel? This shiny, Puritan surface. I get no traction here, the not-so-spic-and-span room, tainted with the smell of nerves and viscera, the white-coated technicians, and Diana with that cough of hers, the incessant hacking up. The sputum, the phlegm, the thick saliva, the paper-white masks, the dry, clinical touch—such are the wages of outgrowing your use, if you ever had one to begin with. Not commodifiable, that's for sure. The vial, syringe—the liquid. The needle thin as spidersilk. The shaving of the flesh before it pricks. It travels in.

Shouldn' be long now. Say bye-bye.

Thangod.

Every story must come to an end, Tomás, even my tongue-wagging, these thousand and one vignettes, reduced to this coffin of a room with hush-hush, accoustical tiles overhead, the eggwhite of my eye below, held as I am an inch or two from the surface, the egg-white of the eye, mirrored back darkly in the stainless—certainly that can't be me.

Peacoat, I read you—

—It won' be long now.

The backflow of blood the muzzling the full blown universe, bearded with ice. An Atacama of the north, burning cold, formed entirely of H2O. Inclement and jagged white world, coming into focus behind the glass shine, why did we never see this before? Here on Mars, the frozen planet, this place of exile, of the weary, the marginal, the unnumbered vulnerable, there is evidence of water literally everywhere we look, stand, but none of the stuff is remotely evident—I only wanna speak t' Peacoat says Bradford.

Not you, Jake.

Why not both a us?

Let it alone, Jake. Everything'll be OK. Pastor Billy and I are overdue for a one-on-one.

But—

—Don' worry.

Peacoat hugs Jake warmly before he turns and stalks up the street, away from the river and lake, though I remain, unseen as usual, especially outside where Pastor Billy always argued I belonged. Sisters Pauline, Marnie, Cathaleen, Jeanette, and Nancy sit ringed inside with heads bowed, there through the broken window, praying for Peacoat's salvation we're told.

When should I come back? Jake hollers from a distance.

Peacoat'll find you!

It's halfway between late afternoon and early evening, the salmon-colored hour, not quite day or night, which still comes early this time of year. The three of us shift from foot to foot, the two men-folk with their arms folded, and all of us snorting. We then shift like cattle around the side of the house toward the back, the moist, frozen air condensing in huge puffs below our noses, pouring out our mouths. Behind us the ice is cracking up, wailing with asylum voices, caged inmates about to be set free. This deadly tentacle of the Shagaran, the eastern branch, started to rise some time ago, condensing now into a solid flow. I can see it inching up the trees, still naked, the flouncy tendrils of last years undergrowth at their feet, as black as Peacoat's pubic hair against a sheet. All of nature caught with its pants down, the hairiness of its legs and backside. Once covered in a green frock, its clothes have been ripped away, exposing its privates for the world to see. As though nature had something to hide from god and Bradford. Nature, me, such as we've been constructed, fallen only in the minds of men, or so at least Jake tried to say early on at one a the bible sessions, contradicting Peacoat, and by extension Bradford, before he was prayed into silence. The boy learned to mum though, and ultimately drank the Kool-Aid.

For a time.

Peacoat's mummed now as well, it appears, toggling from foot to foot, sheepishly and peevishly both. I've never seen this side of him before, his warrior past on the rise.

Don' be angry.

I'm not *angry*!

Bradford massages Peacoat's shoulder the way he always does, kneads the muscles under the canvas collar, the one that's fading. It's no longer the army-issue green it once was.

C'mon, I can tell y'are. But don' be. I just wanna talk t' you, brother t' brother—y'know, heart t' heart.

Bradford catches me nearby, casting an eye slantwise as though I were a fiend, beyond feral. There's another look on his part, verging on resignation, a tangled knot of pleasure and horror. I admit that when Jake started to lead a path out of here I was torn in my allegiances, don't ask why. In my heart of hearts I knew I belonged to him, to Jake for sure, yet neither could I stand the idea of splitting from my Peacoat, abandoning him under the circumstances, given the vibe I got. It didn't help that he was encouraging me in his way, apparently having changed his mind about me at some point in the course of our time together, like some kind of light switched on. He was gesticulating gently, reaching his hand toward me—I'm no simpleton.

Good old Mollykins.

So I stayed. Now the three of us are moving as though we're being drawn magnetically across the yard, at a glacially slow but steady pace, the way a body always inclines toward water, toward liquidity as it were—we seek the direction of a flow. Or a floe as the case may be, a floating island to land on, however unsteadily. As if compulsed, Bradford draws Peacoat toward him with his massaging hand, embraces then addresses—

—My dear Brother!

Peacoat clears his throat, encased in this show of affection, he slants like a fish congealed in ice as if waiting patiently for a thaw, for Bradford to unbosom him. Then he wriggles free.

What *gives*?

What d'you mean, What gives, Brother?

I don' understand what this is all about.

Don' understand what?

Everythin'. All this. What we're doin' here.

Bradford, having gone silent all of sudden, almost feline, batting a birdie of unknowing for some time while Peacoat reveals himself in the process more and more as not-Peacoat, so far as I've known him, Peacoat who is always as resigned as a post-Contact Native in the face of so much fire power in the pastor's presence, though shape-shifting now, a process that started some time ago that has only become more noticeable in the time leading up to this moment. In fact his demeanor has been undergoing a freeze vis-à-vis the Reverend, solidifying into a perturbation, to the point that he simply starts peeling away in Jake's direction.

I know what goes on b'tween you two—

Peacoat halts, swivels his head, his eyes a pair of drones.

That'd be nothin'. S'far as you're concerned.

Bradford eyes me as if to say, You know their secrets! You seen it all. Everything—hell, you prolly inspired 'em, you fallen thing!

Don' tell me *nothin'*! I seen where you two been with my own eyes. I can' begin t'imagine what the eyes a god has seen.

That'd be nothin'.

Then it's somethin'.

Peacoat scrapes the earth with the heal of his boot, inscribes a black rut in the white snow, drags a patch of grass that falls in a heap, there atop the earth. Two furrows appear between his brows, mimicking the line he's made with his foot. He glances at me in a plea for silence.

I don't know what you see in that boy—I mean he's trouble. His feet are planted in the world, clear as day. But you're blind t' it. He's gonna be your ru'nation.

How would you know about what I see or don' see?

Sometimes the devil has such a hold black begin to look like white an' white like—

—It's all in your head!—that's what this is.

It's a falsehood, the kind th' devil put on, like it was a mask.

That's a terrible thing t' say—I'm sure Jake's not—

—That boy, I'm telling you. The reverend rubs the stubble on Peacoat's cheek with the back of his hand. His feelin's for you. They ain't normal.

The sun's waned considerably already and Bradford appears in a melancholy light, the saddest hues of the day, just on the cusp of graying. The cold, wet air congeals in stout puffs below our noses, pouring from our nostrils. The ice of the Shagaran cracks continually and moans—again I notice the floes inching up the trees that reach toward the sky, similar to the ones in the painting over at the museum, the ones Jake couldn't go a fortnight without reseeing.

To accuse Jake of such a thing—what does it even mean?

The boy's in lust. He ain't like you'n me.

What would you know?

Bradford's trembling. Truth be told, it seems some kind of ice is cracking in him, not unlike these floes, though I'm not entirely sure if it's from the chill or something else. He's quaking, though not like Sister Pauline when she's visited by the spirit. In fact I fear he's about to rattle apart at the level of sinew, muscle, and bone, to the point he'll dissolve, a case of quick liquefaction—

—Are you OK?

No, Brother, I am *not* OK!

Well then what is it?

I'm deeply disturbed!

By what!

By what I've seen!

Peacoat peers at Bradford with flat-out derision, as if to say, You weirdo—

—I've seen it all, these many months, the many times you two checked into that place a impurity. I know why you wen' there.

You don't know noth—

—*Save* yourself!

From what?!

From whatever demon lurks between you two—!

Bradford claps Peacoat's wrist with a talon grip and Peacoat gestures to flee, but he halts himself, looks at me as if to say, Molly!—Do something!

I eye him back, charge the reverend in an effort to catch him off guard, cause him to loosen his grip, but he kicks me in the side with the heel of his shoe—

—Confess an' god'll forgive you!

But there's nothin' t'—

—You lie!

Bradford juxtaposes his face close to Peacoat's, who leans back then looks away, but Bradford grasps his chin, swings it around, hardens his gaze and then just as quickly softens. You like—but never mind. Never mind all that. I'm not here t' discuss water over th' dam. What I rully wanna talk about is th' future.

He's trying to hold it together—I award him an A for effort.

Save yourself!

But I don' need savin'—I'm already—

—Then save me, Brother!—he interrupts his scheduled program, falters and is unable to continue, as though he's tossed his prepared script into the river, the flow of blood surging, he presses his lips hard into Peacoat's then staggers away—

An age passes.

—There!. . . . Are you happy?—

Bradford's hand jiggles to the point of vibrating off Peacoat's jacket, who recoils from his grasp—but the reverend persists. It becomes clear that what has just slipped out is less an impulse than a vision he's dressed like a doll in the attic of his brain, alone and in total privacy, an image he'll paint for Peacoat come hell or high water, a mural of the possible, one I believe he's done a good deal of fussing over in the span he's spent trailing us, rendering a scene of some kind in elaborate, one could say dainty detail—he will impart it, sketch the whole image for a flabbergasted Peacoat who is pulling away from Bradford's renewed grip. In any case it's apparent the clever soul of words that otherwise never fails him when he's in god's collar now hightails away, rendering him as mute as me. And yet he tries.

—You and me. We could be *hap*py together.

You an' *me?*!

Why *not?*

But you're more like an unc—

—Don' say it!—Don' respond! Gimme a chance—

Bradford advances on Peacoat with renewed force, the prying eyes peeking out the window at the back of the house be damned, yanks Peacoat next to him, again he tries to kiss him, but Peacoat overpowers, thwarts him, then peels away. Again Bradford redoubles his efforts until the situation commences to lose its footing. The world goes rumble-tumble, including Peacoat too all of a sudden having stepped too far back, ignoring the crack and rustle of brush on the river's edge, nature's detritus that should have acted like gravel on a freeway berm, the pebbles that call you when you've fallen asleep at the wheel—Caution! You've gone too far! Peacoat tumbles into a frozen mix that moves with a power he can't resist—he reaches his hand out, toward the shore, but the shepherd of men seems to have opted to sacrifice this troublesome stray. He tramples Peacoat's hand as it reaches for a hold, gives the shoulder and forehead a nudge, away and away. Peacoat tries to claw what came toward him, but Bradford puts an end to his effort.

I'm saving the both a us! he yelps.

But—

—I'll pray for your soul!

The situation having gotten out of hand, I witness Peacoat lulled in slow motion into a situation he can't undo, so I gesture toward the reverend, impose on him to wake up from whatever spell he's under, but he recoils and again I receive a foot in the ribs for the effort. I fly off balance, nearly joining Peacoat in the soup, the implacable flow of the Shagaran.

I run to alert Jake but he's nowhere to be seen, so I hightail back—but to what? To a mute duel, two souls drowning in different ways, eyes darting frantically, and, conversely, blankly, if determinedly, glowering in some kind of actionless combat, a waiting game, though I know nothing good can come of this. I stamp my feet, cry, whimper, parallel to where Peacoat floats, I say, boy, you're playing with fire. Get outta there, for pity sake!—I mean, I intuit things.

He's in a total daze now, the current drifts him farther out and away, his head barely bobbing above the surface of the ice, Peacoat joining the ranks of the frozen, elevated only a pip, squeezed between the chunks and clods of ice. Traveling. Bradford's kiss, it has a force.

I'm cold, the reverend shivers at last. Again I charge in order to shake him from lethargy, and once again he boots me toward the edge of the river. Fallen thing, he spits.

Peacoat mumbles, his eyes questioning mine, as though for a moment I'm not some mindless adjunct of Jake, a mere shadow—in that state he saw me, I'm sure. Trembling to the core. It seems too many lights have dawned on him all at once, a horrid immanence, and in a twinkling a lifetime of insights condense then drift away, a fertile and productive life that will never take root, for him or Jake the way it might have, a fullness bludgeoned by a river. Bottom line, he's slipping. The body of believers, present in the person of Bradford like *le droit de seigneur*, sits now, heads bowed in Bradford's kitchen at the back of the house as the lord of heaven and despiser of nature is rivering Peacoat northward toward the lake, in the cracking, moaning ice, a weakened Peacoat peering dully at straws, at the brittle stems of last year's ragweed yarrow and queen ann's lace, slowly released from the bobbing In a final burst of energy Peacoat tries to save himself, his body, that reviled thing in Bradford-speak that useless husk that god hates In the time Peacoat has known Jake he's come to resuss it his body as though it were less a prison of the soul than the opposite That is he's come to realize that Bradford has had it exactly backwards all along that as the philosopher says the body is in fact the prisoner of the soul that cultural limit wall bulldozer understanding reversing milleniums, dragging as wisdom realizations limned or limbed from so many moments of flesh against flesh such a simple act occasioning a break between him and Bradford drifting as that dynamic did there below the surface invisible though not unnoticeable at any rate as these things so often are to Bradford most of all who I believe in retrospect sought to maintain a respectability there on top so to speak while underneath just below the surface a knowledge simmered not visible to others but imbibable so to speak he and Peacoat together once Jake had been sent packing. There are the eyes, filling up thousands of pages, notating, glossing, mute eyes now turned articulate, a slomo-thrashing mass of intensions, not the least among them the urge to remain afloat. Peacoat mumbles, Jake. I look one last time toward the reverend, hoping for a miracle never mind a change of heart, but all I witness is his back through the window, repudiating Peacoat and me, me alone now like Peacoat above the water, and yet the two of us, we're moving toward our undoing along the back of a series of properties along the mouth of the Shagaran, we meander along though no one is thrashing wildly with any vigor whatsoever now, and yet still I gaze back, invoke the pastor or anyone else who might give a fig—Molly, Peacoat mutters, his lips blue. My Molly. With his eyes he invites me to stay with him just as I invite you Tommy, to stay with my boy who I turn over to you as loquacious silence approaches, a quiescence that will speak in its own way across millenniums, in a voice that will be both vacant and present, an obtrusive reality that has no existence and yet can't be ignored to you and that group you're with there by the museum I turn him over as you jog off now, the bunch of you, to Wren's chickens and Donald's new-greening sycamores lining the street, his latest coup at city hall, telescoping a career in print, the power of the word, while I join Peacoat in the flow working through the veins, the river pulling us both along it mothers us both it even warms us now that hoar life skulks away he we're complaining less about cold and me about firewater turned freezing in the veins the two of us cease our kvetching as my pal Marks called it, about this and that, when the river finally adopts us as her own. I'm with you still, Peacoat, my brave And you with me To stand so helpless and mute with so much to say and no one there to listen but all of that foreclosed, subject as we are to bigger powers the two of us we drift Away and yet away we float His head now bobbing up then disappearing, resurfacing, his hands having long ago given up their thrashing, the two of us drifting I abandon the idea of rin tin tinning anything now of saving anyone myself most of all just come quick whatever it is

Peacoat's head tilts back, rests as though against a pillow or his mother's breasts when only minutes in the world the great big breast of nature oozing possibilities, the shoulders of a peacoat below the nostrils lips and jaw open near the waterline like carp at feeding time I watch the slow metamorphosis underway the fishy transformation once a land creature now we two turn our sights to the great lake ahead relinquishing the vimvigor the will to preserve any erstwhile state that ebbs from us In flows another resolve like some ordinary run of the mill mammal was it bovine eons ago that decided to quit the land take its chances in a waterworld some relative of the porpoise or the whale because no form is immutable We join you there Peacoat and me both usher to our undoing sinking under the surface not to roil it any more or pay it any indignity after all rivers don't like to be so clogged Somewhere in the world below

a secret deal is cut and we're handed over Tommy as again
I hand you over to my boy with whom you're birthing a life
Peacoat and me together now cradled in a transaction of
another kind of birthing from the Shagaran to the lake the
Eries claimed until such time as their spirits see fit to yield
us up and me now nothing but a stone or bare matter into
which you like the goddess of love must breathe lif—

Acknowledgments

As with most things, it takes a village to write a novel, which is certainly the case with *The Lede*. I'm grateful to many people for their insight, guidance, encouragement, and suggestions, including Lynn McGee who years ago, decades really, recognized the seed of a novel when I shared what would become the first chapter. I'd also like to offer special thanks to Linda Warren, who braved not one but two early incarnations of the work, as well as other early readers, who made their way through the full manuscript when it was decidedly a work in progress. They include Jamie Brunson, Allison Danzig, Kirsten Moser, Channing Sanchez, Hrvoje Slovenc, Jene Teague and Christopher Warren. Their feedback was invaluable. I'd also like to thank Nat Kimber for her generosity, experience, and wisdom in knowing how to talk about *The Lede*; her advice made all the difference.

A shout-out must go to the students in my queer and post-humanist lit courses who not only struggled with but came to own a difficult body of work, to the point of opening my eyes to things I hadn't seen on my own.

And I'd like to express abundant gratitude to Don Mitchell and Ruth Thompson at Saddle Road Press for not just recognizing but saying yes to Molly, for making the novel possible at all. Beyond their helpful insights they softened the edges of a process that can be daunting for a debut novelist. There's a know-how and kindness between them that inspires and moves me.

Many thanks to Sonia Sanchez-Cuesta, my guru in all things Spanish. And to Michele Karlsberg of Michele Karlsberg Marketing and Management. I'm so grateful for all your help. I'd like to express my gratitude as well to Sarah Smith of TRO Essex Music Group, and to Patrick Stewart of Easy Song.

Finally, I want to be mindful of the non-human persons who've been speaking to me my entire life, albeit in another idiom than the one most humans are accustomed. Along with Jacques Derrida I'd like to extend the philosophy of Emmanuel Levinas in affirming each has a face as much as any human animal, and for that reason deserves not only ethical treatment but endless gratitude.

About Donald Mengay

Donald Mengay grew up in a suburb of Cleveland, Ohio, where he worked in a factory for a time and managed a bookstore. He began writing fiction in his early twenties. He taught Queer and Post-Humanist Lit at the City University of New York for over thirty years, as well as English at the University of Paris, Nanterre. During his years teaching he  published several articles of queer criticism in academic journals that include among others *Genders, Genre,* and *Minnesota University Press.* He also co-published a book entitled *Dis/Inheritance: New Croatian Photography,* from Ikon Press. *The Lede to Our Undoing* is his debut novel, the first in a trilogy. He lives in Santa Fe, New Mexico.